Once Upon an Earl

Linen and Lace - Book One

Rosie Chapel

First printing 2016
ISBN 978-0-9945053-9-2

Ulfire Pty. Ltd.
P.O. Box 1481
South Perth
WA 6951
Australia

www.rosiechapel.com

Cover artwork by JF Holland
Images Courtesy of Period Images and Deposit Photos

Other Books by Rosie Chapel

The Hannah's Heirloom Sequence
The Pomegranate Tree - Hannah's Heirloom - Book One
Echoes of Stone and Fire - Hannah's Heirloom - Book Two
Embers of Destiny - Hannah's Heirloom - Book Three
Etched in Starlight - Hannah's Heirloom - Prequel
Hannah's Heirloom Trilogy - Compilation - Kindle only

Prelude to Fate

Regency Romances
Once Upon An Earl - Linen and Lace - Book One
To Unlock Her Heart - Linen and Lace - Book Two
Love on a Winter's Tide - Linen and Lace - Book Three
A Love Unquenchable - Linen and Lace - Book Four
A Hidden Rose - Linen and Lace - Book Five

His Fiery Hoyden - A Regency Novella

Contemporary Romance
Of Ruins and Romance
All At Once It's You

Anthologies
The Highway Man's Kiss - Once Upon A Love Anthology
Heart Rescued - Tales for the Season Anthology
Luck be a Pirate - Kiss My Luck Anthology
Finally Home - Tempting Fate Anthology
Love Kindled - Building Love Anthology - TBR Dec 2018

Dedication

This book is dedicated to all who believe in 'happily ever after.'

Acknowledgements

Grateful thanks to Julie for caring enough to create this beautiful new cover! I am in awe.

To my long suffering proof readers Moira and Janet, profound thanks for your tireless efforts in keeping me on the straight and narrow editing-wise

Although I recently updated the covers on my Regency series, I remain forever grateful to my sister, Helen, who created the gorgeous originals.

The Linen and Lace Clan

An exclusive club, only accessible to the fortuitous few. Those who - no matter their differences in money, title, background or position - marry for love. In an era when status, influence and wealth are bolstered under the guise of marriage, you are like rare gemstones - admired and envied. May your mutual respect, and true affection for one another, be the beacons by which you navigate the rough and the smooth of life's journey. Therefore, whether your clothing be of the cheapest linen or the finest lace, may the blend of either or both bring the richest and happiest union.

Once Upon an Earl

Linen and Lace - Book One

Chapter One

Autumn 1817, somewhere in Hampshire.

Once upon a time, there was an Earl. Yes, of course he was tall, very handsome and far nicer than the average member of the aristocracy, and currently enjoying an ordered ~ although it must be admitted slightly boring ~ existence, dividing his time between his sprawling country estate and parliamentary committees in London. Wearied and somewhat jaded from his time on the battlefield, he saw no necessity to change the status quo preferring the company of his estate staff and his horses to that of the social set. Although he knew that eventually he must choose an eminently suitable wife, as yet he had no desire to be so encumbered. Neither did he imagine ever finding a woman who would captivate his soul, to the exclusion of all others.

Then the storm blew in and in a heartbeat all his calm assurance was turned completely on its head.

Giles Maximilian Trevallier, fifth Earl of Winchester, was more than a little vexed. What had he been thinking? It was lunacy trying to outride this storm. Why on earth didn't he stop at the last inn he passed? It would only have delayed him one night. The light, already bad, was fading rapidly, and the tempest continued to rage all around him. It was getting worse, not better. Surely it should have blown itself out by now? This had been going on for hours.

He ought to have stayed in the city, but estate business required his attention, and could no longer be put off. Frustrated with himself and this awful weather, Giles leaned low over the horse's back hoping his thick cloak would prevent him from getting completely soaked.

It was cold now too — so cold the rain was turning into sleet. He needed to get home and soon. As his horse galloped along the road, familiar landmarks rose in his vision and he realised he was less than two miles from home. Jagged lightning illuminated the darkening sky and as the thunder crashed he questioned his sanity again for deciding to brave this ride. Thankfully his horse, Bronte, was not in the slightest perturbed by the storm and kept up a fast pace.

He reached the fork in the road, taking the left marking the boundary of his lands, but when he turned, he noticed a huddle of something in the middle of the track. It looked as though someone had dumped a pile of old clothes. Angry, both at this wanton littering of his property and that he would have to stop and move it, Giles reined in his horse and dismounted. Cursing, he kicked at the pile, grunting as his foot came into contact with something solid. Assuming it to be a piece of wood, he leant down and lifted the material. It covered a body.

Horrified, he took a step backwards, then got an even greater shock as the bundle moved. It wasn't dead. Who or what, the heap of dirty red material covered wasn't dead. The pile shifted, as whoever was underneath tried to stand up. Giles stared as it morphed into a tiny woman, white as a sheet, obviously in pain and with an air of fragility about her. Well, he did kick her, he guessed. She stared at him, confusion clear in her face.

"Where am I?" Her voice was barely a whisper, yet he heard her over the cacophony raging all around them.

"Near Whiteoaks," Giles replied, as though this would explain everything. She shook her head, her expression blank.

"Where is that? Oh dear, I must have lost my way. I'm so sorry, I didn't mean … I just needed to … I thought … had to rest." She turned away and started to hobble back towards the fork in the road. She had gone less than five yards when she stumbled, collapsing onto the grass at the side of the track, and remained motionless.

Completely baffled now. What was she doing, a woman alone in this weather? No sign of a carriage or horse or a chaperone. What was going on? Giles waited to see whether she was going to get up, his head trying to come to grips with what his eyes were seeing. Realising she was not, he walked over, dashing the water off his face and shook her shoulder gently. There was no response. He lifted the cloak, which was absolutely drenched and saw that she appeared to be unconscious. Not surprising really given how frail she looked.

There was nothing for it, he couldn't leave her there, she would die of exposure. Gathering the slight woman into his arms, Giles lifted her carefully up onto his horse and then climbed up behind her, holding her to him with one arm, catching the reins with the other. The sleet was turning to hail, and he urged Bronte onwards, sighing with relief when the huge wrought iron gates, signalling his driveway and thankfully open to admit him, appeared in the gloom.

As they slithered into the courtyard, his head groom ran out of the stables to help him with Bronte. The man gaped in astonishment, as his master slid off his horse, lifting down what looked like a bundle of rags, cradling them gently. Giles grimaced.

"No, I haven't lost my mind, Will. I found it … this … her, by the fork. She seems ill, confused. I couldn't in all conscience leave her, especially not in this weather."

Will grinned and taking Bronte's reins turned towards the stables, throwing over his shoulder. "You wait 'til you get her in there, my Lord." Nodding towards the main house. "All those women like nothing better than an excuse to cosset someone."

Giles chuckled and agreed, carrying the woman, who weighed no more than a feather pillow, in through the kitchen entrance.

The kitchen was full of people preparing the evening meal, he was expected, and so the house was a hive of activity. No one was in the least surprised when their master came striding through the back door; he generally used the domestic entrance when he returned from riding, aware his staff had enough to do without him adding to their work by trailing mud from the front of the house. He was an unusual man in that, despite his position, he rarely stood on ceremony and maintained a very good relationship with all of his employees from the butler right down to the scullery maid.

What did surprise them was what he held. The woman still hadn't revived, and Giles was becoming rather concerned.

"My Lord?" questioned Ellen — or Mrs Grey to the staff — his housekeeper, her eyebrows raised.

"I found her on the road, Ellen, she does not wake and is soaking wet. Can you do something?" Not usually so helpless, Giles found himself at a loss with what to do next. Dealing with unconscious females wasn't something he came across — ever. Oh, except those who chose to swoon at balls and those he avoided at all costs.

The women in the kitchen swarmed around him. Ellen pulled the hood back revealing a woman's face as pale as a ghost, with dark shadows under her eyes and what appeared to be a rather nasty bruise along her cheek.

"Please, will you carry her upstairs, your Lordship? The Rose Room is closest and is already made up." Ellen bustled out, shouting orders to her maids — towels, hot water, and nightclothes — everything she would need to make their unexpected visitor comfortable. Giles followed, thankful he would be able to hand over this lady to people far more competent than he.

As they entered the bedroom, the woman in his arms stirred. She was shivering now and her lips were a worrying shade of blue. Her eyes flickered open for just a moment and as she stared up at Giles, he was drawn into their green depths. His breath caught, and he had the oddest feeling he should recognise her. As the woman relaxed against him, he dismissed the notion as nonsense, and continued to hold her until the bath was filled, unwilling to place her anywhere while she was so wet. Ellen added salts to the warm water, the delicate scent permeating the room. Then she came over to where Giles stood, dripping all over the floor, his discomfort obvious.

"Leave her with us, your Lordship, we'll sort her out." Ellen smiled and, relieved he could relinquish his burden, Giles tried to stand the woman down. Still barely conscious, her legs buckled and she crumpled to the floor. He moved to pick her up, but Ellen waved him off saying they would look after her, and would find him when they were done. He walked out of the room, strangely bereft without her in his arms and could not help glancing back at this petite stranger now being fussed over by his staff, as they began to peel off her wet clothes.

Averting his eyes, he hurried along to his own rooms where his butler, Thomas, had drawn him a bath also. Suddenly aware of how cold he was, having stood around in wet clothes for what seemed like an age; Giles quickly divested himself of his own sodden attire. Then he gave in to the luxury of a good soak, washing off the dust of the day and letting the warmth of the water banish the chill from his bones. While he lay there, he mulled over the events of the last hour or so, struck by the incongruity of it all. How had this woman ended up, utterly alone, virtually on his doorstep, yet seemingly without a clue as to where she was?

Unable to answer any of his questions, he pushed them aside. Getting out of his bath, Giles dried and dressed quickly for, despite the fire burning in the grate, the room was cool; the temperatures outside plummeting. When he was not entertaining a house full of guests, he did not require Thomas to assist in his dressing, and simply shrugged into a shirt and breeches.

At the last minute, he swung a banyan around his shoulders, for although he felt he ought to try to dress a little more formally while this guest was in his home, the need for warmth outweighed his compliance with etiquette. He'd be surprised if the woman would be able to join him for the meal anyway.

Strolling downstairs, he entered his haven — the library, which he also used as an informal study — and where he usually relaxed until dinner was announced. Thomas followed him in, holding a tray on which stood a glass of brandy. Thanking him, Giles asked his butler how the ladies were coping with the guest. Thomas shook his head.

"They have yet to come downstairs, my Lord. Would you like me to check?"

"No, leave them to it. We'll get into trouble if we interfere."

Thomas grinned, nodding sagely. "You may be right, my Lord. I will ask Mrs Grey to report to you as soon as she is finished. Dinner will be served in half an hour. Is there anything else you need?"

"Thank you, Thomas, not at the moment."

Thomas bowed and left.

Giles picked up the brandy, swirling the amber liquid gently round the crystal glass, mesmerised as the glow from the fire caught the facets. Lost in thought, it was several moments before he realised that someone was knocking quietly on the door.

"Come." Mrs Grey poked her head around the door and he called her over. "So, what can you tell me, Ellen?"

"She is quite unwell, my Lord. I think we should summon the doctor." Ellen was fidgeting, a trait so uncommon to her that Giles began to feel quite anxious.

"Why do you think that to be necessary, Ellen? What aren't you telling me?"

"Well, my Lord, she is terribly thin and we are unable to warm her. I fear she may have caught a severe chill being out in the cold and wet. Everything she was wearing was saturated right through and her shoes have barely any sole on them. It seems as though she may have been walking for days. Also…" Ellen hesitated.

"All right, Ellen, out with it," Giles growled.

"My Lord, she is badly bruised, as though she has suffered a beating, and there's one more thing."

"Well?"

"She was clutching this." Ellen opened her palm and handed her master a strange trinket. Rolling it in his hands, Giles realised it was a clasp, one used to hold the edges of a cloak together. Nestling in the centre of the intricately carved surround was a deep red stone, which appeared to be a ruby and would be worth a fortune if it were. More likely it was a piece of costume jewellery, a mere frivolity.

"Thank you, Ellen, I will keep this safe until the lady can explain herself. Is she awake yet?"

Barely, my Lord, she seems to be slipping in and out of consciousness, another reason why I think we should call Doctor Elliott. I worry that there may be more going on here than meets the eye." Giles nodded almost absently, he was still staring at the clasp, sure he had seen this before as well. *What was it about this stranger?* "My Lord?"

"Yes, Ellen, by all means send for Elliott. Just make sure that whoever goes takes the carriage. The weather is atrocious; it is too awful to venture out on horseback. I will go and see this woman now, I assume she is not well enough to join me for dinner?" Ellen blinked, obviously working out how to tell him in the politest way possible, he was out of his mind. "Sorry, Ellen, I wasn't thinking straight." She smiled and excused herself, hurrying to organise one of the men to go and fetch the doctor.

Giles sat for a few more minutes enjoying his brandy, the aromatic liquid warming his throat and his stomach. *A fine aperitif,* he thought. Then he hauled himself out of the huge leather chair he had been sitting in and went to check on his guest.

Chapter Two

He climbed the stairs two by two, his long legs stretching out as he made his way back to the Rose Room. Knocking quietly on the door, he waited and was admitted by Sally, one of the housemaids.

"She's resting now, my Lord." Sally whispered. "She might talk to you when she wakes, but she hasn't said a word yet."

"Thank you, Sally. Please, stay here with me."

Sally smiled and nodded, taking a seat in the corner of the room. Giles walked over to the bed and got his first real look at the woman he'd rescued from the side of the road.

She was tiny, her countenance — elfin-like. Long dark lashes rested on cheeks that flared red with fever, but the rest of her face was white, too white, and an angry bruise along her jawline marred the delicate features. Her hair was dark, a rich chestnut brown, falling in riotous curls over the pillows and down onto the covers. *It must reach her waist,* Giles thought, frowning as he noticed more bruising along her arms as though someone had held her too tightly. This needed further investigation. Her hands were those of a gentlewoman, soft skin and slender fingers tipped with perfectly manicured nails. These weren't the hands of a servant or anyone who did manual work.

Giles drew a sharp breath and turned to Sally.

"Where are her clothes?" he asked quietly.

"Mrs Grey took them to be laundered, Sir, they was in a terrible mess."

"Were," corrected Giles, absently.

"Sorry, my Lord?" Sally looked confused

"It's 'were' in a terrible mess, not 'was'." Sally blushed and apologised. Giles brushed it aside, sorry to have picked her up on her mistake.

In a time when many of the gentry went about their lives unaware, or more likely uncaring, that schooling was unavailable to most people, Giles Trevallier went to great lengths to help anyone in his household improve their lot. His father, a man ahead of his time, believed everyone, regardless of status, gender and rank, deserved an education. Setting up a schoolroom in one of the old stable blocks for anyone wanting to better themselves, he conducted lessons in elocution, reading, writing and arithmetic — a tradition Giles continued, proud that Whiteoaks was more than just the country seat of an earl.

Dragging his mind back to the current problem, Giles asked, "What were her clothes like, Sally? Were they of good quality?"

"Oh yes, my Lord, they were. Bit torn, mind you, and ever so muddy and wet. Maybe a trifle out of date and quite simple though, not like the flounces some women are starting to wear these day." Sally bit her lip, aware she might have overstepped the boundaries of propriety with her last comment. Giles merely grinned.

"Do not worry, Sally, I happen to agree with you. So, we have a lady of refinement, but one who is a little old-fashioned. One, who was wandering the roads on her own, seemingly lost. It is a conundrum, isn't it?"

"And what about the brooch, my Lord? 'Tis a beautiful thing so 'tis."

"It is, Sally. Maybe she will tell us when she wakes."

All the while they were talking, he stared at the woman in front of him. He was troubled by her fragility, and there was something about her that made him want to reach out and stroke her hair, or hold her hand. Shocked at the nature of his thoughts, Giles stood quickly and, as he did so, the chair scraped on the wooden floor. The noise jarred through the silence of the room and the woman in the bed shuddered. He remained motionless, praying he hadn't disturbed her, but his hopes were in vain as she moved restlessly and her eyes opened. He was struck again by how green they were and was once more hit by a jolt of recognition.

She looked up at him, her expression one of utter bewilderment.

"Where am I? Who are you?" Panic coursed through her when she realised she was in a strange bedroom and a tall man — one she didn't know — was staring at her. Swallowing, she tried to push herself away, but did not have the strength to move. Suddenly a young girl appeared from behind the man.

"It's alright, Miss. I'll help you sit up. This 'ere's his Lordship, he brought you in. You were all wet and he didn't want to leave you out in the storm." All the while she was talking, Sally was plumping pillows and lifting the woman up on them, tucking the bedclothes around her and generally making her feel comfortable.

The woman glanced around at the unfamiliar room. She felt very tired and her head ached. Swallowing hurt her throat and her chest was tight. Oh no, she couldn't be ill, she had to … now what was it she had to do? She knew it was important but she couldn't remember. Her hands fluttered in her anxiety and she looked up at the two people by the bed. She tried again.

"Where am I? Please tell me." Her voice was barely a whisper, yet both Giles and Sally could hear the huskiness in her voice brought on by the chill running through her.

"You're at Whiteoaks, Miss, his Lordship's country estate."

The woman looked no less confused. "Where is this Whiteoaks?" she rasped. Giles and Sally looked at each other flabbergasted, everyone knew Whiteoaks, didn't they? Apparently not, the woman didn't appear to be feigning.

Giles sat back down and told her Whiteoaks was in Hampshire, not far from the New Forest. She muttered something about it not being far enough, but didn't elaborate. Then Giles asked the question, the answer to which they all wanted to know, and even though he had no clue as to her social standing, erred on the side of caution when he spoke.

"My Lady, please, will you give us your name?" He spoke calmly, his voice warm, inviting her trust. She looked at him and swallowed, opened her mouth, then closed it again. Her eyes widened and a look of such terror appeared in them, it was all Giles could do not to pull her into his arms.

"I can't remember! I can't remember! I don't know my name. How can I not know my name? Oh no! What do I do?" Had her voice not been cracked and broken, she would have shrieked the last few words, her expression going from bewildered to wild in a split second. "I have to go. I must leave. I can't stay here." Tears pouring down her face, she threw back the covers and made to stand up, but her strength gave out and she collapsed on the floor. Giles looked at Sally in consternation and, without thinking, gave into his earlier instincts and gathered the woman up off the floor into his arms and rocked her as he would a child.

"Hush, sweetheart, hush now, everything will be alright. Just relax, we will sort it out in the morning." She stiffened in his arms, and struggled to free herself, but Giles kept rocking her, crooning nonsense, anything to soothe her. He never recalled what he said; it could have been nursery rhymes for all he cared. He just wanted her to calm down, to cry out her panic. She sobbed against his chest, soaking his shirt. Obviously, today was his day to get wet Giles thought ruefully. Slowly, very slowly, her tears subsided and she became calmer; still Giles held her. As she settled, however, he noticed her breathing was strained; he could hear the ruckles in her chest and wondered what was taking the doctor so long.

After what seemed like an age, he realised she had fallen asleep, her head nestled against his shoulder and it felt as though she had always been there. He knew he should put her back to bed, but he didn't want to let her go. *What the dickens was wrong with him?*

"Sally," he whispered. Sally came to stand next to him.

"Yes, my Lord?"

"Let us try to get her back into bed, without waking her. She is very distressed and if she has truly lost her memory, we don't want to scare her anymore." Sally nodded, and between them they managed to lie her down. Sally filled a bowl with cool water and brought a cloth. Giles took it from her and, rinsing the cloth, carefully wiped the woman's face, then her hands. Her head felt hot and her cheeks had lost none of the redness they noticed earlier.

She began muttering incoherently and they listened hoping she might tell them something to help identify her. It was very garbled though, the only words they could make out was something about her father, some documents and a carriage.

Nothing of which made any sense at all. Baffled, they gave up and just watched her.

About an hour later, the doctor arrived, full of apologies explaining he'd been tied up with another case. Giles told him all he knew of his guest — scarcely anything, by which time Ellen had joined them, telling them what they discovered when bathing her.

"She seems terribly bruised doctor, more than just from falling and…" she hesitated looking over at Giles.

"Come, Ellen, what didn't you tell me?"

She blushed and continued in low tones. "I think she might have been abused."

"In what way, Ellen?" Giles waited, a cold trickle running down his spine, but his housekeeper was unwilling to voice her opinion in front of him. She shook her head.

"All I will say is that there are marks which cause me concern. I would rather let the doctor check her out before I say anymore.

"Let me examine her, Giles," said the doctor gently. "I can see she has a fever, we need to treat that, and I will determine what other damage has been inflicted on her while I'm checking her over. Trust me," as Giles made a reflexive movement, "I will be careful and discreet. I will come and find you when I am done. Go and have your dinner." Ellen and Sally ushered him out of the room. He could hear the woman still muttering and was loath to leave her, but he had no choice.

Giles made his way to the dining room where his meal, which looked very tasty, was served, and tried to eat. His appetite had left him however, all he could think about was the woman upstairs so slight and so frail. Why would anyone hurt her? He couldn't understand what it was about her that had him so wound up; pondering over whether her distress had anything to do with that clasp, the one Ellen had handed him. Maybe that would help her remember who she was and why she was here.

Finishing his meal, Giles went back to the library, to find the fire was still burning merrily and a tall goblet of hot chocolate standing on his desk. He found this drink preferable at night; it warmed him more than tea and sleep seemed to come more easily. He wasn't sure, however, he'd be able to sleep at all tonight. Tacitly thanking Thomas, Giles drank deeply, savouring the rich flavour and waited for the doctor to come down. He tried to look at the papers on his desk, but was unable to concentrate, so in the end just sat in his leather chair and waited for Theo.

He was nodding off by the time Doctor Elliott knocked and stuck his head around the door.

"You awake, Winchester?"

Giles roused himself and waved his friend in. "Come in, Theo. What can you tell me? Would you like a drink?" The doctor nodded his thanks and Giles pulled the bell. Thomas appeared almost immediately, Giles asking him to bring two more hot chocolates as well as two whiskys. They waited until Thomas returned with the drinks, then once the butler left the room, Giles repeated his question.

"What can you tell me?"

Theo Elliott stared at his friend, steepling his fingers together, before he spoke, almost contemplatively. "Your guest has not been well treated of late. Her body is covered in bruises and I think it is likely that at least two of her ribs are cracked — possibly broken, it is difficult to determine; her ankle is sprained and she has bronchitis, which may develop into pneumonia. She is a very sick young woman." He paused and Giles interjected —

"That must be why she couldn't walk, she damaged her ankle. No wonder she fell, poor thing. What of the other fear?"

"I think Ellen was overly concerned. While there are marks, which I grant you might at first glance look to have been caused by an attempt to ruin her, after closer examination I think it more likely she landed awkwardly on something. There is no sign of the damage I would expect to see had it been worse. Giles, this woman may have been walking for days. I certainly don't think she's eaten a decent meal in quite some time." Theo stopped and took a sip of the hot chocolate. "Ellen mentioned a clasp or brooch or something, apparently the woman was clutching it? Giles nodded. "It must be very important to her, she was holding it so tightly, it has cut into her palm. I have cleaned and bandaged the wound but we must make sure it does not become infected."

Giles stared into the fire, watching the flames dance up the chimney while reflecting on his friend's words.

"She must stay with us, we can look after her, there are enough women on my staff not to raise any questions. Nobody even knows she's here and for now I would like it to remain that way. I will make enquiries and see whether I can trace who she is. She doesn't remember her name, you know."

Theo nodded. "Sally told me. It may be as simple as shock. It appears she is trying to get somewhere or away from something, and whatever that is may have caused her mind to shut down, but her illness could also play a part. Let's deal with one thing at a time. Hopefully, as she recovers all the other things will slot into place."

"Do you recognise her, Theo?" Giles asked curiously.

"No, why?"

"She seems so familiar to me, as though we have crossed paths before, but for the life of me I cannot recall who she is or where we met."

Chapter Three

As the wind howled around the building and the hail lashed against the windows, the two men tried to work out how Giles could possibly know this woman. They came up with nothing. Giles and Theo grew up together; went to school and then university together. They knew each other's friends and colleagues, and neither could recall ever having met the lady before.

Eventually accepting they were getting nowhere, Theo turned the conversation to the treatment he would be providing for Giles' guest. She was quite ill and it was likely the household would endure sleepless nights before they knew whether she would survive. They needed to give her a name too, until she could remember her own; they couldn't continue to call her 'guest,' it was ridiculous.

Giles suggested his friend stay the night. The weather had worsened and there was always a room made up for Theo. The doctor was easily persuaded and the two men relaxed in the warmth of the study, enjoying each other's company for the remainder of the evening, accompanied by excellent conversation, a fine port and a platter of cheese.

It was quite late by the time they retired. Theo checked on the woman twice during the course of the evening. She was in the throes of fever, but Ellen and Sally were with her, making sure she was tended to properly. A bronchitis kettle hung over the fire, the steam with a touch of menthol permeating the room, its pungent vapour helping the woman's breathing, which had become laboured.

Giles peered around the door before he went to bed, asking whether they needed anything else. Theo shook his head, they could only watch and wait. The fever would take its course; they just had to hope she was strong enough to fight it. Ellen said she and Sally would sit with her overnight, so she wasn't left alone.

Acknowledging he was in the way, Giles thanked them and made his way to his own bedchamber. Shedding his clothes he realised how tired he was. A long day in the saddle as well as the worry of what to do about his unknown and very sick visitor, made the thought of his comfortable bed most inviting, and he fell asleep as soon as his head touched the pillow.

Sometime in the middle of the night Giles was awoken by screams. Aroused from a deep slumber, it took him several minutes to work out where he was and who the devil could be making such a racket. Then he remembered and, pulling on a warm dressing gown, ran along the hall to the Rose Room. The room seemed full of people, but in actual fact there were only four; Ellen, Sally, Theo and the woman in the bed to whom the doctor was trying to administer something from a vial, which Giles assumed to be laudanum. The woman was thrashing so much, however, that Theo was having no success.

Giles strode over to the bed and looked down at her, she was still screaming from whatever terror stalked her dreams turning them into nightmares. Her hair was damp with sweat, her face so pale she looked more dead than alive. Her frail body was wracked with tremors and her cries sounded raw from the throat infection as well as the screaming. It was a pitiful sight and he could not bear it. Without pausing to think and mindful of her broken ribs, he scooped her up as gently as he could. Then just as he had done earlier, held her to him rocking her like a child, crooning softly and trying to break through the fear holding her in its grip.

The other three stared at him in shock. His behaviour was less than appropriate, yet what other choice did they have. The woman was very ill and she needed to be calmed before they could hope to give her the medicine that would help her sleep without nightmares. Giles sat down on the edge of the bed and swung his legs up, settling himself against the pillows, still rocking and crooning. Eventually she began to settle down. Her screams died away, leaving shuddering sobs in the aftermath. Still Giles cradled her, talking to her about everything and nothing. His housekeeper and housemaid gaped at him, while Theo took the opportunity to get the woman to drink some laudanum. She swallowed it without protest and without opening her eyes.

She was muttering again as before; it definitely seemed to relate to her father and those documents, but also, as before, nothing was coherent enough for them to make any sense of it. This along with her name would have to wait. While Giles held her, Theo checked the woman's temperature. She was burning up and, in an attempt to lower the fever, the doctor placed cool damp cloths on her wrists and forehead as they watched for the opiate to take effect.

The tremors subsided, and the woman in Giles' arms began to relax, her head falling against his shoulder. He waited until her breathing steadied, then tried carefully, to place her back on the bed. Even in her state of oblivion, his movements seemed to panic her and she clung to him, her slender fingers fisting around the material of his dressing gown. She never opened her eyes or seemed conscious of her actions, but he did not want to disturb her again.

"It's all right, Theo, I'll stay here, I don't want to cause her any more distress. If this is the only way we can get her to sleep, I am happy to stay. Maybe Ellen or Sally will stay too, so propriety is observed. I would not want to place anyone in an awkward position. Moreover, if she wakes and finds me holding her, she may take fright."

Ellen said she would stay, and shooed Sally off to bed. The young girl was almost asleep on her feet and she had duties enough to worry about the next day.

Theo made sure he had done everything he could and gave instructions for them to call him should her condition worsen. He believed the dose of opiate should keep her asleep for several hours and hoped, by the morning, her fever may have broken. Giles thanked his friend, who took himself off to bed. Ellen, tutting under her breath at the situation, nevertheless fussed around for a few moments, plumping up the pillows behind his Lordship, placing another under the arm in which the woman rested, giving him extra support.

Giles wasn't overly worried; the woman was no weight. He shuffled against the headboard and brought up the blankets, so they covered both the woman and him. The fire was blazing away merrily making the bronchitis pot bubble and steam. Only two candles remained lit, the light in the room dim, yet cosy. Giles thought about the woman in his arms and wondered how long it would be before they knew who she was. A mystery indeed. He looked down at her, she seemed so vulnerable, yet she was running from something or someone. She could be a murderess for all he knew. Even that thought did not stop the wave of protectiveness flooding through him, and still that strange feeling he knew her.

It was a long night. Several times the woman woke, battling some inner demons that would not let her rest, as well as the fever, which had her burning hot one moment and shivering with cold the next. It seemed to Giles as though she was too weak to fight the infection, and he barely slept a wink for fear she would slip away while he held her. He was most relieved when the dawn finally broke and she was still breathing.

As light began to filter through the drapes and into the bedchamber, highlighting the soft pinks in the room, the woman in his arms stirred. He nodded to Sally, who had taken over from Ellen less than half an hour previously, allowing his housekeeper to snatch a little sleep. The maid came closer so the woman would see her if she awoke, and would not panic at finding herself in the arms of a man she did not know. The woman murmured, her voice croaky, her words unintelligible, her dark lashes fluttering against her cheeks, yet her eyes remained closed.

They held their collective breath as she seemed to come to wakefulness, but then with a huge sigh she turned and seemingly unaware of what she was doing, snuggled against Giles' chest, her small frame fitting neatly into his large one. Her breathing settled into a more natural rhythm and she slept on. Giles felt his own breathing hitch and his heart was not beating quite as steadily as usual. He gazed down at her now peaceful countenance, fighting not only an absurd desire to kiss her, but also the notion she was where she should be, and that he had been waiting his whole life for this woman to be wrapped in his arms.

Shaking his head to clear it of such nonsense, Giles contemplated his life. He never thought to wed, even though he knew it was expected. He was supposed to marry a suitable woman, one who would look good on his arm at balls and other social functions; preferably one who could hold a conversation, but he had no mind to do so. Those of his friends who were married did not seem overly content, more resigned. He had enough to do on the estate and in London. He did not need to worry about some hapless female who was unable to function without a man, or who was looking for one with a large purse, which she could fritter away on dresses and hats.

Giles' parents married for love and he grew up in a happy home, one in which both parents enjoyed being with each other and their offspring and, in fact, were rarely apart. As children, he and his two sisters were not palmed off onto nannies; their mother brought them up, teaching them, caring for their ailments, playing with them. It had been a home where their lives were always intertwined and where the children knew they were secure in the love and support of both parents.

This was Giles' example and he would settle for nothing less. He had not yet met a woman who made his breath catch or his heart beat faster, one without whom life would not seem worth living.

Until yesterday.

The woman in his arms was causing havoc with his emotions and he had no idea why. Pushing these disturbing thoughts away, he asked Sally whether she would mind ringing for some coffee. He needed his wits about him and he had not had enough sleep; coffee would have to do. As Sally went to do his bidding, Giles shut his eyes, just for a minute he thought, and was immediately asleep.

The woman blinked, the light was different in the room, it must be daybreak. Her head was throbbing and her throat felt raw; her breathing seemed less restricted, but her chest ached. She still had no idea where she was, but she felt safe and warm. Turning her head carefully, she nearly yelled out in shock as she realised she was lying in the arms of the same very tall man whom she remembered from the last time she awoke. Shoving her fist into her mouth to stifle the cry, she stared up at him, studying his features in the half-light.

His black hair fell in an unruly mess as though he kept running his hands through it, this and the light stubble shadowing his jawline, combined to give him a slightly piratical appearance. There was not an ounce of excess fat on his body. She could feel the muscles through his night attire and was startled by a sudden urge to trail her fingers over them. The beat of his heart, steady and strong, was comforting and a wave of emotion she could not define washed over her as, even knowing that she should not be there, found herself unable to move. The man looked exhausted and she had no wish to disturb him. Deciding she would worry about everything later, she drew the bedclothes a little higher, covering her shoulders and giving the man extra warmth, then tucking her head under his chin, went back to sleep.

Sally watched this little tableau unfold; her interest piqued at the behaviour of his Lordship and their guest. Despite declarations to the contrary, it seemed to her as though they knew each other, that they had known each other for a lifetime, but at a subconscious, rather than conscious level. Smiling to herself at such flights of fancy, Sally turned her attention to the room, picking up all the cloths and towels, used overnight to cool the woman while she fought the fever. Collecting bowls and water jugs, the young girl was just about to take everything down to the kitchens, when the door creaked open and Lucy, one of the kitchen maids, came in with a tray on which stood a pot of steaming coffee, two cups and a plate of freshly baked drop scones.

Whispering her thanks, Sally took the tray and asked Lucy to take the pile of cloths and stack of bowls downstairs. Lucy nodded and asked how the lady was, adding that everyone was worried about her. Sally gave her an update and promised to come down with a more detailed report once the doctor had checked their guest. The heady aroma of the coffee woke Giles, who was disoriented for a few seconds, momentarily forgetting where he was and that he had a woman asleep on his chest. Sally placed the tray on the bedside table and pressed her finger to her lips, pointing at the women.

Memory flooded back and he knew he should lay her onto the bed where surely she would sleep more comfortably. Plus, his body ached from sitting in the same position for so long, he needed to stretch his limbs. He took a sip of the coffee savouring the rich flavour. Then, placing the cup back on the bedside table, said —

"Sally, please would you help me? She seems much more relaxed and I think she would sleep better lying in bed rather than curled up on me. She can't possibly be comfortable, especially if her ribs are broken."

"If you pardon my saying, my Lord," Sally grinned, "she has slept like a baby since you have been holding her, far better than before her nightmare. Seems you have the magic touch."

Giles smiled back, thinking that in any other household Sally would probably be reprimanded for being too familiar in her conversation with the master of the household. He was glad his staff felt comfortable enough to say what they felt, while maintaining their utmost respect. "That's as maybe, but I need to move too. I am losing the feeling in my legs."

Sally giggled as, between them, they managed to lay the woman on the bed properly, settling her comfortably against the pillows and covering her back up with the sheets and comforter. They studied her for a moment; she was obviously still quite unwell, but Giles thought her skin felt less clammy and her breathing not quite so laboured. Telling Sally he'd be back shortly, he went along to his own room to freshen up and dress.

Once he'd completed his morning ablutions, Giles flung back the curtains and opened his window, letting the chill air circulate throughout the room. The weather looked bright and clear, the storm had finally blown itself out. He gazed out over his lands. Below him in all their splendour lay the formal gardens kept in perfect order by Samuel and his staff. Beyond them as far as the eye could see was the Great Park, liberally scattered with elm, ash and oak leading to the dark pine forest, which flowed out to the boundaries of his land. Sometimes he had to pinch himself to believe it was all his. The estate also included several farms supporting both agriculture and stock, but they were in the other direction.

Giles was proud of his heritage, which could be traced back to the time when the Romans ruled Britain and he wanted to make sure it was cared for properly so it could be handed down to his next of kin in good order. Next of kin! Didn't he mean his heir? That could only happen if he had a son, yet he had no intention of marrying. Refusing to be dragged down that track, Giles leaned against the window frame, breathing in the morning air. Autumn was upon them, yet generally the days were not overly cool, snatching the last gasps of summer before the winter chill held the country in its thrall.

It was as though the storm had washed the skies, the air was heady, like champagne and the light, soft. The harsh blues of the hot summer days had faded to a gentler hue, and the beauty of the land spread out in front of him made Giles itch to go for a ride. He knew Bronte would need to rest but his stallion, Zeus, would love a good gallop across the countryside. However, he had a knotty problem to deal with first in the guise of the woman in the room along the hallway. He needed to know how she was and whether they had managed to arrest the fever. Then he needed to know *who* she was, how she got here, and what about that strange clasp?

Chapter Four

Sauntering downstairs, he went along to the kitchens to see whether anyone could be persuaded into making him an early breakfast. Sarah, his cook, was bustling about banging pots and pans in what looked like a very dangerous manner, but he knew better than to comment on it. Sarah was an institution and her cooking legendary, but she had her own ways and he would never dream of upsetting her. She had been with the family since she was a young girl, before his parents' marriage.

When he was a child, Giles and his sisters played in the servants' halls, getting under the feet of all the staff who never told them off or shooed them out. He loved the smell of the kitchens; there was always bread or cakes baking, or maybe a joint roasting in one of the huge ovens. There was usually a cat or three, intended to keep any rodents out of the pantry, but more often than not were too lazy or too comfortable to be bothered, becoming treasured pets.

Thomas was sitting in the corner, near a low table, polishing boots. He glanced up as the door swung open and stood; Giles waved him back to his seat.

"Carry on, Thomas, I do not wish to disturb you. I was just wondering whether my wonderful Sarah could manage a couple of eggs for me, maybe on a slice of toast." Giles winked at Thomas as he said this and waited for Sarah to tell him off. He didn't have to wait long. Sarah turned and, placing one hand on her hip in feigned indignation, wagged her finger at him with the other.

"What are you doing down here, my Lord? You know fine well you shouldn't be in the kitchens; it isn't right." Giles merely grinned and repeated his question. "Well, I'm sure you and the doctor will want a decent breakfast after all that going on last night. I'll get on to it right away." Her tone changed, gentling to one of concern, "How is the poor pet by the way, my Lord? Mrs Grey said she was right poorly."

"She sleeps now, Sarah, but I fear she has not eaten properly for many days. Maybe some of your famous porridge might help get her appetite back on track." Giles smiled his most winsome smile and knew Sarah would go out of her way to find something that the woman upstairs would find very palatable. Sarah nodded, muttering to herself about men thinking they could just walk into her kitchen and expect her to drop everything and cook eggs.

"Thank you, Sarah," said Giles and, ignoring her mutterings, walked around the table to give her a big hug, "I do appreciate you, you know."

"Get on with you, my Lord." Sarah spluttered, blushing to the roots of her greying hair and batted at him, without any visible effect. Giles grinned and left while the going was good, hearing Thomas chuckle as the door swung closed.

Retracing his steps, he went back to the Rose Room and knocked quietly. Ellen opened the door, looking as tired as he felt, and Theo stood at the bedside examining the woman, who appeared to be fast asleep. Giles frowned; surely she should have been disturbed with all the noise a waking house created.

"Theo?" His friend turned at Giles' entrance and motioned him over. "She sleeps still? There was a moment during the night when I thought she might awake, but nothing came of it." Ellen joined them, saying —

"Sally tells me the woman awoke for a few moments at dawn. Apparently she nearly cried out when she realised that she was sleeping in your arms, but then settled. It seems she felt comfortable and safe."

Giles smiled rather sheepishly. "It was the least I could do. For some reason I seem to be able to calm whatever night terrors she has; one night of lost sleep is worth it."

Theo looked at his friend, and at Ellen. "I hope that was your only night of broken sleep, my friend, but she is not over the fever yet, it still runs through her. I think you may resign yourselves to one or two more nights of disturbance before she turns the corner. Broken ribs and bruising aside, lack of nourishment over what might be an extended period means she is not wholly able to fight any infection and she needs to build up her strength." The doctor sighed, "I wish I knew how she came by such injuries. They are quite severe and she seems to be a woman of standing."

Giles nodded his agreement. "Sally said her clothes were quality and her hands do not show signs of manual work. The whole thing is a mystery. We have to hope she can remember something when she eventually wakes up."

In silence, the two men contemplated the woman in the bed. As though aware of their scrutiny, she stirred and as they had done the previous evening, everyone in the room held their breath. Giles stepped quietly away, so if she did wake, she wouldn't feel crowded. As he did so, there was a knock on the door and Lucy popped her head round saying she had a tray of food for the lady, and that breakfast was about to be served in the dining room. Giles whispered a thank you and took the tray. Lucy bobbed a curtsy and fled back to the kitchens.

The woman showed no real sign of waking but Theo was worried about how long it had been since she ate. As Giles placed the tray on the bedside table, the doctor suggested they leave Ellen and Sally to wake her and try to persuade her into some breakfast, while they two went and partook of theirs. Giles nodded, albeit reluctantly, and after a couple more instructions to Ellen, the two men walked down to the dining room.

Breakfast was a casual affair at Whiteoaks. Plenty of eggs and toast, coffee or tea, and some fresh seasonal fruit. Simple and filling. Unless he had a house full of guests, Giles did not like fussy meals. Plain yet tasty was all he required; and as Theo was a friend, a regular visitor to the house and classed as family, there was no need of formality. They chatted while they ate. Theo was concerned about the woman and was loath to leave her, but he had rounds to make and one or two people had call on his time. Giles convinced him that as long as he left instructions, they would manage. Ellen and Sally took most things in their stride and it gave them someone to cluck over, instead of him.

After breakfast, they sat for a long while over a second, then a third cup of hot coffee. Eventually Theo dragged himself out of the chair, remarking that he would check her one last time before going about his duties. Giles nodded, saying he would see him in the stables as he fancied a ride and would accompany the coach as far as the fork in the road, the place where he found the woman the previous night. Was it only last night? It felt as though he had known her longer than that. Striding upstairs, he changed into his riding habit and boots, and called to Thomas that he was going out on Zeus.

Theo met him at the stables, mentioning the woman was awake and eating, and although barely enough to fill a sparrow, it was better than nothing. Giles was tempted to go and see her, but decided a ride would be more beneficial. He needed to clear the cobwebs and a brisk gallop in the mild autumn air would do him more good than watching a sleeping woman. Zeus was saddled ready and, after mounting the huge stallion, Giles trotted alongside the carriage while it rumbled along the roadway. When they reached the fork, he waved off his friend, and Theo shouted that he'd return by evening. As the carriage disappeared around the bend, Giles dismounted and spent a few moments surveying the area where he came upon the woman.

He took his time, making sure he covered a goodly amount of ground. He had no idea from which direction she had come, so it was pointless going any further. Just as he was about to give up, he spotted something almost buried in the long grass winking in the sunlight. Walking over, he noticed a reticule, which although completely sodden appeared to be of good quality. The design was simple, but the chain looked to be silver, and the delicate stitching suggested it was made for someone of the upper classes. He did not open it — it was not done to go through a woman's possessions — but he wondered whether there was anything within that would help them work out who she was.

Tucking it into his jacket, he then forgot about everything else except for being out for a ride. He clicked Zeus into a gallop and the horse flew across the Great Park. It was weeks since he had been home and he missed Zeus who wasn't the most pleasant tempered of mounts and definitely not suited to gentile rides around the parks of the capital. Bronte was his city horse, but Zeus was a dream to ride when allowed his head. Giles rode for over two hours, returning to the stables tired and windswept, but much the better for it. Dismounting, he walked the horse over to the trough and let him quench his thirst, then led him into the stables and rubbed him down.

Giles found it very cathartic to brush his horses, the action soothing; he loved to listen to the gentle nickering of the animals, and to smell the warm hay. In fact he was happiest in the stables than anywhere. He understood his horses and they responded to him. Far less complicated than people. Eventually he was done and, patting Zeus on the flank, left him munching hay in his loose box. On his way out of the stables, he talked softly to his other horses as he passed them, then retraced his steps up to his bedchamber to wash off the horsey smell, before going to see how his guest fared. They still had no name for her and he mulled over this while he washed and changed. Thomas took his riding clothes and boots to be cleaned, while Giles pulled on breeches, a white shirt and a waistcoat.

Checking to make sure he looked presentable, if rather casual, Giles strolled along to the Rose Room. Maybe they should call her Rose; it seemed as good a name as any. Knocking quietly, he waited to be admitted. The woman was sitting up in bed, leaning against the pillows, while Sally brushed her hair. Dressed in a diaphanous nightgown, probably one of his mother's, which all but drowned her, she looked terribly pale and fragile.

Giles walked over to the bed and asked, gently, how she was feeling. She gazed up at him, a little frown creasing her brow and replied —

"Thank you, your Lordship, I am quite well. I must not intrude any longer on your hospitality and would ask that my clothes be brought to me, so I may continue on my way." Her voice was very croaky and Giles imagined her throat must hurt from the effort of speaking. He listened to her request in astonishment.

"Good lady, I do not think you understand the extent of your injuries. I imagine that 'quite well' is wishful thinking. You have a badly sprained ankle, many bruises, at least two cracked ribs and a severe chest infection. Have you even remembered your name?"

"Of course, I am…" she stopped and stared at him, then tried again, "…my name is…" she clamped her jaw tight in an attempt to stop her lips from quivering. Her eyes darkened in panic and Sally leaned over the bed, laying her hand on the woman's arm.

"Do not fret, Miss, it will come to you. His Lordship is correct mind, you cannot leave just yet. Let us look after you and when you are well, we will see you safely on your journey." The woman turned to listen, her panic subsiding at the quiet words.

"How can I not know my own name?" she asked, clearly perplexed. "It is something you carry for a lifetime."

"Is there anything else you can remember? Such as where you are from? Where you were going?" Giles asked gently. She concentrated for a few minutes then shook her head.

"I can't remember anything." She lifted trembling hands to her head and Giles could see tears forming in her incredible eyes. She blinked them back and inhaled a sharp breath trying to regain some control. As she did so, she started to cough, the bout wracking her tiny frame. Sally tried to soothe her, but she was unable to stop the agony flooding the woman's chest as the attack ratcheted through her damaged ribs.

Unable to catch her breath, the coughing and the pain in her chest proved too much and the woman fainted dead away. Giles watched, feeling helpless, as Ellen checked her pulse, managing to slip a drop of laudanum between the woman's pale lips hoping this would give her some respite. They had to find out who she was, and why she was travelling alone, on foot with no luggage, for surely she must have family who were missing her. Thankfully, the opiate worked quickly and the woman's breathing steadied.

Giles remained for a few moments making sure the woman had indeed calmed down and was sleeping as naturally as possible. Motioning to Sally and Ellen, he drew the two women into the hallway.

"Please, can you listen to her in case she mutters in her sleep, she may give us information which she otherwise cannot recall. Also, I have found her reticule but have not opened it. I will bring it to her when she next awakens; hopefully it contains something that will help us."

His housekeeper and maid nodded and he left them with their charge.

Going down to the library, he noticed Thomas had placed the newspapers on his desk. Giles had the city papers delivered as well as the local ones and, making himself comfortable in one of the huge wing-backed chairs near the fire, he scrutinised them all closely on the off-chance there might be any mention of a missing woman. Nothing. He read the broadsheets cover to cover and none contained anything remotely resembling a missing person's report.

He did notice, however, there was an in-depth article in one of the more reliable papers regarding the belief that French operatives were infiltrating the English aristocracy. This was apparently an attempt to uncover the identities of any who might have been involved in clandestine operations for the English government during the recent wars, with a view to apprehending them and removing them to France for trial. Giles realised that 'trial' was a euphemism for summary execution and, knowing several people who were involved in such operations, shuddered at the thought of what might happen should they be discovered. He just had to hope the gossip among the *ton* didn't include secrets best left uncovered.

Chapter Five

Pushing this all aside for now, Giles turned his attention to the mountain of estate business awaiting him. How it managed to accumulate at such a rate when he had only been away a couple of months was beyond him. Running his hand through his hair, he sat down at his desk, concentrating on the matters at hand. As an estate owner, he was responsible for the upkeep of all the buildings on his lands — the farms, cottages, barns, sheds, workshops and so forth.

On top of this, were the carpenters, bricklayers and mechanics employed to keep everything running smoothly. Each season required different programmes of land management such as clearing ditches, planting or felling of trees, maintenance of paths, tracks and roads. Some jobs were short term, some were year round and Giles was responsible for the well-being of all whom he employed in whatever capacity. For most, their only income was whatever they earned from working on the estates, without which many would not be able to provide for their families.

Giles was a conscientious employer, however, and despite the fact that much was manual labour and often rather monotonous, there was always enough to keep everyone under his protection busy. He was blessed with exceptional stewards who managed the day-to-day running of the estate as well as the farms. By the time he read through their comprehensive reports, he was satisfied everything was as it should be.

He jotted down a few things he wanted to check on himself such as the provision of chopped wood to be distributed amongst all of his tenants, either on the farms or in the village. Winters here could be brutal and the estate always provided fuel for the fires, sorely needed when the chill set in. The husbandry of both animals and trees was key to the success of his farms and he took a personal interest in every aspect of his lands.

He was so engrossed in his work, he forgot to ring for lunch, and in the early afternoon Thomas knocked on the door to check whether his master would like a light meal. Thanking his butler, Giles stretched his stiff muscles, rubbing his hand round the back of his neck. Thomas reappeared almost immediately with a platter consisting of a large slice of cold meat pie, pickled vegetables, fresh bread and cheeses, and a hot coffee. Giles inhaled everything; savouring the coffee, before taking the tray back to the kitchens himself.

Used to her master's ways, Sarah merely thanked him, remarking that their guest managed to eat something for lunch — a poached egg and a little bread. Not enough in Sarah's opinion, but it was better than nothing. Giles nodded, grinning, and made his way up to the Rose Room to see how things were going.

Sally was there, sitting by the bed reading out loud from a book, even though the woman under the covers appeared fast asleep. Looking up as Giles entered the room, Sally put her fingers to her lips.

"I think she's asleep, my Lord, but reading seemed to calm her, so I just carried on. I like this story, and I don't mind."

Giles lifted up the book to read the title 'The Sylph', undoubtedly one of his sister's books left behind when she married. Apparently a popular book amongst the ladies, but he had no clue what it was about and really did not care to find out. While they were talking, the woman in the bed began tossing and turning, her cheeks flaring as her temperature was rising again. Sally muttered that she'd been like this all morning, hot cold, hot cold. It was all they could do to keep her comfortable.

"Sarah tells me she ate something at lunchtime."

Sally nodded. "Yes, my Lord. She had most of a poached egg and a few squares of toast. Not much, but more than she had last night. Maybe we need to think about soup, it can be digested much more easily than bread."

Giles agreed, saying he would have a word with Ellen when she came back. Between them, using damp cloths, they managed to cool the woman down, but by now her nightdress was soaked. Unwilling to leave Sally to deal with this on her own, yet knowing he shouldn't be there while his maid changed the woman's attire, Giles shifted his weight from foot to foot self-consciously for a few minutes. Understanding his anxiety, Sally smiled and said she could manage. A relieved Giles hastened through the door, bumping into Ellen on his way out.

"I think Sally may need a hand, Ellen." He muttered and shot off down the stairs and across to the estate office, trying to ignore the rush of emotions the frail woman in the bed stirred in him. He spent the remainder of the afternoon going over estate business with his three stewards before Theo stuck his head round the door sometime after five, saying he was going up to examine their visitor. Giles said he'd join him shortly, and proceeded to conclude the discussions the four men were having regarding one of the farms.

Dawdling across the courtyard, whistling and hands in his pockets, Giles ruminated about the woman lying in his Rose Room. He still reckoned he knew her from somewhere, but try as he might he could not place from where. Taking the stairs two at a time, as was his habit, he knocked on the bedroom door to be admitted by Ellen. Theo was listening to the woman's chest and Giles could hear her wheezing from across the room. Theo was very gentle with her, checking her over very quickly with a minimum of fuss, but as he turned to greet Giles, he was frowning.

"What?" Giles asked his friend.

"She is getting worse, not better. I think maybe yesterday's drenching was the final straw. As I mentioned last night, she has little reserve to fight such a serious infection. I wish there was a decent hospital close by that I could remove her to, but the best ones are in London. I doubt she will survive the journey."

Giles looked at his friend in shock. "She is that sick then?"

Theo nodded. "I have rarely seen someone so unwell. I fear we may lose her yet." As Theo uttered these words, Giles felt as though he had been punched. He could not countenance the idea this woman was going to die in his house. They had to keep trying everything.

"I refuse to let her die." Giles said quietly but firmly. She is a guest in my home and I am willing to try anything at all to help her survive." Theo stared at him, unsure what had prompted this; it seemed more than simple concern for a sick

44

visitor. They fell into a discussion about treatment. Theo was a clever man. He trained at St Bart's and was of the opinion that traditional remedies also had their place. He was against bloodletting, as he had never seen it applied with any success and often consulted with apothecaries regarding the efficacy of herbal medications. As they were talking, there was movement from the bed and all heads turned to the woman, who was watching them intently.

Giles went over and asked how she was feeling. She shook her head, and Giles surmised this meant she wasn't feeling the best. He explained to her that she was seriously ill and they were trying to decide the best treatment. Theo added his opinion and the woman listened, her brow furrowed as she tried to concentrate.

"White willow," she whispered. Giles looked at her, not sure he'd heard correctly and asked her to repeat herself. With a huge effort she did so, "White willow," then paused, as a memory flickered but skittered off before she could capture it. Another breath. "Elderberry and garlic." The four standing around the bed just stared at her. She nodded and spoke again. "Blend in hot water or wine, works wonders." Then, "For my bruises, arnica, rubbed on." Theo was jotting this down. He had heard of these remedies but was astounded that a gentle-born woman would have even the slightest knowledge of such things. He started to ask her a question, but the effort had been too much and she slipped back into unconsciousness.

Giles, Ellen and Theo stepped outside the room, talking in the hall so they wouldn't disturb their guest.

"Can we get hold of these things?" Giles demanded. Theo nodded,

"Assuredly. I am simply in awe she would even know of them. They are old remedies, not used much nowadays. I had forgotten about them, but I am certain I can find them locally. I will go straight after breakfast on the morrow."

Thomas appeared to tell them dinner was to be served in ten minutes if that was acceptable. Giles thanked his butler, confirming they would be down shortly.

Poking his head into the bedroom, Theo ran his expert eye over the woman, but she slept. Her breathing was relatively steady, despite the wheezing and her colour not too high. He believed he could relax over a meal for an hour or so. Asking Ellen to call him if anything changed, Theo followed Giles down the stairs.

Sitting in the dining room, the two men waited until the meal had been served and their glasses filled with a rather tasty, full-bodied red wine before they continued with their discussion. It kept them going throughout dinner and well into the evening. Theo checked on the woman several times, but it seemed she had fallen into a stupor. At least she wasn't tossing and turning, but she was very deeply asleep, and now Theo was starting to worry she may never wake from it. He shared his fears with Giles who still stubbornly refused to accept she might not recover.

"What is it about this woman Giles?" Theo asked his friend as the evening drew to a close.

"I don't know, Theo," Giles replied, "there's just something about her, as though my finding her was meant to be. I'm still certain we have met before." He paused. "Oh I know that seems absurd, but it keeps niggling at me and I'm damned if I'm going to sit back and let her die." Giles' voice had risen in his frustration and he took a deep breath, getting himself under control. He shook his head. "If only we knew her name."

Theo grinned at Giles, commenting maybe it was her striking eyes and pretty hair that dazzled him. Giles was about to refute this hotly, when he caught Theo's lips twitching, realising that his friend was needling him. He relaxed suddenly and laughed.

"Hark at me, pragmatic lord of the manor all upset over some chit he doesn't know."

Theo wasn't fooled for a second but diverted their conversation away from the woman, asking Giles about the estate. That kept them occupied for the remainder of the evening and it was late by the time the two men turned in. Giles accompanied Theo to the Rose Room to check on their guest, but Ellen said she hadn't stirred.

Giles was exhausted and expected to fall asleep quickly. He found he couldn't, however, concern for the woman along the corridor playing on his mind. In the end, after trying to settle for a couple of hours, he got up and, pulling on his dressing gown, padded along to where she slept. Knocking quietly, he entered. Ellen was sitting in a chair near the bed; Sally had gone to get a well-earned rest.

"How is she, Ellen?" he asked in undertones. His housekeeper shrugged her shoulders.

"There doesn't seem to be any change, my Lord. She sleeps still, she has not moved since she spoke earlier this evening. Her breathing is somewhat easier and she hasn't had a repeat of the night terrors like last evening, but she is so frail." Ellen bit her lip, not wanting to say what everyone feared.

"I know, Ellen, you all think she will likely die but I will not give up on her. If we can get her through this night and Theo can find those ingredients, maybe they will mitigate the symptoms, allowing her body to start healing itself." His words were harshly spoken and he could have kicked himself; Ellen did not deserve to be spoken to in such a way. He apologised, something Ellen waved aside.

"Do not fret, my Lord. We are all worried."

Giles, smiled slightly and accepting, tired as he was, sleep would elude him a while longer, stayed with Ellen, the two of them chatting as they kept vigil. Sometime in the dark reaches of the night the woman stirred, muttering unintelligibly; at least it seemed to be unintelligible until Giles realised that she was speaking French. He stared at Ellen — French? Was she French? Her English was excellent and she had no accent, but right now she sounded as though she had been born and raised in Paris.

Ellen shifted uncomfortably, the same thought racing through both of their minds. Giles' recalled the newspaper report. Were they inadvertently harbouring a French spy?

Chapter Six

Giles shook his head, impossible! He refused to favour such an idea. There was another, perfectly reasonable explanation for her ability to speak French. It could be that a family member was French, or that she learned it at her governess' knee. Maybe her father was an academic and taught her the language so she could translate texts. Under no circumstance was she a spy.

While all this was running through his head, the woman roused, muttering and moving restlessly, hectic colour flaring up her cheeks. Arms flailing, hoarse cries tore at her throat as whoever or whatever it was tormenting her thoughts returned to plague her. Ellen tried to wake her to no avail, and unable to watch her suffering, Giles simply repeated his actions of the previous night. Lifting the trembling woman into his arms, he talked to her in soothing tones, rocking her until she calmed down. It took some doing, her nightmares refusing to relinquish their grasp, but eventually her cries quietened, her shudders slowed and her body relaxed.

At one point she opened her eyes and looked straight at him for what felt like a lifetime, although it was probably less than a minute. He couldn't tell whether she recognised him or even realised he was holding her but she obviously felt safe with him for her lips curved into a brief smile as sleep reclaimed her.

Ellen was watching him, eyebrows arched, silently asking what on earth he thought he was doing. He grinned diffidently.

"This helped last night; she slept while I rocked her. It seems to allay her fears. Surely it is better for all of us that she sleep than spend all night tossing and screaming." He winked at his housekeeper. "Don't you trust me, Ellen?" Ellen tried to glare at her employer, but failed. He was right; if this was the only way she could get a decent rest, this is what they would have to do. Giles shifted his position on the bed, getting comfortable; the woman never stirred. He remembered her reticule and again speculated as to whether it held anything that might help them.

Ellen returned to her chair and the two continued their conversation, until weariness claimed Giles and he fell asleep. The rest of the night passed uneventfully. Giles woke at dawn, the woman in his arms still fast asleep. Her colour was less fevered, her breathing not so laboured and he finally dared to hope she might pull through. With Ellen's help, he laid his guest carefully back onto the bed, drawing the bedclothes over her and making sure she was tucked in. Her chestnut hair was splayed riotously over the white pillows, dark eyelashes and the angry bruise on her jawline stark against her pale cheeks. He stared at the woman for long moments, recognition teasing at his consciousness, but refusing to be pinned it down. Storing it away for now, he told Ellen that he was going to wash and dress, suggesting that since she had barely slept for the better part of two days she might like to retire to her chambers to snatch some sleep herself.

Ellen made no comment, knowing all she'd be doing would be sorting herself out for the day ahead. Catching up on sleep was a luxury she did not have time to indulge in. She managed some rest during the night and hopefully, if the woman lying so peacefully in the bed was on the mend, she could chance a proper night's sleep tonight.

Wise to his housekeeper's reasoning, Giles pulled the cord by the bed. Sally arrived barely two minutes later, knocking softly and slipping in to take over. Giles mentioned that Ellen needed to sleep and no one was to disturb her. Sally nodded and Giles ushered his exhausted housekeeper out of the room, watching as she dragged herself along the corridor to her own quarters.

"I mean it, Ellen, I don't want to see you until at least midday. You are no good to anyone in this state. This house will not fall down around its ears if you are unavailable for half a day."

She turned and smiled, thanking him, before disappearing through the door connecting the staff's quarters to the main house. Giles stuck his head back into the Rose Room.

"Sally, if Mrs Grey gets up before noon, you have my permission to take her straight back to bed. We don't need her to take ill as well."

Sally grinned and said she would make sure his wishes were carried out. "The lady seems less poorly this morning, your Lordship. Did she sleep?"

"After a fashion. She had night terrors again but we were able to calm her down. I agree though she does seem slightly better this morning. Thank you, Sally, I will be back soon."

Giles walked slowly along to his bedchamber, mulling over his next move with this unknown visitor. They desperately needed to know who she was and why she was travelling on her own and on foot. He let ideas play around his head while he washed and dressed, digging out warm clothes, for the house felt chilly, the weather finally on the turn. Lastly, he pulled on a pair of winter boots, then made his way downstairs to the kitchens. His staff was already bustling about preparing the meals for the day, and he checked with Sarah about a small bowl of porridge for their guest.

"Apparently she ate it all yesterday, so maybe try her with a larger portion today. Theo says she is malnourished so we need to tempt her tastebuds."

Sarah asked how their guest was faring, so Giles gave all who were in the room a quick update, then left them to it, telling Thomas he was going for a walk, requesting breakfast be served in about an hour.

The morning was very cold, the first frost of autumn turning the grass white and covering the trees in an icy gauze. Giles was thankful for his heavy coat as he strode out along the footpaths. The sun was beginning its journey across the sky, slowly erasing the long shadows that clung to the earth in a vain attempt to hold onto the night. Falling leaves created a carpet of colour and the air was crisp. Giles loved this time of year. He loved the vaporous morning fog and the frosty ground. He loved the smell of bonfires in the air and the change in the light. Recently one of his sisters gifted him a newly published volume of poetry and his favourite was about autumn, the writer calling it the season of mists and mellow fruitfulness, which seemed to Giles the perfect description.

An hour later, he walked into the dining room to find a hot breakfast awaiting him. He tucked in, going back for a second helping, before taking a large cup of hot coffee through to his study. Thomas had placed the daily papers on his desk and Giles scanned them absently, his mind running over the other tasks he needed to attend to that day. As he was glancing through the papers, an article caught his eye. A fire in one of the fashionable London streets left at least three dead and several injured. The name of the street was familiar and he realised it was less than half a mile from his own city residence.

He read the snippet carefully. The house, owned by a Viscount Ashbourne, had been gutted and although it was presumed an unattended candle had been the cause of the blaze, there seemed to be some question as to the veracity of this. The staff who survived swore they doused all the candles. It was unclear who was killed in the blaze; three bodies had been recovered but they were burned beyond recognition. However, after questioning the staff and neighbours, three men including the Viscount had not been seen since that night. The only other family members were a son and a daughter, ages not noted and whereabouts unknown.

Giles re-read the article, unsure what it was about it that nagged at him. He knew of the Viscount as they met occasionally on parliamentary committees, recalling he had even visited his house once or twice. Further, although Ashbourne was one of the few peers who were actively trying to resolve the problem of poverty, Giles didn't believe this alone was enough to warrant an attempt on his life. That there appeared to be children, who were missing also, bothered him.

Perusing through the rest of the paper, Giles' attention was drawn again to the issue of French operatives. The garbled mutterings of his visitor played through his head and he wondered whether a trip to the city was in order. Pushing the papers aside, he tilted back in his chair and rested his feet on the edge of the desk. He'd only just come home and did not relish the idea of returning to the hubbub of the capital so soon. His mother and sisters remained in the city, looking forward to the usual round of winter parties and events, but he intended to stay on at his estate throughout the autumn and winter. The thought of London in such weather most unappealing.

His coffee long finished and no decision made, Giles got up and went upstairs to check on his guest. Sally told him she ate all her breakfast and drank some hot sweet tea. She was sleeping again, but apparently had not coughed once and her breathing sounded easier. Rather than disturb the woman, Giles simply thanked his housemaid, leaving her to it.

Theo — who owing to several other patients requiring his care, left very early — arrived about an hour later and went to examine his patient before coming to find Giles, who had returned to his study and was buried in estate matters. Thomas brought in two large cups of steaming hot coffee and a plate of fresh-baked ginger biscuits. The two men discussed the woman in the Rose Room for a little while, Theo being of the same opinion as Sally, in the hope she had turned the corner. He was able to procure the herbal ingredients the woman asked for, and Sarah was steeping them in hot water in readiness for when she next awoke. In addition, Theo managed to find some arnica, the pungent remedy to be massaged over the bruised skin.

They discussed the newspaper articles that were bothering Giles, who also commented that the woman upstairs had been muttering in French the previous night. Theo suddenly snapped his fingers.

"Sorry, I completely forgot, apparently a couple of days ago a carriage was found overturned along the London road about two miles from the Cross Keys," this being the alehouse on the outskirts of the village. "Seems a man was found dead under the wheels."

Giles stared at his friend. There was something very odd going on. To be fair, death by carriage was not all that unusual, but in Giles' mind there was more to it — an upturned carriage; a dead man; a woman soaked to the skin, injured and with no memory; a town house gutted by fire; and French agents.

On their own, each would seem unimportant, but it was their proximity to each other in time that bothered him. As he explained his theory to his friend, it did sound rather half-baked, but the more they talked about it, the more certain Giles became that there was some connection. He just couldn't work out what it was.

Chapter Seven

Both men came to the conclusion, until they knew who this woman was, they were clutching at straws. Giles remembered the reticule and said he would take it to her later in the day along with the strange clasp. Agreeing to return that evening for dinner, Theo went back up to the Rose Room to check on the woman and to make sure the new treatments were ready. Giles said he was going to take Zeus out and ride over to where the carriage had been seen.

Letting Thomas know where he was going, Giles strolled over the stone flagged courtyard to the stables and, saddling his huge stallion, set off across the fields. The sun was high in the sky now, but its meagre warmth had done little to melt the frost and the ground was like iron. The Cross Keys was at the far side of the village on the road that travelled west, but it wasn't far and Giles was there in well under half an hour. Circling the horse in order to take a good look, Giles noticed the carriage was badly damaged and tipped over halfway into a ditch.

Dismounting, he walked around the area, taking note of the rutted ground and the direction the carriage was facing. Just before the ditch, there looked to be two sets of tracks, quite recent if he wasn't mistaken. Had there been two carriages trying to pass and one misjudged the gap, or was it something less benign? He spent quite some time studying everything then, mindful of the icy ground, gingerly edged his way down to the upturned vehicle and peered inside. Nothing to give him any indication as to whose carriage it was — no bag, papers or even a cloak. There were a couple of damp and muddy travel rugs but they had no identifying marks.

Very odd.

Giles clambered back up onto the road and remounted Zeus, trotting along for another mile or so, but there was nothing else to be seen. Obviously the body had been removed and Giles made a mental note to ask Theo whether they had been able to glean the man's identity. Retracing his steps, he travelled the road in the opposite direction on the off chance;

but to his disappointment there was nothing this way either. Just as he was about to turn for home, Giles noticed a flutter of white in a bush off to one side. Nudging Zeus over to it, he saw what looked like a piece of torn cloth coated in mud.

Dismounting again, he carefully unhooked the item, surprised to discover it was actually two sheets of paper stuck together, a heavy vellum like that of a legal document. Tucking it into the breast pocket of his riding coat, he got back up onto Zeus who was pawing the ground in distaste, fed up with all this standing around. Clicking the stallion into a gallop, Giles let the horse have his head. They flew across the ground, Zeus' long strides eating up the miles. Rather than going straight home, Giles swung around the back of the village, allowing his horse to tire himself. It was nearly two hours later before they finally slithered into the stable courtyard, both man and beast panting with exhilaration. Giles, aware he had been out much longer than intended, handed the reins to Will who walked Zeus over to the trough where the stallion quenched his thirst, spraying water over all and sundry. Giles grinned and strode into the house, removing his boots at the door and sliding his feet into more comfortable house shoes.

Shouting a hello to his staff as he walked passed the kitchen, Giles went to his bedchamber and changed, dropping his shirt into the linen basket neatly placed at one side of his wardrobe. Rinsing the dust off his face and neck and retrieving a fresh shirt from its hanger, Giles gathered up the reticule, clasp and papers and hurried along the hall to the Rose Room. Wrapped in a huge dressing gown, the bedcovers tucked snugly around her, the young woman was awake and sitting up, sipping at a hot drink. Her face lit up as he entered the bedchamber, causing his heart to do a weird flip-flop in his chest.

"Good morning, my Lady," he said, "I trust you are feeling a little better."

"Thank you, my Lord, I am finally able to breathe without feeling as though my chest will split in two and have not coughed once this morning. Sally is very pleased with me." Her eyes, though slightly dulled from illness, twinkled as she said this, making Sally laugh.

"You are a model patient, Miss. If I could just persuade you to eat a little more, I'd be very happy."

"I will try at the next meal, Sally," she responded, smiling at the maid. "I'm afraid I cannot promise, but this draft will start to work soon; it is most efficacious. I do not wish to be a burden on your household."

Giles sat down in the chair next to the bed and looked at his guest. He wasn't sure how she was going to react to what he had to say, so was trying to think how best to phrase it.

"You are not a burden, and you are welcome to stay here until you are recovered fully. Now, if you feel up to it, there are one or two things I feel we should discuss. I have discovered items that may or may not be yours. Before we get to them, however, I would like to talk to you about something I read this morning. I do not know whether any are connected to you and one is quite shocking, but if they are, it might help your memory. Are you willing to hear what I have to say?"

She stared at him for long moments, trying to process what he meant. "So you fear what you tell me might be more than I can handle?" she questioned him.

Giles nodded. "If what I have read relates to you, it will be…" he paused, "…upsetting at the very least and I do not wish to impede your recovery. I believe, however, that knowing who you are will help us determine how you came to be here, soaked to the skin and apparently miles from home."

She held his gaze, her astonishingly green eyes penetrating his until he felt that she had reached right into his soul, and for a split second everything around him faded into insignificance. The world righted itself and the woman was speaking. Giles dragged his attention back to what she was saying.

"…so, yes, I am willing to hear what you have to say." Ignoring the fact he missed her first few words, Giles simply acknowledged her response and began to tell her about the newspaper article.

He explained about the fire, which had destroyed a town house in London. He then went on to say three people were found dead in its ruins and the owner of the home was missing, possibly one of the deceased. Before mentioning the owner by name, he went on to tell her about the upturned carriage and the dead man found under it. As he was telling her this, she began to tremble. He watched her closely as he continued to talk, saying that he'd found a reticule, that she was carrying a rather interesting clasp and that he'd discovered some documents stuck in a bush.

He handed her the reticule. She opened it, lifting out a coin purse — which was full — a lacy handkerchief and some soggy looking squares of paper. These may well have been her calling cards, which would have had her name on them. She turned them this way and that, her face registering no recognition of the purse or its contents, passing each piece over to Giles once she examined them.

She heaved a huge sigh and rubbed her hand over her brow in confusion —

"They may well be mine but, unfortunately, I do not recognise them. It seems so very little to be carrying, had I indeed been travelling some distance."

Giles patted her hand. "Do not fret, my Lady. I did however notice that you reacted when I mentioned the carriage. Do you recall something of this?" She wrinkled her nose in concentration, the gesture making him want to kiss it. Determined not to let such impulses distract him, he forced them aside and waited as she collected her thoughts. She spoke so quietly, he had to lean closer to hear her words.

"I remember being in a carriage that seemed to be going more quickly than it should, but I can't recall why. It was jolting badly and I feared a wheel would come loose. There was a man inside with me and another driving." Her voice began to rise, agitation threading through her tones. "There was a second carriage. I-I think it was chasing the one I was in, they were both going too fast. It was raining, the wheels kept slipping in the mud and suddenly I was thrown to one side as the carriage tipped. It rolled and landed with a deafening crack. I fell against the open window. I recall dampness, maybe mud, and that I was covered with something, possibly my cloak. Then I heard another loud noise and wondered whether the other carriage had also overturned. After that — nothing." She started to breathe too quickly, images flooding her mind. "Oh no, what happened? What happened to the people in the carriage with me? You said one was killed. What about the other man? Who were they? How did I manage to get to where you found me?"

Giles took her hand and Sally came over to sit at the other side of the bed.

"Please do not panic, you are safe in my home. We will find out what happened and who was involved and make sure they cannot harm you. No one knows you are here, well only my staff and Theo, and they will not share that information with strangers."

Giles' voice soothed her, the terror retreating for the moment. Her eyes searched his. "What about the fire? Whose house was burnt? You must think I might know or you would not have mentioned it."

Aware of her distress, Giles hesitated, but it was too late, he had to tell her everything. "It was the home of Viscount Ashbourne, Edgar Caswell."

She stared at him, the last vestiges of colour leaching from her already pale face. "No, no, no. It couldn't be." Her whispered denial was enough for Giles. She knew the viscount; of that much he was certain.

Squeezing the small hand that he had been holding for longer than propriety allowed, he said gently, "The viscount has not been seen since the night of the fire and they say he has two children whose whereabouts are unknown."

"Stephen. His son is called Stephen." She stopped abruptly. Then in a tone of complete surprise, "He is my brother. I have a brother." Her face brightened, then darkened just as quickly. "Was he one of the men killed in the fire?" Giles couldn't answer that. "If he is my brother, surely I should know my name?"

"Maybe this will help," said Giles, giving her the clasp. The woman held the splendid piece, her fingers tracing the setting. She stared at it for quite some time before murmuring something about it being a gift from a grateful soldier. Giles was perplexed; it didn't seem like something a soldier would wear. The sunlight through the window caught the facets of the red stone and it flickered, sending ruby sparks shimmering across the coverlet on the bed. She rolled it around in her palm and then suddenly she froze. She was still for so long, Giles started to worry. He was just wondering whether he needed to shake the life back into her when the woman lifted her head, her eyes locking with those of the earl who gazed at her with such concern.

"My name is Willow."

Chapter Eight

Giles gaped at her. *That couldn't be right. Surely she was jesting. Willows were trees.* He began to think this guest in his home was losing her mind, that whatever happened traumatised her to such an extent, all reason had left her. He started to speak but she shushed him maybe rather curtly, causing Sally to gasp at this perceived discourtesy. Giles shook his head; he didn't want to interrupt her train of thought, worried she might clam up on them.

"My mother wanted to name me Willow. She said that willow trees never broke, that even in the worst storm they might bend but they never snapped. She wanted me to be like that. She said life had a funny way of throwing obstacles in your path and sometimes they might seem onerous enough to break you. A willow would only lean and as the adversity passed would once again stand tall," she revealed, whimsically. "She was half French and an artist, possibly a little eccentric, maybe that was part of it." The woman, Willow, looked at Giles, her head cocked to one side as she recounted this. "Stephen and my father call me Billie, it is less…frivolous. Also, I'm not tall like a willow tree and totally unrefined, so Billie seemed a better fit."

Without warning, she gurgled with laughter, launching into a tale about something that happened in her childhood, demonstrating just how un-willow-like she was, but halfway through she burst into tears; deep racking sobs, shocking both Giles and Sally who were laughing along with her as she described her exploits. The sobs set her off coughing and, without thinking, Giles gathered her into his arms, running his large hand down her back trying to steady her breathing. It was several minutes before Willow was able to recover her composure, shrinking back into herself as she did so. Unconsciously, she nestled against Giles while he calmed her, but now gently disentangled herself, feeling rather lost without his arms around her. Confused by the direction her thoughts were taking, and determined to read nothing into her host's actions, she took a deep breath and banished it to the back of her mind, trying to concentrate on the matter at hand.

Sally came around the bed and poured another glass of the draft Willow asked them to concoct for her, helping the distraught woman to sip some of its contents.

"I'm so sorry, I'm so sorry, I do not know what came over me." Her voice was stilted. "I am a guest in your home, it does not behove me to cry like a baby."

Giles watched her as she spoke, recognising that she was hanging onto her control for dear life and a touch of sympathy would set her off again. Willow bit her lip, and it was all Giles could do not to drag her back into his arms and kiss her until the light came back into her eyes. As it was, he did nothing of the kind and sat quietly, unwilling to break her train of thought. It was more important to get the information out of her than worry about all the other emotions swirling around.

"So, let us talk about what we know," he said, infusing practicality into his tones. "Your name is Willow, you are the daughter of Viscount Ashbourne and you have a brother called Stephen. Both these latter two seem to be missing. You were in a carriage accident and maybe you banged your head when it rolled over. This or getting thoroughly drenched might explain your loss of memory. We need to find out how you came to be so badly bruised though and how you managed to be out walking for such a long time when the carriage was only a mile or so from the village, but we can leave that for another time. Oh, and we have these papers."

Giles leaned across to the bedside table and lifted the frayed paper, having been able to pry the sheets apart without tearing them. Most of the writing had disappeared, the ink dissolved by the weather, but a few words remained. Willow studied the papers, turning them over and over, trying to guess what had been written on the pages. There were a few words, which might become more distinguishable once they could be read in a better light, but three seemed somewhat clearer. One was obviously 'Cornwall,' then two, that were possibly 'ruin' and 'cliff,' however this was only a best guess; some of the letters were blurred.

"Anything?" asked Giles. She looked at him, confusion clouding her eyes.

"I'm not sure. I feel I should know what Cornwall means. Something is teasing at the edges of my brain, but I cannot hold on to it." Mystified, she dropped the papers onto the bed, resting her head in her hands. Giles took the documents, placing them in the bedside drawer along with the reticule and its contents. Then he picked up the clasp that Willow had placed beside her on the bed.

"I think we should put this in my safe," he said, "it is too costly a gem not to be secured." Willow nodded, relinquishing the clasp with obvious reluctance. "Trust me, Miss Caswell," Giles said softly. She smiled shyly at him and then asked hesitantly.

"Please, would it be too much of an imposition to ask that you call me Billie, rather than Miss Caswell or Willow? Miss Caswell seems much too formal a title for someone who has been languishing in one of your guest rooms for the last two days and I always think my mother is going to tell me off when I hear my proper name."

Giles grinned and said he would be happy to, and Sally added that she thought it a lovely name. Billie, as she would now be called, smiled again, but was looking rather fatigued. Giles was worried they had overtaxed her.

"Maybe we could talk again about this later? There are other things I feel I must discuss with you, but I can see you are tiring, so I will leave you to get some rest. I will also try to find out everything I can about the fire; maybe your father and brother were not home when it happened." He wasn't sure whether he believed that, but he felt his guest needed something to cling to. Also it seemed probable someone was indeed following her and they needed to find out why. Billie stared at him while he was speaking and again he felt that jolt of recognition, but he had never met anyone called Willow, of that he was absolutely certain. He could not figure it out. She let out a tremulous breath and snuggled under the covers. Her eyelids were already drooping and before Giles stood up, she was asleep.

"I believe she will get better now, my Lord." Sally said. "I think she was fretting over who she was and even though her memories might be frightening, at least she has them. Now she knows who she is, and she thinks someone might be after her. If she had not recalled this, she could be in danger, unaware until 'tis too late."

Giles agreed and the two of them talked quietly about keeping a close eye on Billie. As they were talking, Ellen appeared and they updated her on what had happened. Ellen frowned, concern written all over her kindly face.

"Poor mite. So, it looks as though she's lost her father and her brother and someone else is after her. I wonder where her mother is. How on earth are we going to get to the bottom of this?"

"I am hoping, as her memories become clearer, she might recall what the men in the carriage looked like and be able to give us a description of them. I am going to send a letter to my man in London and ask him to make enquiries into that fire and also the Caswell family. We need to know whether this fire was an accident or whether someone deliberately targeted them. Billie's mother is half French, which explains the mutterings last night, but there are those who are searching out anyone who worked for the government during the war and this French connection might prove rather perilous." The two women nodded their agreement. "Anyway, I'm going to have a quiet chat with the rest of my staff while you two lovely ladies get on with whatever you need to get on with. Thank you very much for all your help, you are invaluable to me." Both women blushed. Giles was a good employer and he was quick to praise. Still after a long couple of days it warmed the heart to hear it.

"Get on with you, my Lord," bustled Ellen. "I thought I heard Thomas saying something about hot coffee in your study." She hustled her master along the corridor and Giles complied, grinning wickedly as he went down the stairs taking two at a time as usual. He strolled into the kitchens, asking whether it was convenient to have a moment of their time. Waiting until everyone was settled, he proceeded to tell them about Willow. It took a little time as, inevitably, the staff had questions, but eventually he covered everything. He did warn them not to say anything about her to anyone, not even to their friends in the village, as they could inadvertently be overheard telling others. He wanted to keep Willow's whereabouts under wraps until they knew with whom or what they were dealing. Then he went over to the stables and had the same discussion with Will and the rest of his estate staff. Satisfied he had done all he could for now to keep his guest protected, he went back to his study where a fresh cup of steaming hot coffee waited.

He spent some time drafting a missive to send to his man in London, an old army friend who had undertaken some investigative work for him in the past, very trustworthy and discreet. Giles paid handsomely for his services but it was well worth it, especially as he was happy to recommend the man to others of his friends should they suddenly have a sensitive matter that required a delicate touch. Once finished, he laid it on the platter ready to be collected with any other mail.

Absorbed in scrutinising the financial aspects of his estate, lunch came and went. Giles ate whatever it was Thomas brought him with little regard for what was on the plate. He drank several cups of ambrosial coffee and didn't realise how late it was until Theo was announced.

"Theo! Come in, come in." Giles met his friend with a firm handshake. "Have you been up to see our guest yet?"

"No, I thought to see you first. Any news to share?" Giles updated his friend on what had happened and that they finally knew their guest's name. "Hmm, she appears to be Ashbourne's daughter. I have met him a few times, a good man. Have you seen anything else in the newspapers about whether it was his body in the fire?" Theo questioned. Giles shook his head. "Interesting, so they still have not identified any of those who died, or if they have it is not public knowledge. Neither do we know who was killed in that carriage accident, although I have a written description so I can discuss it with — what did you say her name was? — Billie? Curious sort of name for a girl that. This tale is becoming more intriguing by the day."

Giles grinned explaining Billie was short for Willow.

"Good lord, that's even more peculiar." Theo chuckled. "Right, I shall go and check up on Billie," shaking his head. "That is going to take some getting used to."

Saying he'd follow his friend in a few minutes, allowing the doctor time to examine his patient without interference, Giles concluded his business and finished the last of his coffee. Ringing the bell, he informed Thomas, Theo would be joining him for dinner, and then went upstairs to see how Billie was doing.

The bedroom was warm, the fire blazing merrily and a bitter aroma hung in the air. He noticed Ellen was massaging something over Billie's bruises; he assumed this must be the arnica. While Ellen worked, Theo was carrying on what looked like a very serious conversation with Billie, who was looking up at the doctor in rapt attention. Giles felt an odd sensation run through him, a flicker of something — was it anger, jealousy? — gnawed at him. Perturbed by the direction of his thoughts, he ignored them and caught the end of Theo's question.

"...does that sound like anyone you might know?" Billie chewed on her bottom lip, concentrating on the person Theo was describing, the absent-minded action drawing Giles' gaze to Billie's mouth and he imagined rubbing his thumb over its soft pink plumpness. Forcing his mind back to the conversation, Giles was unnerved by his reactions when in the company of this young woman. Honestly — what was wrong with him!

Billie was running through some names, her voice, still very husky, pausing on each one, trying to decide whether any was the person who had been with her in the carriage. Giles approached the bed and listened. In undertones, Theo explained to his friend, these were the staff Billie remembered being part of their household, although some still eluded her. As she said the names Banks and Havers she paused, her brow creasing in concentration, but she shook her head and continued. A few more names followed, some immediately discounted as they belonged to women. She paused again and went back to Banks and Havers, rubbing her forehead distractedly.

"These names are bothering me. I think Banks was our driver and Havers was one of our grooms. Banks, I can understand, he always drove our coach, but why would Havers be with me? Ordinarily, he would normally be working in the stables. Oh, this is so confusing. My brain feels as though there is a fog in it. There are so many things lurking, but I cannot make them clear." Billie looked up at the two men, her expression one of utter frustration. "I'm sorry, I don't think I am like this normally." Both men chuckled and Theo patted her arm.

"Do not worry, Miss Caswell, things will come back to you. I do not think there is any lasting damage to your memory. You just need to get well and let us know when you recall any other details."

She smiled at the doctor a little tremulously. "Has there been any more news about the…" she trailed off, unwilling to voice her fears about the burnt house and the bodies discovered therein.

"Not yet," replied Giles, "although I do have someone looking into it for me. I will let you know when I hear anything." He wondered whether this might be a good time to ask about her mother. Billie was watching him, her eyes reading his indecision.

"What is it, my Lord?" Giles wavered, still not certain he wanted to cause her any more unhappiness. "Please, whatever it is seems to worry you. Even if it is uncomfortable news, I would rather know."

"It is not news as much as a question you may find hard to answer." Giving up and taking the risk he asked, "Where is your mother? Is there a way we can get a message to her? If so, we could arrange someone to escort her here safely." Billie smiled wistfully.

"She is dead. She died nearly seven years ago when she was in France.

Chapter Nine

There was a long moment when no one spoke, then Giles apologised for reminding her of such a sad time. Billie was still staring at him, but her eyes were glazed; she was lost in memories and he wasn't even sure she heard his words.

"She was so beautiful, very tall with dark auburn hair, which glinted red in the sunlight. She was always there for Stephen and me when we were children. Papa was often away, but she never left us with a nursery-maid or governess in order to accompany him. Sometimes we all went. We travelled quite a lot when I was younger, mostly between here and France." Billie went on to describe their life, which seemed idyllic, living in a small French chateau on the banks of the Seine not far from Paris. Visits to the French capital, parties at their home, long days playing among cultivated grounds or riding horses. As she spoke, her gentle tones wove a spell around them, conjuring up happier times.

"Papa worked for the English government, I believe — well he still does — before the war, maybe something to do with the diplomatic corps. He met Maman at a ball when he was in Paris. She was the daughter of a French Vicomte with whom Papa had business dealings. We came back to England when I was twelve years old. It was too dangerous for us to stay in France. Maman had to return maybe three years later; her father was dying and asked for her. We never saw her again. Papa received a letter telling him she died after being thrown from her horse."

Billie looked at the two men who were listening closely to her story and she frowned at her thoughts, her face a mixture of sorrow and confusion. "It was very strange though. Maman was an excellent horsewoman. Her family had bred horses for years and she knew everything there was to know about them. It must have been something very bad to unseat her. Papa was unable to go there and bring her body home. The letter said she had been buried in the family mausoleum. He was devastated."

She stopped abruptly, not wanting to say anymore, feeling her long buried grief welling up. Pulling herself together, she straightened her shoulders, and brought her attention back to her host and the doctor.

Giles and Theo were looking at each other, several things running through their minds. They had a nobleman with political connections in Paris before the war, married to a French woman who had died in questionable circumstances. A home that mysteriously burnt to the ground, possibly killing said nobleman and his son. A dead carriage driver, a missing groomsman, and the daughter of the house finding herself lost in the middle of the countryside, injured and sick, with little memory of how she came to be there. It sounded like the plot from a Greek tragedy.

They realised Billie was waiting for them to say something. What was there to say? They had no answers for her. Giles was uneasy about the circumstances surrounding the death of her mother, and wondered whether there was more to it than a simple riding accident. Too many odd things were happening to this family and he was starting to think that they might well be related to the war and the intelligence service. Unwilling to share his suspicions quite yet, Giles said —

"Let me see what information my man in the city can turn up. There is no point speculating until he has had a chance to investigate. I appreciate this must be very worrying for you, Miss Caswell, but rest assured we will get to the bottom of whatever is going on. In the meantime, you need to concentrate on recovering. Do you think you might like to join us for dinner this evening?"

Unable to help herself, Billie glanced down at the night shift she was wearing. "Thank you, that sounds rather lovely, but I am afraid I do not have much of an appetite and I have not ... my clothes ... I don't know..."

Ellen, who had finished rubbing in the ointment and was tidying up the room, interjected. "My Lord, if Miss Caswell feels up to it, maybe we could find one of Lady Helena's dresses? They might be rather long, but I'm sure we could manage."

Giles smiled at his housekeeper gratefully. "Thank you, Ellen, that sounds just the ticket. There you are, Miss Caswell, problem solved and do not be concerned about your appetite, just eat what you can."

"What about the clothes I came … arrived … err … had on when you found me?" Billie asked diffidently. "Maybe I could wear them?" Ellen shook her head.

"They may need a little longer before they are presentable, Miss. They were sodden wet and very muddy."

Billie sighed. "It seems I am in your hands, Mrs Grey." Turning to Giles, she continued, "Thank you, my Lord, you are too generous. I hope Lady Helena will not mind."

"Lady Helena is in town with my mother, no doubt spending my hard-earned coin on a whole new wardrobe of dresses for the winter season." Giles replied, amusement playing around his mouth. "I imagine anything left here she considered unfashionable. Please help yourself. Ellen and Sally will assist."

Billie blushed rather becomingly at this, feeling at once warmed by her host's generosity while at the same time embarrassed she had nothing to wear — nothing at all. How was it that she was so far from home without a trunk or, at the very least, her valise? Try as she might, she still could not remember.

Noticing her disquiet, and feeling an absurd desire to comfort her, Giles knew he needed to remove himself, and pronto. His proximity to this elfin-like creature was doing very peculiar things to his body, and if he didn't walk away he would not be responsible for his actions.

"Hopefully, Theo and I will see you at dinner. We eat at seven." He bowed and, without waiting for a response, left the room quickly. Billie watched him go, unsure what it was about this man that made her feel so safe when he was close, yet despite there being two other people in the room with her, oddly alone when he left. No time to ponder this for Ellen was speaking to her.

"Do you think you can manage to accompany me to Lady Helena's rooms, Miss Caswell? It will be easier to choose there rather than I bring a whole pile along. There is a good mirror and we will be able to see which colours suit. I can lend an arm for support."

Billie nodded and got out of bed, shivering a little as her bare feet touched the cool floor. Ellen brought a thick dressing gown into which she wrapped Billie very snugly, and laid out a pair of warm slippers for her feet. Finally, a walking stick the housekeeper found in a cupboard in the hallway, was pressed into Billie's right hand. Then, suiting her suggestion to action, Ellen tucked Billie's left arm under hers and, mindful of her sprained ankle, helped the young woman to hobble along the maze of corridors to the far end of the large house and into a very feminine room.

"Oh, how lovely." Billie gasped. The room was decorated in shades of blue and cream, the fading afternoon sun highlighting the luxurious materials of the drapes and the rugs. Ellen lit several candles brightening the room further, and moved to a huge wardrobe, opening the doors to reveal a multitude of dresses in every colour imaginable. Billie sank onto the pristine bed, dumbstruck. She knew, even if she could remember everything, she had never seen so many dresses in her life.

Ellen smiled at Billie's reaction. Lady Helena loved clothes and as the youngest daughter, had been rather indulged. Glancing at Billie, then back at the dresses, Ellen chose several she thought might appeal to their guest. Billie's dark hair and green eyes begged to be accentuated by vibrant colours. Before Billie had a chance to look at the gowns, Ellen had whipped off the dressing gown and ushered her into the first one. It was of deep turquoise, in fine velvet, the classical style with its empire waistline flattering Billie's delicate features.

It was ridiculously long, but Ellen told her not to worry about that, plus it needed a bit of tucking here and there, the clever fingers of the housekeeper making sure the line of the dress did not alter. The simplicity of the design was offset by a touch of lace at the neck and some intricate embroidery along the hemline and sleeves. Two more gowns, one in emerald the other a dramatic russet, both in silk were included along with a couple of simple wool dresses in softer shades, the warm material more suitable for everyday wear. Then Ellen added underclothes, chemise, stays and petticoats — all exquisitely made.

Billie started to feel rather overwhelmed by it all; she had no intention of staying here long enough for all these clothes to be worn. She only needed a couple of dresses to get her through the next few days until she was well enough to take her leave without seeming impolite. She definitely wouldn't need anything as gorgeous as these gowns, but how could she explain this to Ellen, who was obviously in her element, and without appearing ungrateful?

"Excuse me, Mrs Grey, isn't there a morning dress I could borrow? These are so fine, I hardly think you need to alter such beautiful dresses when I may wear them only once…" Billie's tone was hesitant and rather pensive, suddenly feeling quite sad that she would have to leave this warm and friendly place. Shrugging that aside, she straightened her shoulders. "…and I don't think I could wear stays at the moment, my ribs…" faltering as she saw Ellen's expression. "Please, don't think I'm not grateful. I am, very much so, but I will have to leave soon and then these dresses…" Billie stopped speaking, biting her lip and feeling useless tears well up in her eyes. She would not cry; she could deal with whatever life threw at her, she was after all, a willow.

Ellen came over to where Billie was sitting.

"My dear, these *are* morning dresses. Lady Helena's ball gowns and evening attire are in her dressing room." Billie gaped at the housekeeper who stifled a laugh. "Now, come along, let's get you back to your warm bedroom, I've kept you too long away from the fire." Gathering everything in her arms and refusing Billie's offer of help, Ellen led the way back to the Rose Room. By the time they reached it, Billie was shivering. Ellen dropped the clothes on a convenient chair, hustling their guest back into bed, drawing up the sheets and blanket and tucking the luxurious comforter up around her chin. Ellen checked the fire and collected the pile of clothes and before the housekeeper had left the room Billie was fast asleep.

Ellen roused the young woman a couple of hours later, by which time Billie was feeling much less wrung out. The thought of an evening making polite conversation was daunting, but it would be churlish to refuse. His Lordship was kind enough to have a doctor treat her and allowed her to stay in his home, not to mention the clothes. Oh those clothes — Billie was still quite overcome by it all.

Sally appeared at the door with some hot water so Billie could freshen up, the scented water clearing the young woman's groggy head, and going a little way to removing the smell of arnica from her skin. The maid helped her dress, then spent some time on her hair. Catching the rich curls into a loose bun and sweeping Billie's fringe neatly off her forehead, leaving a few curls to frame her face. Completing the look, Sally threaded a ribbon, the same turquoise as the dress through the coils of the bun, letting the ends trail down Billie's neck.

Satisfied, Sally turned Billie so she could see herself in the long mirror. The young woman gasped — that couldn't possibly be her? She looked positively elegant and the dress fitted perfectly, its simple lines flowing softly to her ankles, flattering her slender frame.

"How did Mrs Grey manage this?" Billie asked the maid, stunned by her reflection. "She must have magic fingers." Sally chuckled.

"Mrs Grey loves sewing and Jane helped. The two of them could make a dress like this in half a day if they had no other duties. Very clever they are."

"I am in awe. I will thank her myself when I see her, but please pass on my gratitude for her help. This is above and beyond."

Sally smiled and said she would. "Now, Miss Caswell, 'tis time for dinner. There won't be a gong tonight, as 'tis just family, but I think they will be waiting for you in the library." Billie looked a bit flustered, having no clue where any of the rooms were, but Sally was way ahead of her. "Come, I will show you where it is." With one last glance in the mirror, and checking her hair was still in place, it having a tendency to fall out of any style it was twisted into no matter how tightly fixed, Billie picked up the walking stick, thankful of its support, and followed the maid down the stairs to the library.

Chapter Ten

Sally left her at the library door, and feeling unaccountably nervous not to mention a little out of place, Billie paused for a moment, smoothing her hands over her skirts. Then taking hold of herself, she knocked quietly. Thomas opened the door and, as she stepped over the threshold, Billie was mesmerised by the warm ambience of the octagonal-shaped room. Unsure quite what to do, she just stopped and soaked it all in. Heavy curtains in a dark bronze brocade-like material framed the large bay windows, which filled two of the room's walls, and several candelabra were arranged on every available surface, casting soft light over the space. The doctor and the Earl were leaning over a huge desk positioned at one side of the room totally engrossed in what appeared to be a map. A huge fireplace graced the wall opposite the desk, its flames crackling merrily, sending sparks up the chimney and creating lively shadows over the walls, which were lined with books.

Billie let out a delighted sigh and, leaving her stick at the door, involuntarily — if not rather unsteadily — moved towards the bookcases, her eyes running over the titles when she reached the first shelves, Greek mythology, and classical literature. She moved to the next shelf, Chaucer, Petrarch, and Thomas Malory. The list went on. Billie was captivated, her fingers stroking the spines as she murmured their titles. Suddenly she realised where she was and, mortified for being so forward, intended to slide back over to the door before anyone spotted her, but as she turned saw both men staring at her in amazement.

"Please forgive me. I saw the books and I couldn't help … what?" She frowned uncertain now. "What's wrong? Am I dressed incorrectly? Have I smudged my face?"

Theo got a hold of himself first.

"No, no, Miss Caswell, it's just…you look…" the doctor stumbled a little.

"…absolutely beautiful." Giles completed the sentence, his eyes locking with Billie's and for a moment it was as though they were the only two people in England, never mind the room. Billie felt everything begin to spin and her heart hammered in her chest. By sheer force of will she regained a modicum of control, but struggled to look away from the tall Earl whose gaze held her spellbound. Nerves made her giggle, the sound echoing through the room and bringing them back to earth. Giles bowed, asking Thomas to bring in drinks and the moment was gone.

"Thank you," Billie stammered, still rather dazed by the reaction of the two men and her host's smouldering stare. "This is all Mrs Grey's handiwork and of course Lady Helena's gorgeous dress. I do not think I have ever worn anything so fine. I hope I don't ruin it," the last said in rueful tones. Theo raised an eyebrow in question. "I think I'm a bit of a tomboy," she elaborated. "I think I rarely have need to dress up and my usual clothes tend to be much harder wearing than this." The two men were puzzled.

"Did you not have a Season, or a debutante ball?" asked Giles. "Your father is a viscount, surely he would have wanted you to be introduced into Society?"

"Oh, yes I remember having a Season. In fact I think I've had more than one. It was all rather tiresome." Billie's face crinkled in recollection. "I fear I do not care for Society and all its rules. You have to be so accomplished, be able to converse about nothing at all, smile simperingly at everyone, while trying not to look as though you are on the hunt for a wealthy husband. Listen politely to rich matrons as they point out the assets of Lord so-and-so or Duke whatshisname." She shuddered in distaste. "I can speak two languages, and understand both Latin and Greek. I can read and write, I love history and geography. I want to travel and see antiquities in their place, not in a book. I hate needlepoint, and cannot paint to save my life. I play the piano and have a tolerable voice, but hate being presented as some kind of performing animal."

Billie's voice rose in her agitation. "I have managed to avoid being handed over to some man like a piece of furniture to be admired from afar, and I have absolutely no intention of allowing anyone to decide the rest of my life for me." She wound up, standing in front of the two men, all not quite five feet of her, hands on hips, face flushed, eyes flashing green fire, and her unruly hair already beginning to fall out of its confined bun.

Giles and Theo gawked; her attitude was so unlike anything they were used to hearing that they weren't quite sure how to respond. Billie bit her lip, fearing she had gone too far, remembering how often her mother warned her to think before she spoke. Then she noticed Giles' lips were twitching and Theo was obviously trying not to laugh. She released a breath she did not realise she was holding, and smiled somewhat self-consciously.

"Oh, I do beg your pardon. Maman was always telling me not to let my tongue run away with my words."

Giles chuckled, he couldn't help it, she looked like a naughty child caught sneaking into the kitchens for cake. Theo joined him, the two men laughing wholeheartedly at the image Billie conjured up. Billie relaxed, glad she hadn't upset them, grinning in relief. The conversation slipped easily into mundane matters, and soon Thomas announced dinner was served.

Giles offered Billie his arm and shyly, she curled her fingers around his sleeve. They crossed the wide hallway to a room at the far side. The dining room was a study in refinement. A long mahogany table polished until you could see your face in the surface, napkins in a rich creamy colour — matching the lacy table runner — were placed neatly alongside the delicate china. As with the library, the room was lit by a multitude of candles, and warmed by a roaring fire in another massive hearth. The chairs were of a simple design, yet gracefully crafted, each seat made comfortable with cushions of striped cream and burgundy. Billie sighed in pleasure at the scene, as Giles escorted her to her seat, pulling the chair out for her.

During the meal, the three of them chatted animatedly about this and that. Billie managed to eat more than she thought she would, but still not enough. Kind enough not to draw attention to this, Theo asked to hear more about Billie's life in France, while Giles talked about the estate and upcoming winter events. As dessert was served, without thinking and forgetting their guest was a woman and not normally privy to such topics, the two men fell into a discussion about current politics and the issue of foreign agents. Billie listened to them, fascinated, before suddenly realising she knew something of what they were talking about. Dredging through her mind, she remembered her father talking about a similar thing with Stephen and that they had grave concerns. She let these thoughts roll around hoping to pin them down, but they kept skittering off.

Giving up, she brought her attention back to the conversation, trying to stay awake, weariness overtaking her. It was, after all, only a little over forty-eight hours since she had been carried in, near death. However, even knowing that it was not the done thing to fall asleep at the dining table, Billie no longer had any say in the matter. Desperately trying to stay awake long enough to get back to her room, she bit the inside of her lip and pinched her thigh. Nothing worked.

"Sir, my Lord, I'm sorry, I..." she never finished her sentence, exhaustion claimed her and, as she pushed her chair back intending to leave with as much grace as possible, she slid rather elegantly to the floor, the turquoise velvet puddling around her. Giles leaped from his seat and hurried around the table.

"We have kept her up far too long, Theo," Giles said, grimacing. "How could I have forgotten she has been so ill?"

"I do not think it will do her any permanent damage, Winchester. I suspect she is merely over-tired."

Giles swept the tiny woman into his arms, cradling her to his chest. She was very pale, but breathing easily. Her head lolled against his shoulder and he could feel her heart beating a little faster than it probably should be, which didn't help his own heart one jot. Carefully, he carried her back to the Rose Room, Theo following close behind. Sally was already in the room. The bed was turned down and the blazing fire had warmed the room thoroughly. Theo re-hung the bronchitis kettle over the flames, adding a few more drops of menthol. He didn't think Billie was going to relapse but thought it wise to be cautious.

Giles laid Billie on the bed and left Sally to undress her and tuck her in. The woman muttered something, but none who heard her could work it out. She tossed a little and then settled, sinking deeper into sleep. Glancing at the clock on the mantle, Giles realised it was later than he imagined; they had been talking for over three hours. No wonder she was tired. The two men, satisfied that Sally had everything in hand, left her to it and returned to the library for a nightcap.

The next morning, Billie did not stir until quite late, but when she did, she was none the worse for her late night, managing to join the two men again for dinner in the evening. Giles arranged for it to be served earlier than the previous night, and Billie was able to return to her chambers at a much more respectable hour for one still recuperating.

The following days fell into a routine. Once awake, Ellen or Sally helped Billie dress for the day and, after she ate a light meal, helped her downstairs. If she had to spend hours on her own while Giles saw to the business of his estate, Billie preferred to do so in the library. It was always comfortable and the view from the huge windows was breathtaking.

Built on a slight rise, the house had a commanding view out over the gardens and to the Great Park beyond. Billie often curled up on the window seat and just admired the scenery, entranced by the colours in the autumnal light. The weather had turned much colder, heavy frost hung from the trees for most of the day, and coated the grass in white crystals. Winters in Billie's memory were spent either in France where the climate had been rather milder, or in London, where all she could remember were grey days and slushy pavements.

During these quiet hours, something about Cornwall continued to tease at her memory until one day, more than two weeks after she had arrived at Whiteoaks and while she was engrossed in Petrarch's *Letters to Laura*, images began to form in her head. A house standing on a cliff edge, white sands below, a village nestled near the sea at the bottom of a winding road and soft salty breezes lifting her hair. But where it was or when she was there was lost to her. Where was this place? She needed to describe it to Giles and Theo; there was a chance that they might know.

Frustrated at how long it was taking for her memory to return, Billie laid the book on her lap and leaned back against the window frame. She was feeling much better, although her ribs still pained her when she moved awkwardly or suddenly. She wasn't coughing as much and the other symptoms of her illness were dissipating rapidly. Even her hand healed up, much to Theo's satisfaction. Good food, proper rest, and the feeling of being safe all contributing to her well-being.

Her thoughts strayed to Giles, as they often did. Unexpectedly, this man had somehow broken through her carefully erected barriers, haunting her days and disturbing her dreams. She was very much afraid her feelings were becoming more than they should be. Her heart beat faster when he was close, when he made her laugh with some silly anecdote, even when discussing whichever book she was reading. Sometimes, she was aware he watched her when he thought she wasn't looking, his expression unreadable as though trying to discern who she really was. She suspected he considered her to be a spy. For all she knew, he might be right — she couldn't remember.

She knew she had to leave before it became too hard. If only she was only able work out the Cornwall link, she could go there. Maybe that was where she was heading when the carriage upturned. Her travel clothes had finally dried and were now in pristine condition, hanging in the wardrobe in the Rose Room. Ellen found several more suitable dresses from Lady Helena's collection and, with the help of Jane, altered them to fit Billie, telling their guest to leave her own clothes until she was well enough to carry on with her journey.

So wrapped in her own thoughts was Billie, she did not hear the door open, nor the sound of the Earl's footsteps across the magnificent rug. She was wholly unaware of him until he was standing right in front of her. She jumped, yelping in shock when he spoke, his deep voice asking whether she would like a hot drink, the book landing with a thud on the floor.

"Oh, my Lord, please forgive my carelessness." She slid off the window seat and picked up the book, checking it for damage.

"I'm sure it will be fine, Miss Caswell." Giles responded, his eyes glinting with amusement, gently taking the book out of her hands and placing it on the desk. "I came to ask whether you would like to join me for a hot drink."

Billie smiled up at him and nodded. "Yes please, that would be lovely. Have you finished your work for the day?"

Giles confirmed this was the case, suggesting that after they enjoyed their drinks, she might like to accompany him on a short walk. "You haven't seen any of the grounds yet, except through the windows, and the day is not too cold. I have no doubt that Ellen can find a warm cloak for you."

"I have my own cloak now, my Lord. I'm sure it will be adequate."

Giles ignored this, knowing said cloak was rather lightweight, and in no way suitable for the chill autumn air. Thomas appeared and Giles requested two hot coffees and maybe a slice of cake if Sarah had any going spare. Thomas smiled, replying that he was certain Sarah would have something tasty for them. Billie watched this interaction with interest. Giles had such camaraderie with his staff, yet they in no way abused it. She said as much while they were waiting for their drinks, Giles having manoeuvred his guest over to the large wing-backed chairs circling the fire. Giles explained his father's philosophy about looking after the staff. How he tried to give all under his protection every opportunity to better themselves, and that he, Giles, was simply continuing what his father started, adding if it were not for his staff, the house and estate would fall apart. He respected all they did for him and he believed it was reciprocated.

Billie was astounded, finding his sentiments sat well with her, confirming what she already thought she knew about this man who took her in, knowing nothing about her, but ensuring she received the best of care. A moment or two later, Thomas brought in the coffee and some very decadent-looking cake.

"I will definitely need to take a turn around the gardens after this," Billie gurgled as Giles handed her a slice, "I can feel myself getting fat just looking at it." Giles glanced at her sharply, wondering whether she was begging to be complimented, but she wasn't even looking at him, concentrating on trying to eat the luscious cake without dropping crumbs everywhere.

This diminutive woman constantly surprised him. She didn't seem the slightest bit interested in him as a prospective husband; she could hold her own on any topic of conversation, even current affairs, often asking the most insightful questions. She was intelligent, funny and irrepressible not to mention the most beautiful woman he'd ever seen. She intrigued him. He wanted to know everything about her and when they were in close proximity, he had to work very hard at not whisking her into his arms and kissing her soundly. Realising that Billie was asking him a question, he forced his attention back to her, trying not to give into his baser instincts.

"...and that maybe it was somewhere you knew of?"

"Beg pardon, my mind was elsewhere for a moment. Please would you say that again?" Giles asked apologetically. Billie repeated what she said about the house in Cornwall, describing the little fishing village, the cliff and the view. Regrettably, and knowing how much she wanted him to be able to tell her where it was, it sounded like every fishing village along the long Cornish coastline. Trying to let her down gently, he explained this, asking her to let him know if she recalled any more details. "It may be that the name of the place will come to you soon and if you try not to think about it all the time, it might just pop into your head. I shall mention it to Theo, in case it seems more familiar to him, but neither of us has visited Cornwall for many years."

Billie nodded, accepting he was right, but Giles could see that she was disappointed. "I know 'tis hard, but I'm sure it will all come back to you in the fullness of time." He paused, "Now, Miss Caswell, do you feel ready for that walk?"

Billie smiled and said she was very much ready. As they stood to go and get their cloaks and outdoor boots, she reached out to him, then aware of how it might look let her hand fall, saying —

"Please, my Lord, I realise you do not know me from a bar of soap..." Giles smothered a laugh, "...but I have been living here for two weeks, we talk all the time and you have been endlessly kind, making sure I am well looked after. Would it be too much to ask that you call me 'Billie'? 'Miss Caswell' sounds so formal and stilted." She beseeched him with her extraordinary eyes, staring up at him as she made her plea. It was beyond him to deny her anything she requested.

"I would like that very much, but only on the proviso you call me Giles." She started to protest and he raised his hand "No, madam, the same applies. If you continue to call me 'Sir' or 'my Lord,' I will go back to addressing you as 'Miss Caswell'." Blushing at his words, Billie agreed, putting her hand out towards him. He looked at her askance.

"Shake on it." She smiled. He smiled back and gripped her small hand in his large one, feeling a frisson run through him as he did. He gazed down at their entwined hands, unwilling to let go relishing even this, so small a contact. He lifted his eyes back to Billie's and found her watching him, her own eyes darkening. Involuntarily, he leaned towards her and she tilted her face to read his expression. Her lips parted as she ran her tongue over them; he heard her breathing quicken, and his heart drummed against his chest so loud to his ears that he was certain she could hear it too.

Billie stared up at Giles. His chiselled features softened in the firelight, his eyes such a deep grey, and those perfect lips that really needed to be kissed. Shocked at the sensual nature of her thoughts, Billie started to speak but her mouth had gone dry. She tried to moisten her own lips, but nothing seemed to help. She could feel the air crackling as though a storm approached, and was most surprised not to see the flicker of lightning.

Did she want this?

Chapter Eleven

Oh yes, she most definitely did. Even if nothing else came of it, even though she had to leave this wonderful place likely never to see him again, she wanted to feel his lips on hers, knowing the memory of one kiss would be enough for a lifetime of nothing. She tightened her grasp on his hand, squeezing his fingers, willing him to lean just that little bit closer.

The same yearning was consuming Giles: his need to kiss this delicate woman whose hand he held and whose face intruded into every thought, was becoming nigh on impossible to ignore.

Propriety however, already out of the window since she had no chaperone, dictated he let her go and escort her around the gardens, as was their plan. He couldn't move and her eyes continued to draw him in, until he felt as though he was drowning in their emerald depths. He heard a groan and realised it was him. Was she pulling him towards her, or was he imagining it? Then he heard her mutter —

"Oh, please just kiss me," a shocked pause, "Oh my goodness, did I say that out loud?" Billie dropped her gaze, heat stealing up her face. Giles smiled his slow smile, his eyes still holding hers as he touched a finger to her pink cheek.

"I desire to do so more than anything, but are you sure?" he murmured. "I really shouldn't," hoping she wouldn't push him away.

"I really don't care," came her whispered reply. Gently, Giles stroked her jawline and with one finger resting under her chin so she could not look away, grazed her lips with his, feather-light.

Sighing, Billie placed her free hand on his chest, her fingers brushing over his waistcoat. Warmth coiled around her stomach and her heart began to beat way too fast. New and interesting sensations fluttered along her spine and she took a step closer, wanting more. They were touching now. Billie could feel Giles' heart, delighted that it seemed to be beating as erratically as her own.

Still holding hands, Giles wrapped his other arm around Billie moulding her to his body. She was so small, he was afraid he might break her. She moved against him, her free arm circling his waist, her eyes never leaving his. He took possession of her mouth again revelling in the softness of her lips. She responded, tentatively and Giles realised that this might well be her very first kiss. Determined not to frighten her, he let the intensity of his kiss grow slowly. She moaned against his mouth, then drew a sharp breath, bringing her hand up to her face in consternation.

Cheeks flaming, Billie stammered, "I am so sorry, I don't know … I've never … can't seem to help…" but Giles simply hushed her and, letting go of her hand, lifted her, carrying her over to sofa alongside the window, where he sat, settling Billie on his knee. Running his fingers through her riotous curls, totally destroying her neat bun and, cupping the back of her head with his hand, Giles brought her lips back down to his. Their kiss deepened, becoming more passionate. Giles shifted slightly never loosening his embrace, but beginning to trail his lips down her neck to the curve of her throat, scattering kisses across her shoulder, and as the warmth in her centre threatened to burst into flame, Billie felt she might lose control completely.

Unable to stop herself, Billie slid her hands up his neck, tracing his cheek before threading her fingers through his dark hair, pressing her body into his, wanting every part of her to be touching every part of him. Her body felt as though it was melting and she knew without a shadow of a doubt that if Giles had a mind to take this to its anticipated conclusion, she had neither the will nor the inclination to stop him. The very moment this thought raced through her consciousness, cool air cut between their faces as, taking a ragged breath, Giles lifted his head, his eyes burning with a hunger she knew must be reflected in her own.

"Don't stop," she breathed.

"I must, sweetheart."

"Did I do something wrong?" Bewildered.

Giles groaned. "No, my love, but I have no wish to ruin you and if I don't stop, that might be exactly what happens. You are under my protection, in my care, and although it is not proper that I take advantage of your situation, I find I am unable to help myself. You have cast a spell over me; desire for you possesses my every waking moment. I want to kiss you until you are begging me to make love to you, yet I am hampered by the most annoying case of respect for your good name."

Did he just call her 'sweetheart' and his 'love'? Billie's head was in such a whirl, she wasn't certain what she was hearing, but she was almost positive he had.

"I'm not entirely sure anyone cares about my good name, or if I have one whether I want to keep it." She said, then — "Oh my, that wasn't very ladylike was it?" Giles laughed gently, dropping a kiss on her forehead. Billie bit her lip aware she might have overstepped the bounds of acceptable behaviour. Sighing, she continued, "I am at a loss here. I wanted that kiss as much as you did; what is wrong with a few kisses?"

"Because I fear I will be unable to stop at a few kisses, it seems I am powerless when it comes to you. I believe we have something between us and I would like to court you properly, but I cannot do so until we know whose permission I must ask." Billie stared down at her hands resting lightly in her lap.

"So, what do we do now?" she asked, in a low voice. Giles took one of her hands in his and lifted it to his lips, turning it at the last minute, kissing her palm, sending shivers right down to her toes.

"We go for a walk."

Several minutes later, with Billie bundled up in so many layers she wasn't sure she would actually be able to put one foot in front of the other, never mind take a brisk walk around the grounds, the two met at the bottom of the stairs. Giles ushered her through the hallways to the back of the house and out into the rear courtyard, the same one through which he carried her dripping wet that first afternoon. He stuck his head into the kitchens as they passed, informing Thomas they would be out for a little while, and asking to please have their slippers warming on the hearth for their return.

Then they were outside. The day was sunny, but the chill air made Billie gasp. She shoved her hands deeper into the muff Ellen procured from somewhere, very glad of Lady Helen's winter cloak and matching hat. Mindful of Billie's sprained ankle, which although much better still caused her some discomfort, they walked slowly around to the gardens and onto one of the paths that ringed them. The ground was hard. Here and there in the shadows frost lingered, but where the sun's warmth kissed the earth, green grass glimmered, carpeted with leaves of burnished red and bronze and gold, the trees themselves almost bare.

"My Lord," Giles raised an eyebrow, "sorry — Giles. I know this sounds very childish, but would you mind terribly if I kicked through the leaves?" He looked down; her face was bright with mischief and a longing to be carefree for just a little while.

"It is not my right to object, Billie. You may do as you please." His words, though rather formal, were softened with a grin, which she returned before hastening as fast as she could manage towards the inviting piles of leaves. At first she held back, not wanting to look like a complete hoyden, but the utter pleasure of being in the fresh air after being confined to the house for two weeks soon won out and she forgot about being on her best behaviour. Using her good foot, she kicked leaves all over the grass, trying not to wobble over as she did so, twirling in the sunlight, gathering huge handfuls, and tossing them with gay abandon, calling for Giles to come and join in.

Billie's cheeks grew rosy, her laughter filling the quiet air. Such unaffected joy was contagious and as Giles watched her, he realised t he could never let her go. She had touched his heart in a way no other ever would, and the thought she might choose to leave, to say goodbye, nearly felled him. He needed to find her family, discover whether her father or brother had survived that fire and what, if anything all this had to do with a house in Cornwall. Most of all, despite knowing very little about her, he knew that he wanted her to stay in his life forever.

Too quickly, the light began to fade as the day waned, the colours morphing from vibrant hues into dull greens and greys, quieter but no less arresting; and as they chatted on the way back to the house, their warm breath hung like gossamer clouds in the cold air. Not really looking were she was going and as they stepped off the gravel pathways onto the flagstones leading to the courtyard, Billie slipped on a patch of ice, her feet shooting out from under her and she felt herself falling. Giles reacted quickly and, before she hit the ground, caught her, his hands spanning her back and curving under her arm. Billie cried out as the sudden action sent an agonising twinge lancing through her side where the cracked ribs were still healing.

"Billie, are you alright?" Concern laced Giles' tone as he slowly righted her. It was not very long since she could scarcely get out of bed; maybe they stayed outdoors too long.

"I think so…" she panted, pain slicing through her, spots dancing in front of her eyes, "…it's just my ribs, the jolt…" she found it difficult to speak and it hurt to breathe. "Cannot breathe, need to sit down." Without thinking and instructing herself not to faint, Billie moved to sit on the cold stones.

Giles shook his head. "Not here, my sweet. Come, let me help you inside." Giles wrapped one arm around her shoulder and carefully they walked the few steps around to the back door. Will appeared from the stables and Giles motioned towards the door. In quick understanding, Will had the door open and held it while his master virtually carried Billie into the warmth of the house. Billie's head was spinning and her body didn't seem to want to behave, pain still coursing through her side. She gripped his arm.

"Please, Giles. Please wait a minute. I need to get my breath." Her voice cracked, and Giles realised she was trying not to cry.

"Hey, love. Don't cry, it will be all right" He removed the hat and muff, and lifted the cloak off her shoulders while she stood gasping. "Please accept my apologies; it was not my intent to hurt you." She waved a hand at him in a vain attempt to convey that she was fine, and replied in staccato sentences.

"Not your fault. Forgotten about ice. Not concentrating. I'm sorry for spoiling such a lovely walk." They lingered for a few moments, waiting for Billie to start breathing properly again and then Giles, seeing how pale she was, asked whether she would prefer to return to her chambers rather than go to the library.

"Oh, no the library, please, if you do not mind," she replied shyly. "I love that room and I have no wish to see my chamber until bedtime; I am fair sick of it..." then realising she probably sounded ungrateful. "...but that's not to say 'tis not a lovely room, it is. 'Tis just, I've spent so many days there, a different scene is welcome." Abruptly, Billie stopped speaking and bent her head in embarrassment, aware her tongue was running away with her words. Giles chuckled and she peeked up at him through her lashes. He didn't seem unduly perturbed, so she risked a proper glance. He was grinning. Relieved she smiled back, rather wearily assuring him she was fine to walk now.

Giles led the way to the library and, finding a large blanket, tucked Billie into one of the huge chairs, fetching the book she was reading earlier, from the desk.

"I will be back soon, I have some things I need to attend to. I think Theo may join us for dinner tonight as well." Billie smiled and thanked him, asking whether she should change. He shook his head, saying it would not be necessary. Placing two more huge logs on the fire and checking whether there was anything else she needed, Giles took his leave.

Billie snuggled into the chair and opened her book, but her side still hurt and her mind was on the events of the afternoon. Her body trembled when she remembered the feel of his lips on hers, the way his hands stroked her back, the look in his eyes — as though she was the only woman in the world. Was there any chance they could make this work? Did he really care for her, or was she just convenient? She thought she understood him well enough to know that he wasn't a capricious sort of man and that it was unlikely he flitted from woman to woman. What if he had a mistress? The thought of him with another woman hurt her heart, but she had no claim on him. He hadn't even told her he loved her, just that he wanted her — was it the same thing? She didn't think so. Her thoughts started to tumble around her head. She couldn't hold onto any of them and suddenly she was asleep.

Chapter Twelve

It was well over an hour later before Giles returned to his guest. She was still fast asleep in the chair, her face, no longer pale, was flushed from the exertion of the afternoon and the heat from the fire. Unwilling to disturb her, he sat in the other chair, a large tumbler of whisky at his elbow and a broadsheet on his lap, to all intents and purposes engrossed in the news contained therein. His mind was on the woman in the chair next to him. He had received a letter from his man in London and the information therein was troubling.

They had identified two of the bodies from the fire at Viscount Ashbourne's house and Stephen was definitely not one of them. The identity of the older man still eluded investigators. Maybe they would never know; the body was severely burned. However, a large signet ring with a distinctive crest on it had been discovered under the body suggesting in all likelihood that the dead man was indeed the viscount. Stephen had completely disappeared and rumours had begun circulating that Billie, angry with her father for thwarting a budding romance, had set the fire herself before running off with her lover to Gretna Green. Preposterous though the rumours were, and despite there being absolutely no grounds for such accusations, scandalous gossip always found willing ears.

Giles was absolutely certain that Billie had never taken a lover, her behaviour when she kissed him, while somewhat unrestrained, was still very much that of an innocent. Neither could he be persuaded she would intentionally hurt anyone, never mind her own family regardless of how angry she may be with them. He believed the whispers began because no one had seen or heard from Billie since the night of the fire. Rumours, however, had a nasty habit of becoming accepted, regardless of what the truth actually was, and thus it was now imperative they try to get to the bottom of why she was in that carriage, so her name could be cleared. Otherwise it was possible a whole other group of people might soon be hunting her.

He watched Billie as she slept, her breathing steady, her head pillowed on her hand. He knew he should wake her — it would soon be time for dinner — but he was enjoying being able to observe her unnoticed. Her black eyelashes swept over her pink cheeks in a sooty curve. Her chestnut hair, begging for someone to wind it between their fingers, spilled over her shoulders, glossy curls long since escaping the neat style she started the day with, his heart thudding in recollection of its silky weight under his fingers. The blanket had slipped down, exposing her slender form, encased in a fine wool morning dress of a deep claret colour — another of Helena's cast offs — but which suited Billie far better than it ever suited his sister. One of Billie's slippers had fallen off and her stockinged foot peeped out from under the blanket, offering Giles a glimpse of her delectable ankle.

Shuddering he told himself to get a grip, lifting his gaze away from temptation and as he did so, glanced at Billie's face, straight into her remarkable green eyes. His heart missed a beat and he fought to appear detached. Unfortunately for the household, his sudden change of demeanour set off a chain of events that might have had dire consequences if not for the quick actions of one of his staff.

"Good afternoon, Miss Caswell, I trust you had a restful nap?" His formal words and disinterested tone caused Billie to glance at him in bewilderment.

"I feel quite relaxed thank you, my Lord," she replied, emphasising the last two words. Giles smiled contritely, remembering their agreement.

"Do your ribs still hurt?"

Billie stretched tentatively and took a deep breath. She winced as she felt the bruises, but no worse than they were before she slipped.

"It seems I have suffered no ill-effects." Politely, a frown beginning to form.

"No thanks to me."

"You saved me from falling flat on my backside, my Lord. Please think no more of it." An uncomfortable silence fell, leaving Billie even more perplexed. What happened to cause such reserve between them? They were having such a lovely day. She rubbed her forehead distractedly, running her mind back over the last couple of hours; nothing stood out as being cause for his attitude. Determined to reclaim their gentle friendship, if nothing else, she grabbed the bull by the horns.

"What have I done to upset you, my Lord? We were enjoying a perfectly delightful afternoon, now you treat me as though I am a little-known acquaintance. Have you perhaps discovered I am a spy and have murdered several people, including my family?" She spoke in jest, but she was so close to the details contained in the letter that Giles blanched and did not reply.

Scrutinising his face, Billie read his expression, watchful now, and he detected hurt lurking in her eyes.

She straightened her shoulders.

"So, one minute you wish to court me, the next you think me so capable of harming others, I would burn my family alive?" Dismay laced her words and she paused, trying to retain some equanimity. "Fine, I am grateful for your honesty. At least I know your true feelings before it is too late. I will take my meal in my chambers tonight. I have no wish to sully your reputation." Her voice was hard, emotionless, and she thought her heart was about to shatter.

Giles started to speak, but she raised her hand, determined to get this over with.

"I do not wish to hear it. Maybe you should hand me over to the nearest magistrate. I'm sure they will find an excuse to hang me quickly enough, saving them the trouble of discovering what really happened." Billie gulped realising it might come to that, but she was beyond caring. She stood up, the blanket slithering to the floor, pooling around her feet. Appalled at the notion anyone, let alone Giles, might consider her so unscrupulous, Billie's temper spilled over, swamping her anguish and her eyes flashed green fire. "Thank you, my Lord for your generous hospitality. I will ensure I am gone before word gets out you harbour a criminal." Her hair whirled around her as she spat out the words, then drawing herself up she turned to leave the room with as much dignity as she could manage.

Giles could do nothing other than gape at her.

At the door she paused and looking back at him, said in a sad little voice barely discernible over the gentle hiss of the fire. "I thought I knew you," and was gone.

Giles remained pinned to his chair, stunned by her words. *Why hadn't he interrupted and told her what happened? Well, because she didn't give you a chance,* his rational side reminded him. *Did he go after her? No, he should let her calm down, then find her and explain. What did she mean by 'before it is too late'? What if she decided to leave? No,* he argued with himself, *she would wait until morning. She surely would not risk travelling in the dark — would she?*

Billie stumbled up to her chambers, anger and distress fighting for control while tears poured down her cheeks. He suspected her a murderess! That she killed her father! Oh God! She asked him to kiss her. What was the matter with her? He would think her nothing better than a strumpet — completely forgetting his tender words following that wonderful moment. What did she do now? She had to leave. There was no way she could remain here if the man she had come to respect, the man she had come to care for, believed she had killed her family. There was no recovering from this. Her heart ached and, she could no longer deny that from which she had been hiding. She loved him; she would never love anyone else. In two short weeks he had stolen her heart and it would be his forever. That kiss, that earth-shattering kiss, would indeed have to last a lifetime.

Pulling herself together, Billie changed into the clothes she was found in. They would suffice until she made it home, or had to purchase some more. She ruminated on the issue of money as she dressed; realising she would probably have to sell the clasp, then remembered Giles held it in his safe. She would have to leave it, and hope once she found her brother and they proved she was innocent, someone might come back to retrieve it for her. She didn't think she could bear to see Giles again. She took her bedraggled reticule out of the drawer in the bedside table and removed the coin purse. Counting the money, she realised she probably had enough to hire a wagon for part of the journey, which was of some relief.

She tried to write a letter, but didn't know what to put. She wrote his name, scratched it out, tried again and in the end she just added a single word. Never one for thinking a plan through, something to which anyone who knew her could attest, Billie didn't stop to consider that maybe Giles hadn't meant what she thought he meant, or that she had overreacted in any way at all. Nor did she wait until she had eaten; she just knew she had to get away, that she couldn't face him anymore, the belief he deemed her capable of deliberately harming anyone, more painful than any cracked rib or sprained ankle.

No, rather than behave rationally as a woman of nearly two and twenty years really should do, and demand an explanation from Giles, Billie simply swung her cloak around her shoulders, shoved her feet into the boots that might, if she was lucky, last a few more weeks and went quietly down the stairs. It was dark outside and she didn't really know which way to go, but she recalled them saying the carriage overturned somewhere near the Cross Keys, which she understood to be at the far side of the village. If she could find it and follow the road, she thought it might take her to Cornwall.

Having absolutely no idea Cornwall was several days ride away and that the weather was about to get even colder, Billie left the place that had been a haven for her and into the frigid night air. She shivered, but set off, determined to get as far away from Whiteoaks as she could.

Unbeknownst to Billie, Jake, the stable boy, spied her slipping out of the back door to step out in a rather resolute fashion along the path towards the gate. Bemused by someone walking in the dark and not at all sure what was going on, he mentioned it to Will, who immediately went to find Giles. His master was still sitting in the library staring into the fire. Will knocked and after Giles invited him to enter, explained what Jake had seen.

"Hell's teeth, but, she is the most exasperating woman!" Giles ground out. "Now I have to go and save her. Again!" Yelling for Will to fetch him a torch, Giles ran up to his bedchamber, pulling on his warmest cloak and sturdy boots. Back down the stairs and into the kitchens, Giles asked Sarah to have some hot coffee brewing, saying their guest had got it into her head she was no longer welcome and had taken her leave. His staff stared at him dumfounded, not sure whether he was joking.

"No, I am deadly serious. I will explain what prompted such a muddle-headed idea later, for now I need to get her home." His staff jumped into action. Thomas went to stoke up the fire in the Rose Room, and then did the same in the library. Sally and Ellen made sure the bedding was drawn up, sliding the warming pan between the sheets, and there were plenty of extra blankets on hand. Will, two torches in his hand, was outside waiting for the earl, along with Jake and one of the gardeners, Samuel. He handed one to Giles and the four men hurried along the path that led out of the estate.

Fear leant urgency to Giles' footsteps. He was concerned, not only for Billie, but also whether anyone had worked out where she was and were watching for an opportunity to take her. Why, oh why did he let her walk out of the library? He had every chance to stop her and tell her he didn't believe the information, but he let her go. He could kick himself, and probably would later on, but not until they had her back safe and sound.

It was bitterly cold. Billie realised her cloak was next to useless against such bone-chilling weather, but she wrapped it tightly around her body, hoping that by walking briskly she would warm up. The sky was clear, the stars breathtaking and she stopped at the main gate to stare up at them, trying to locate Polaris, the North Star. She read quite a bit about astronomy and knew once she worked out which direction was north, the rest was easy, Cornwall being to the west. Finally spotting Polaris, she judged which way she needed to travel and turned along the road towards the west. The moon had not yet risen, but there was just enough light from the stars to make out the road.

She trudged on, the events of the last two weeks swirling around in her head. Her world had been turned upside down and, still unable to recall much of her life before Giles found her, for a short while she felt part of something. She had come to know and like all the staff at Whiteoaks, a sentiment they seemed to reciprocate. Quietly, and without venturing any further than the stables, Billie began to learn about the estate, and how it was run. Pestering the gardeners and the grooms with all sorts of questions, for no other reason than it helped her to know Giles. No, she refused to dwell on it. It was behind her now. Her priority was to find her father and brother, even though she couldn't remember what they looked like, hoping that when she saw them she would recognise them.

The village was quiet. Billie worked out that it was probably sometime after seven o'clock, maybe they were all at home enjoying a warm dinner or at the public house downing a beer. Her traitorous stomach rumbled, reminding her she had not eaten since luncheon. *Oh Billie*, she thought fretfully, *you never think, do you? Why didn't you wait until after dinner, or better still after a good night's sleep and some hot breakfast?* Even accepting she would not have slept, both of these ideas were eminently preferable to the one she chose to follow. *Nothing you can do about it now*, she remonstrated with herself, *just pretend you're not hungry.*

The four men were not far behind her, their long legs carrying them over the frosty ground much more quickly. However, they did not know which route she took when she reached the fork in the road and they wasted precious minutes trying to decide where she was headed. All at once, Giles remembered Cornwall. It was to the west; would she be able to work that out? As they stood there trying to decide which way to go, Giles leaned against the fence mulling over their options. Glancing up at the night sky, a thought struck him. Thinking out loud, he ruminated —

"Tonight's misguided exploit aside, Billie is an intelligent young woman. Do you think there is any chance she knows about the stars and how you can use them to guide you?" The other three chewed this over for a few minutes, until Will snapped his fingers.

"Yes, my Lord. I think she might. A few days ago when she was talking to me in the stables…" Giles looked at his groom in amazement. "…oh, she often pops in for a chat and to spend time with the horses, I rather think she's a soft spot for Bronte."

Samuel was nodding. "Aye, she comes to see me most mornings, afore I start, while I'm having me cuppa in yon scullery and talks about the gardens, asking what plants and herbs we grow. She has prodigious knowledge of herbs, my Lord." Giles could not have been more surprised had Samuel suddenly grown two heads. It seemed his guest had managed to become part of his household without his knowledge.

"Anyway, my Lord, as I was saying, when she was in the stables the other day, she was talking about some constellation or other, named after a horse and you can see it in autumn." Will continued, ignoring Samuel's interruption.

Dragging his attention back to the quest at hand, Giles nodded, feeling a little more positive.

"Yes, that would be Pegasus. Thus, if we accept she can read the night sky, we must also accept she has worked out which way is west, and that she has probably set off for Cornwall." The other three men gaped at him.

"What? Cornwall? Has she any idea how far away Cornwall is?" spluttered Will in shock.

"No, sadly I don't believe she does. And if we don't find her, she will likely die of cold or from something else I would rather not contemplate. We must find her and soon. This way." The four men set off, following in Billie's wake.

Chapter Thirteen

Billie was drained. She had not allowed for the fact, as a result of being so sick, she lost much of her stamina. She remembered vaguely, that usually she was quite fit; she rode horses, and walked a lot. She had, however, spent much of the afternoon dancing about the garden, not to mention all that wasted emotional energy what with being kissed and then her altercation with Giles. She should never have asked him to kiss her — ah but then she wouldn't have the memory of it. Oh, it was all too confusing.

For the first time since she stomped out, all righteously indignant, she faltered. Looking around her she registered how lonely it was, out here in the darkness, but it wouldn't do to stand still, it was too cold. She considered returning, and trying to sneak in unnoticed, but Giles' face swam across her vision and she knew it wasn't possible. Shivering a little, she stamped her feet in an attempt to get warm and then, both mentally and physically, straightened her back and forged ahead.

Maybe an hour later she was still walking, but was so tired that she could barely put one foot in front of the other and her ankle was throbbing. She was done in and decided, quite sensibly she thought, that a short nap would help. Frost was forming on the trees, the rime coating the walls along the roadway luminous in the moonlight and the grass was crunching underfoot. At any other time, the frozen beauty of the landscape unfolding before her, would have entranced Billie — now she didn't even see it. All she cared about was sleep. Where on earth could she rest?

Near a gate into a field, she noticed a large stone block sticking out at an angle to the rest of the wall. Not realising this was the bottom rung of a stile, she huddled onto it and tucking her cloak around her, leaned her head against the wall — a dark shadow the only sign she was there — and slept.

Not very long after Billie curled up on her ledge, four men came towards her, torches blazing. Giles was starting to think they were going the wrong way, because they had not seen any footprints for a while. Giles, Will and Samuel walked straight past Billie, but Jake hesitated, perceiving there was something different about the look of the wall.

"My Lord," he whispered. Giles turned, waiting. Jake put his fingers to his lips and pointed. Giles went over the wall and lifted his torch. The flickering light illuminated a tiny figure tucked into a cloak, almost hidden from view. All that distinguished her from the darkness was an ear around which a strand of chestnut hair curled, and the smooth rise of a cheek. Giles stood for long seconds, so relieved they chanced upon her he wasn't sure his legs would obey him and actually move. Will asked whether His Lordship wanted him to go and fetch the wagon, or even Zeus, so it would be easier to transport her home. Giles didn't think they could wait that long.

They debated what to do and then Giles asked that Will go with Jake to fetch the wagon, while he and Samuel started walking back with Billie. It would be quicker and left each pair with a torch. Will agreed, and whisked Jake along the path as fast as they could go in the moonlight, the two soon disappearing into the darkness. Giles lifted Billie. She was so light that he knew it wouldn't be too hard to carry her all the way home but they had come a fair distance. He was quite surprised Billie managed to get this far; she must have covered at least four or five miles. He smiled to himself thinking how shocked she would be when he told her it was only another hundred and forty or so to Cornwall.

Samuel trotted alongside, holding the torch so Giles didn't stumble. Billie hadn't stirred, which on one hand was a good thing, but on the other made Giles worry that she was already too chilled. Annoyance at her thoughtlessness warred with his desire to shake her awake in order to kiss the heat back into her. Gritting his teeth against more than just the cold, he strode on, his burden weighing next to nothing. Maybe half an hour later he heard the rattle of a wagon and breathed a sigh of relief. Jake and Will must have run all the way home.

As they drew up, Samuel opened the door and Giles was in and sitting down almost before they came to a complete halt. Someone, probably Will, thought to bring a blanket and Giles wrapped it around Billie, desperate to get some warmth into her body, while his groom found a suitably wide piece of road and turned the wagon for home. It didn't seem long at all before they reached Whiteoaks, the light spilling out from the windows welcoming them home. They rolled into the courtyard and Jake ran out of the stables to open the door, pulling the step down. Giles thanked him and hurried into the kitchens. Jake had informed them Billie was found, and all of his household staff was there, waiting on tenterhooks, to see that she was safe.

Giles smiled wearily, affirming they found her asleep, or possibly unconscious but alive. She was very cold, which was becoming a habit with her, and he needed to get her warmed up quickly. Ellen suggested a hot bath, Sally the bed, but Giles thought the library.

"If we bathe her, she will get warm too quickly, and Theo has told me previously this can be detrimental. She needs to warm up a little more slowly than that. I'll take her into the library, it is a cosy room and the fire will help. I know we could put her to bed, but I want her to wake properly and eat something before we let her sleep. As far as I am aware, she has not eaten since luncheon. Thomas, please bring me two hot coffees and two brandies. Sarah, if you have anything like soup or stew, something warm, even porridge would do, that would be most appreciated. Now I must get this young lady sorted out." His instructions given, Giles left the domestic quarters, hastening to the library, noticing to his deepening anxiety, Billie still had not woken, she hadn't even moved.

He nudged open the door and saw, to his surprise, Theo leaning against the mantelpiece smoking a cigar, a glass of whisky in his hand.

"Theo. I am glad you are here, but have I forgotten an arrangement?"

"Well, you did invite me for dinner, which I would not have made anyway as I was called out, so no matter. I was actually just popping in on my way home to see whether you might like to offer me a nightcap, and heard the hullabaloo about Miss Caswell. Decided you might need my assistance, plus Thomas insisted I sit with a wee dram before I set off home." Theo's eyes twinkled and Giles grinned at his friend, giving him the barest outline of the evening's events. Theo was not convinced he had heard the whole story but let it go for now, and gave Billie a quick examination. Her breathing was steady but her heartbeat was very slow. Her skin was ice cold, but he perceived that it might well be starting to warm up. When he lifted her eyelids, her pupils reacted to the light in the room. She wasn't shivering but at this stage that could be good or bad.

Giles pulled one of the wing-backed chairs even closer to the fire and wrapping another blanket around Billie, tucked her onto his knee. He noticed Theo's expression and shook his head.

"Quite frankly, I don't care what you think. It's my fault she was out there and I find myself unwilling to let her out of my arms until I know she is awake." Theo said nothing, merely waited for the explanation he knew was about to follow. Giles gave up and told the doctor what had happened that day, everything, including that he had kissed Billie.

"It's the darnedest thing, Elliott," he concluded. "I very much fear I have fallen in love with her, but now she thinks I believe her to be a criminal and she likely won't forgive me for not setting her straight when I had the chance. I was just so shocked that her words almost exactly matched what Withers wrote in his letter."

Theo chuckled. "I was wondering whether you were ever going to admit you care for her, Winchester. It has been patently obvious to the rest of us almost from the moment you brought her here two weeks ago."

Giles grinned sheepishly. "I just never expected it and I don't want her to feel obliged because she has been staying here. She might already have a husband, or a fiancé. She has enough to deal with. The loss of her memory, the worry over her father and brother, this link to Cornwall, and maybe the death of her mother. I don't want to pressure her into anything else, she might not even return my feelings." He dropped his head, unconsciously resting his chin against Billie's forehead, still rubbing his hands up her arms trying to get heat into her icy veins.

"I think you will discover she is not indifferent to you, my friend." Theo said after pondering Giles' words. "It seems to me, all the pair of you need is some sense shaking into you."

Thomas came in with three coffees, a bowl of something piping hot, two brandies and another whisky. Giles thanked him gratefully; at least his butler was aware of who was in his house at any given moment. Theo thanked Thomas and placed his empty tumbler on the side table. Giles picked up one of the brandy glasses and held it under Billie's nose. Finally they got a response as she moved her head, trying to get away from the aromatic scent. Giles held her firmly, keeping the glass there until she began to fidget. Trusting that she was coming into wakefulness, he placed the glass by his elbow and ran his warm hand over her cheek, cupping her chin.

"Come on, Billie, please wake up, you need to have something to eat and a hot drink." She groaned and snuggled closer into his chest. "Billie, please, you have slept for hours, you must eat." He shook her gently, lifting her away from his body. She shuddered, trying to reclaim the warmth but this time his need for her to wake, outweighed his need to have her in his arms. "Billie!" A little more sternly, "Come now, this won't do." Helplessly he looked at Theo, who merely grinned and went over to his doctor's bag standing on the desk. Lifting out a small vial, he walked over and wafted it under Billie's nose. The effect was instantaneous. Had Giles not been holding her, she would have fallen out of the chair, so quickly did she come round, spluttering in distaste. She turned in Giles' arms and, realising where she was, just stared at him, the misery in her eyes making his heart ache.

"Why am I here?" she asked, obviously puzzled. "I left."

Well that's the understatement of the week, thought Giles, but he didn't say so, rather he replied, "I know you left, you goose, and we came after you. Be grateful Jake saw you walking down the driveway, otherwise you'd likely be frozen to that wall against which we found you asleep."

"Well, that would save the magistrate a job," she muttered, grumpily. Giles wanted to laugh at her expression, but decided it might not be quite the right response, so said nothing and simply gave her the brandy glass indicating she should drink it. She shook her head. "I really don't like brandy."

"I really don't care," came his response, echoing Billie's words of earlier that day. Her lashes fluttered and her cheeks flared as she acquiesced, albeit grudgingly. The spirit coursed through her body, banishing the chill, its strength making her cough. Giles drew her back against him, rubbing his hand along her back until the bout ceased. Then he persuaded her to finish the glass.

"It will do you good, my sweet. Then you can try the hot soup Sarah made for you."

Billie didn't reply, all she heard was the endearment. Was he just treating her as he would a child, one of his sisters, or did he mean it? Her brain was rather foggy at the moment, so it was hard to think straight. A bowl full of something that smelt heavenly appeared under her nose. Billie's stomach growled in response and she felt mirth rumble through Giles' chest.

"Don't you dare laugh at me," she hissed under her breath. He held the bowl, but the effort of trying to coordinate the spoon with her mouth proved too much for the exhausted woman and the spoon splashed back into the bowl. She attempted to get off the earl's lap, muttering something about needing to sleep before she resumed her journey the next day. Giles put the bowl down, turning her so that she faced him.

"You won't be going anywhere, young lady. How on God's good earth did you think you were going to get to Cornwall?" He seemed genuinely interested, so she told him.

"Walk some of the way and maybe a coach for the remainder. I have some coin," she replied coolly

"Have you any idea how far it is to Cornwall?"

"Maybe twenty or thirty miles?" She glanced up at him, hearing Theo stifle a bark of laughter, which earned the doctor a glare. "I cannot understand why it even matters to you, my Lord. I am no longer your concern. You have cared for me and now I am well, so it is fitting I should leave. You know I should not stay under your roof."

Giles bit his lip. She looked so adamant, had he not been half out of his mind with worry he might have let her try it. "My love, it is about hundred and forty miles from here to

Cornwall, further depending how deep into the county you need to go."

"Oh!" The fight went out of her and her shoulders drooped.

"Yes, oh! Now please eat some of this soup before it gets cold. Sarah made it especially for you. We'll worry about Cornwall tomorrow."

Billie shook her head, feeling her surroundings tilt a little. "I'm sorry … can't … so tired … the spoon … heavy…" her voice trailed away, and she began to slide off Giles' knee. He caught her, lifting her to him, and without warning she started to cry, sobbing brokenly about being accused of murder, and her cloak was too thin, and her boots were falling apart, and why was he calling her his love, and she wanted her Papa.

Theo intervened, saying she was suffering from a reaction to being tired, cold and emotionally overwrought, suggesting bed was probably the best option. She had at least woken, even though she still hadn't eaten. All the while Giles held her close, rocking her as he had done so many times before.

"Come on, love. I think Theo is right, the only place you are good for is bed." He carried her up to the Rose Room, which was warm and homely, laying her on the bed. He made as if to leave but she grasped his hand.

"Please don't leave me." She spoke so quietly, he wasn't sure she actually said anything, but as he tried to extricate his fingers, she repeated it.

"I need to let Sally help you undress, sweetheart. I'll come back shortly." A large tear rolled down her cheek. He caught it with his finger, leaning down to kiss her gently.

"Promise?"

He nodded. "I promise."

She sighed then, and relaxed her grip. Giles heard footsteps and Sally came into the room with the bowl of soup. Giles left them to it, telling Sally he'd be back shortly.

Making his way downstairs to the library, he saw Thomas had brought yet more fresh soup as well as hot bread rolls dripping with butter for both Theo and him. They tucked in, enjoying the simple yet filling fare. When they finished, Theo took his leave, saying he'd be back the next day just to make sure Billie suffered no nasty after-effects and, despite Giles remarking it would serve her right if she did, he thanked his friend. He walked unhurriedly along to the kitchens to thank everyone for their help, whereupon Sarah asked what prompted Billie to run away like that. Giles apprised them of what happened, without going into too much detail, for some should remain between Billie and him. As the tale unfolded, Sarah looked more and more aghast and he realised he might be in for a rap on the knuckles.

"Before you tell me off, Sarah, please understand I was already resolved to tell her such a rumour was nonsense, and I certainly didn't anticipate the silly girl would run off in the middle of the night."

Sarah muttered darkly under her breath about that being quite typical of men, then said in normal tones. "Well I'm not sure quite what you did expect, my Lord. Allowing a poor girl, who turned up on your doorstep drenched and bruised, possibly fleeing for her life, with no memory of who she was or how she got here, to believe you consider her capable of burning her family's house down with them in it. Honestly, sometimes you need to remember you are not a child anymore. Your words, or lack of them bear weight now." No one but Sarah could get away with speaking to Giles this way, a privilege of knowing him since he was knee-high to a grasshopper. Giles, suitably chastised, grinned at her fierce expression. "Where is she now?"

"In bed, I hope. Sally is with her and I promised I would see her before I retire for the night."

"Be off with you then, go to the poor bairn. I hope you set her straight before she sleeps." Sarah waved her flour-coated hand at her master, shooing him out of the kitchens, and as the door closed on him, he heard her say to the rest of the assembled staff — "Well, what a pickle."

Still grinning, Giles was back up to the Rose Room in a jiffy. Sally was sitting next to the bed and Billie was apparently asleep, her dark lashes smudged like bruises over too pale cheeks. He raised his eyebrow at Sally and nodded at the woman in the bed.

"How is she?"

"A little distressed, I think, my Lord. She kept saying how sorry she was for the trouble she caused and not to bother with her; it was all rather confusing. I couldn't get her to eat anything either. What happened, do you know? If you do, would you be so kind as to tell me?"

Giles ran his hand through his hair, and for the third time in less than an hour revealed why Billie had left. A man of his status had no reason to explain anything he did to anyone, but Giles was on extremely good terms with all in his household, and they enjoyed an unusually amicable relationship with their master. More than this, his staff needed to be aware Billie might be in danger, as it seemed someone was intent on removing the Caswell family from the face of the earth. He really needed to know who stood to inherit if Ashbourne's children died without issue. Maybe it was nothing to do with French spies; maybe it was all about a will.

Sally nodded her understanding and hesitated. She knew she should stay but she trusted her employer, and it was not her place to demand Billie be chaperoned.

"It's fine, Sally, you may go. I will not do anything to compromise Miss Caswell." Sally grinned and curtseyed, leaving the room quietly, then rushed down to the kitchens to tell the others that in her opinion the earl was in love with Billie. Most of the staff chortled at her, pooh-poohing the notion, but Sarah nodded slowly.

"I think you could be right, Sally, but we'll have to wait and see."

Chapter Fourteen

Meanwhile back in the Rose Room, Giles settled himself into the chair by the bedside, contemplating his guest. She confused the very life out of him. Her decision to flee was thoughtless and juvenile in the extreme, yet he did not know anyone else brave enough to set out for an unknown destination on a cold night at the onset of winter with little money and even less in the way of suitable clothing. In truth, he didn't really know anything about her, not even how old she was, although he guessed that she must be at least twenty owing to her comments about France before and during the war.

The thought he upset her enough to leave his home without care of the consequences worried him, concerned she may do it again. Persuading her, he believed her innocent was critical. Elbows on his knees, his hands hanging loosely between his legs, Giles bowed his head, knowing what he really wanted to do was tell her he loved her, fearing he had missed his chance. He was in unknown territory here, never before having lost his heart to anyone, but at the same time realising, while his nice, neat and orderly existence might well be a thing of the past, he rather welcomed the change. As he was mulling over the upheaval Billie wrought on his life, he spotted a crumpled sheet of paper on the floor. Curious, he picked it up, flattening it on his knee. It was a letter; well, no, more a note. Well, actually it wasn't even a line. She had written his name, then crossed it out, then his family name, then his title and then finished up with 'my Lord'. Underneath, there appeared to be several failed attempts at an explanation. In the end she had simply written 'thank you'. His heart clenched and he stuffed it in his pocket, wanting to keep this sad little missive as a reminder of how not to behave.

Unbidden, he recalled their kiss — had it happened only that day? It seemed a lifetime ago. He remembered what he said to her, and nearly groaned aloud realising this was why she ran. He told her how much he wanted to make love to her, that he wanted to court her, then scant hours later allowed it all to come crashing down, and let her simply walk away. *You are an utter idiot,* Giles berated himself, *what the devil were you thinking?*

He raised his head, his gaze colliding with a pair of deep green eyes watching him from a wary face. They stared at each other. Giles couldn't find the words he wanted to say to bring back her smile, but he felt as though he was melting into her gaze. Billie stretched her hand towards him, resting her fingers on his knee in a tentative gesture. He placed his hand over the top of hers, entwining his fingers with hers. Billie tugged at him. Unsure what she was doing Giles didn't move, so she tugged again, pulling him towards her. His eyes widened at the implication, but he didn't stop her, or remove his hand. She shuffled over in the bed, pulling him still closer, until there was room for him to sit next to her on the covers. Only when he had positioned himself on the bed did she let go.

"I think we need to talk," she said quietly.

"I think we do too," he replied just as quietly. She moved into a sitting position, so they were shoulder to shoulder, drawing the bedclothes up around her to stay warm. They sat in companionable silence for several minutes, then Billie spoke.

"Why did you call me 'my love'?"

"Because to me you are." Honesty seemed the way to go.

"Oh," she hesitated, testing the waters, "but you think me a criminal." It was a statement not a question.

"No, I really don't," he replied, turning his head to face her as he said it, wanting her to know the truth of his words.

"B-but…" Billie stopped.

"Sweetheart, if you had but given me a chance I would have told you why I reacted the way I did. Your words shocked me. They were so close to the details contained within a troubling letter I just received, I didn't know quite what to say and then you rushed out before I could explain. I certainly in my wildest dreams never expected you to leave the house. What did you mean by 'before it's too late'? And why did you run?"

Billie stared at him. This man, who had somehow taken her heart, who kissed her, as though he never wanted to let go, and who had saved her life twice. Could she risk telling him? He had told her. She looked down at her hands folded neatly on her lap and took a deep breath.

"Because you are my love too."

Giles stilled. Everything went quiet; the only sound in the room was the hiss and pop of the wood on the fire as the flames consumed it. The silence stretched out and Billie started to think she said the wrong thing, he didn't mean he loved her at all, she'd misunderstood him and he was trying to find a way to let her down gently.

"I am sorry … I shouldn't have … too forward of … please forget I…"

"You love me?" Giles interrupted her incoherence, shifting on the bed so he could look at her properly, his expression one of hope. She nodded shyly, a rosy glow suffusing her face. "You love me?" It was a question, not a statement. She nodded again. "My beautiful Willow, if you love me why did you flee?"

"You changed. When I woke from my nap, you were distant and cold. You were calling me 'Miss Caswell' again, perfectly polite and correct. Then when I tried to ask you what was wrong, joking about discovering my involvement in nefarious activities, you didn't answer. It seemed the words you spoke earlier meant nothing, that maybe you just wanted something to distract you and I was convenient, right there and ripe for the plucking. I even asked you to kiss me."

Giles groaned, grasping her hand, bringing it up to kiss her palm, causing a quiver to run down her spine.

She paused, the rosy glow becoming a hot flare, remembering her wanton behaviour. Then she gathered herself and continued. "It was already too late for me. So I left. It was rash and thoughtless, but I did not have the strength to face you knowing how you felt…" she paused, then whispered, "…but at least I had that kiss. I could live a life alone on the memory of that one kiss.

Billie's voice quavered and she stopped speaking. It was an effort to admit how much she cared. She was baring her soul to Giles, praying desperately that it wasn't going to backfire. Unable to look at him, Billie let her head drop to her chest, her hair falling all around her face. She could feel useless tears welling up and blinked fiercely to stop them spilling down her cheeks. She sensed movement and Giles, still holding her hand, ran his other under her chin tilting it so he could look at her.

His fingers stroked over her jawline, to cup her neck and entwine into her rich curls, making her legs tremble.

"I love you more than my own life. I will love you forever. You have ensnared me and I fear I will never be able to let you go." His deep voice was gentle, yet compelling.

"Oh!" was all Billie could manage right at that moment — speech quite beyond her.

"I had been watching you sleep, you looked so peaceful, your hair curling around your face," he admitted, twisting one of said curls around his finger while he talked, "it was all I could do not to drag you into my arms and kiss you senseless." Again Billie could feel hectic colour wash up her cheeks. "I knew I could do no such thing, so I forced you out of my mind, trying to detach myself. I obviously did a very good job…" he finished up ruefully, "…because it made you want to remove yourself from my presence as fast as possible."

"What was in the letter?" Billie stared at Giles, needing to know, needing him to say the words she was dreading to hear.

"Maybe we should leave it until the morning; it is rather a long letter containing a lot of information."

Billie wasn't to be put off however. "Why? Do you … do they think me a murderess?"

He could hear the hurt in her subdued question and knew she would not rest until he clarified. "A rumour has been circulating that your father disapproved of your current beau so in a fit of pique, you deliberately set the fire and fled with your lover."

Billie gasped in horror, processing his words, her countenance going from pink to white in a heartbeat. "You were serious before? People do think I killed my family? No, no, no, no, no! How could anyone believe I would commit a heinous act? Not to my Papa, not to Stephen, not to anyone. Are those who started the rumour, people who know me? What on earth have I ever done in my life to warrant such evil thoughts?" Her voice rose as panic threatened to engulf her, the full implications of such innuendo suddenly apparent. "Giles, what do I do? What do I do? They will be looking for me. I can't stay now. They will want to drag me in front of the magistrate. I must find out who really did this. I need to clear my name."

Her terror tore at Giles. He wrapped his arms around her drawing her into his embrace, oblivious to anything else save soothing her fears.

"Everything will be all right, my love. We will get to the bottom of this. You are exhausted and you must rest. Tomorrow we can come up with a plan. My man in London is investigating and he is very thorough. We will find out who did this. Please, you have to trust me." Billie pushed herself closer, needing to draw strength from his body. Her breathing was erratic and he could feel a cough building. "Shhhhh, steady, sweetheart, you don't want to start coughing again." Giles rubbed his hands down her back until she began to calm down, then he cradled her still closer, tucking her head under his chin. They stayed like that for some time until Giles heard her breathing slow and quieten. He kissed her on the forehead before sliding her down under the bedclothes, watching until he was sure she was actually asleep, and then left the room.

He went along to his own bedchamber, and stood looking out over the darkened gardens unseeing. Unaware of the beauty of the night, the glow of the moon highlighting the frosty pathways and making the trees look as though they were sprinkled with diamonds. His mind was tumbling with the events of the day. So much had happened; he should feel as exhausted as Billie. It was the early hours of the morning; midnight had struck long ago, yet somehow he was exhilarated. He wanted to jump on Zeus and ride over the sleeping countryside and shout his happiness to the four winds. *Good gracious, Giles*, he admonished himself, *you sound like a lovesick puppy*. He didn't care and was powerless to stop the broad grin curving his lips. She loved him. Whatever happened, they could deal with it together — she loved him.

Unable to settle, he pulled a thick dressing gown over his clothes, glad of its heavy warmth in the cold of the house, and strode down to the library intent on seeking out a heavy tome that would bore him to sleep. He had been there maybe an hour, said tome doing nothing more than sending his thoughts back up to the woman sleeping peacefully in the Rose Room, when the door creaked open and in crept Billie. She was enveloped in an impossibly large, heavy, wool dressing gown, so long that it trailed along behind her, even though she held it up preventing her slippered feet from getting caught in the voluminous material.

"What on earth are you doing out of bed?"

Billie smothered a shriek when she spied the earl sitting in a dimly lit corner of the room. "I came for my book. You put it on the desk. I woke and you'd gone and I can't get back to sleep," she replied, recovering her breath. "What are you doing here?" Curiously.

"I find I am unable to sleep also. Thoughts of a certain wench are distracting me and I cannot settle."

She giggled and shuffled towards him, the light from the fire creating a halo around her silhouette. "Well, at least we are awake together. Oh, for a cup of hot chocolate. No," as Giles made to ring for Thomas, "Let your staff sleep, I can make it, I know where the kitchens are." Giles gaped at her. She never ceased to surprise him. Ordinarily, the daughter of a viscount should not have the first clue about how to make hot chocolate. "I am quite good at brewing things up," she clarified as she noted his expression. Giles recalled what Samuel said about her knowledge of herbs. That was something else of which he needed to get to the bottom.

"Come on then, since you are so sure, let us go and see what we can drum up." He took her hand and led her through the dark hallways to the kitchens, still warm from the fire that was never allowed to go out. Billie found everything she needed by dint of opening likely looking jars and tins. While the milk warmed and the water boiled, she scraped three squares off a large block of chocolate, adding this to the warmed milk. Then she stirred in some of the hot water, making sure all the chocolate had melted into the mixture. Once satisfied the drink was hot enough, she added a little sugar to sweeten, and poured it carefully between the two cups Giles managed to find.

She curled up in one of the chairs, her fingers curved around the hot cup, inhaling the sweet aroma. Giles leaned against the massive kitchen table, his legs stretched out in front of him. Billie gazed at the earl from under her eyelashes, drinking in his tall physique, unruly black hair and dark grey eyes, which reminded her of a stormy sea, yet were twinkling at her in a most un-sea-like fashion. He knew she was studying him. Her breathing hitched and she lowered her eyes, hearing a quiet rumble of laughter as she did so.

"You don't need to avert your eyes, Billie. I am happy for you to stare at me 'til the end of time." His voice, laced with amusement, caused her head to snap up. Grinning, Giles drained his drink and walked over to the sink, placing the cup in a bowl of water to soak. He filled the milk pan with water, swished it around, poured it out and refilled it. "Are you finished?" Billie nodded, handing him her cup, with which he did the same. Coming around the table to where she was sitting, Giles put out his hand. Billie placed her small hand in his, allowing him to help her out of the chair.

She stood facing him, and everything slowed down. All she could hear was the ticking of the old grandfather clock in the corner; oh, and her heart which was beating so loudly that she was certain Giles must hear it too. His height meant that she had to tilt her head to see his face; she felt like a child next to him. He bent his head and brushed his lips over her hair. Billie swayed towards him, putting her free hand out to prevent herself from falling against his chest. Releasing her hand, Giles wrapped one arm around her back and cupped her head with the other, in much the same way as he had done earlier that day — or was it yesterday now?

"Oh, my love, you undo me." Unable to stop himself, Giles kissed her. Not a gentle sweet kiss, this was a hot fevered kiss as though he was trying to imprint her lips onto his, branding them both. Billie's own lips parted, welcoming his mouth as she gave herself over to the tumult racing through her. Their first kiss rocked her body; this blew her mind. She felt as though she was turning to liquid — she would be a puddle at his feet if he continued like this. Pleasurable quivers ran along her spine as his hands began an exploration of her body. She didn't notice the dressing gown slipping off her shoulders; she was too caught up in the seductive dance his fingers were doing, the capacious nightdress in no way hampering him.

Of their own volition, her hands ran up his arms, tracing the muscles flexing under his clothing, and suddenly wanting more, she pulled his shirt out of his buckskins. She heard him gasp as her cold fingers skimmed over his warm skin, his body trembling at her touch, and she revelled in the knowledge that she had this effect on him.

Their passion was spiralling out of control, and Giles knew he had to stop or he would end up taking her on the kitchen floor. Not the most salubrious place to make love for the first time, well any time really — although — *no, get a grip Giles*, he instructed himself. Reluctantly, he slowed his fingers, breaking the kiss and gazing into Billie's eyes, which were heavy with desire.

"Not here," he whispered raggedly, "not yet. I want us to do this properly. I want to be able to make love to you as often as I can, anywhere we like without fear of interruption or claims of impropriety." Billie was finding it rather difficult to speak, so she just stared at him. "Billie?"

"Hmm … errr." Waiting for the world to right itself, Billie tried again "What … how … what?" Still her words refused to form. So she gave up and simply leaned against him, arms around his waist, her head resting on his chest and breathed him in. She felt a soft murmur of laughter, a comforting sound, and she sighed happily.

"I love you, Giles," she said without thinking. He lifted her away from him and looked down at her flushed face. His smile nearly stopped her heart.

"I love you too, my Willow. Now come on, upstairs with you. I think we should both try to get some sleep."

"I suppose so," she murmured, her legs refusing to comply, and she felt them buckling. Giles lifted her into his arms and carried her up to her bedchamber. "This is becoming a habit, my Lord." She smiled, sneaking a kiss on his jaw as they entered the Rose Room. "I highly approve." His eyes darkened as he looked at her and he surrendered to one last kiss, leaving them both breathless. Then he tucked her in and said goodnight, or rather good morning as surely dawn must be about to break, and brushing her hand with his, left her to some very satisfactory dreams.

Chapter Fifteen

The next morning — well actually it was more like lunchtime before either the earl or his guest awoke, his staff deciding discretion was the better part of valour, leaving them both to sleep undisturbed — Billie woke to the sunlight streaming in through her windows. It was a perfect day and she was missing it. Jumping out of bed, she hurried through her ablutions, slipping into warm clothes before Sally arrived to assist her and then almost ran down to the library. Opening the door, she peeped in, Giles wasn't there, maybe he was in his estate office. Biting her lip, unsure of what to do, she carried on into the room, followed almost immediately by Thomas who must have been watching out for her.

"Miss Caswell, Sarah is preparing some luncheon, would you like it in here, or in the dining room?"

"Oh, in here please, Thomas, thank you so much. This room is so much more comfortable. Please thank Sarah for me too" She beamed at the butler who smiled and nodded, leaving her to it. She wandered through the magnificent room. Billie never tired of admiring the book-lined walls, smoothing her fingers over the leather bindings, tracing the titles. The view beyond the windows today was breathtaking. The frosty ground sparkled in the sunlight, and she imagined it must be very cold. Glancing at the rather ornate ormolu clock, she saw with surprise it was after midday. How very rude of her sleeping so late, especially after causing such a ruckus last night. Not stopping to think, Billie whirled out of the room, nearly colliding with Thomas as she did so.

"Your luncheon, Miss Caswell."

"Thank you, Thomas. It looks divine," retreating back into the library for the next few minutes. Not eating the lovingly prepared meal would be even more impolite. Settling at the desk, swinging her legs under the chair, which was so high her feet didn't quite reach the floor, Billie applied herself to the food with gusto. Game pie, a few boiled potatoes tossed with butter, with a small selection of winter vegetables on the side, and a cup of steaming hot coffee. Maybe rather more than would usually be served at the noon meal, but Sarah knew neither Billie nor the earl had their breakfast, and Billie had not eaten a proper meal for around twenty-four hours. Everything was delicious and, just as she was dabbing butter from the side of her mouth where it very inconveniently dribbled, Giles came in looking devastatingly handsome.

Billie dropped her fork. As it clattered on the plate her hand shot out to steady it, knocking the coffee. She managed to save everything, then tried to stand, tipping the chair over in her haste. Cursing her clumsiness, she raised her eyes to the man still standing in the doorway, his lips twitching with laughter.

"Good afternoon, my Lord." She whispered trying, unsuccessfully, to drop a curtsey.

"Good afternoon, Miss Caswell." His voice was warm like mulled wine, with just a hint of mirth. "I trust you slept well?"

"Eventually." Her own voice husky. "I think Thomas has some food ready for you. Would you like me to ring for it?"

"I have just seen him, luncheon is on its way." Neither moved. They just stared at each other across the room. Billie very much wanted to rush over to Giles, to be lifted into his arms so she could run her fingers through his hair, and was desperately trying to force her feet to stay put. Giles was eyeing her rather like a fox eyes a plump rabbit, and all the while heat flared between them. A knock at the door interrupted the moment, and Thomas came in with a platter of food and more coffee. He handed Billie a fresh cup and removed her dishes. She thanked the butler, saying everything was quite perfect. He grinned and shut the door quietly behind him.

Giles was still standing near the fire.

"Your luncheon, my Lord. Do not let it get cold, it is very tasty."

"Oh, I know exactly how tasty it is," he growled, making no move towards the food. Billie shivered at his expression. Unsure quite what to do, she stayed still and smiled hesitantly at him, running her tongue over suddenly dry lips. Giles groaned, and in three strides she was in his arms. She could do what she wanted to do and entangled her fingers in his unruly mop, tilting her face up for his kiss. He obliged most satisfactorily until Billie thought the room was actually spinning around them. Long minutes passed and still they kissed until, with a sigh, Giles lifted his head. His grey eyes had darkened to black and his expression could best be described as smouldering. Billie giggled, happiness flooding through her, as she batted at him to no discernible effect.

"Giles, I'm not on the menu. Get on with your meal. We have things to discuss."

"Serves you right for being so deliciously edible, my love." He grinned, releasing her so he could eat.

"I'll be back in a moment, there is something I must do," Billie said over her shoulder as she walked towards the door. Giles raised an eyebrow, but she shook her head. "Nothing to concern yourself about. I'll tell you later." Puzzled, but not enough to miss out on his meal, Giles let her go, thinking that the room seemed a little less bright without her in it. Pulling a face at his flummery, he directed his attention to the pie.

A little while later and because she hadn't returned, Giles went looking for his guest. He tracked her down in the stables and, intrigued as to what she was doing, paused to listen.

"...really, I just wanted to say thank you so very much for helping to search for me last night. I acted foolishly and you all risked your lives coming out in that terribly cold weather. I do not deserve such caring friends." Giles heard a murmured reply and had to clench his jaw to stop a laugh bubbling up. She was apologising to his staff. He wondered who else she had spoken to, and retraced his steps into the kitchens where he found Sarah, Jane and Kitty hard at work.

"Sarah, by any chance did…" he didn't get to finish his sentence for Sarah butted in, in her inimitable way.

"Yes, she did. She came in here apologising for the worry she caused, telling us she behaved reprehensibly and could we ever forgive her. I've never heard the like, a lady such as her, begging our pardon."

Giles chortled at the expression on his cook's face. She was all bluster, but he knew she was tickled pink Billie cared enough to explain her actions to his staff, and then to apologise for them. Kitty and Jane were giggling and added how glad they were that Miss Caswell was safe. It seemed his guest had the whole of his household under her spell.

Giles went back to the stables. Billie was still chattering away with Will and Jake, but now she was talking about Bronte. He watched from the doorway, noticing while she stroked the horse's nose, Bronte nuzzled her neck, slyly chewing her hair. Billie kept nudging Bronte, but the horse was determined, making Billie laugh helplessly as Bronte's whiskers tickled her throat.

"Go on, you great lummox," she giggled, "find some hay, that would be far tastier than my hair." Bronte ignored her until Billie gave up and moved away, and if ever a horse could look affronted, Bronte managed it, tossing her head in indignation. Billie took no notice and, thanking the two men again, turned to leave the stables. She saw Giles watching her and stopped dead, wary of his reaction to her spending so long with his groomsman and stablehand. Giles merely grinned and held out his hand. She smiled back, hurrying over to take the outreached fingers feeling a frisson trickle through her as he curled his palm around hers.

"Would you like to make a plan, Miss Caswell?" he whispered. She looked up at him and nodded.

"I really would," she replied just as quietly. They slipped back into the house and along to the library. The minute they were through the door, Giles kicked it shut and pulled her to him, seeking her mouth with his lips, kissing her to distraction. Several minutes later, and in no way satisfied, he deposited her on the sofa.

"What was the why of that?" Billie panted, trying to regain some form of equilibrium and failing dismally.

"I found I couldn't help it," Giles said, his breath too coming in gasps. "You come into this house, use your feminine wiles to captivate my staff, turn the heads of my gardeners and groomsmen, not to mention my horses, and you bamboozle my senses. You are a witch, Miss Caswell, casting your spell over us poor mortals, holding us in your thrall."

Billie gaped at him, trying to decide whether this was a good thing or a bad thing. "Errmmm…what am I supposed to say to that. Have I done something to upset you again?" Quizzically.

Giles realised his desire for her made his tone seem rather brusque. "No, no, my love, completely the opposite in fact. I am simply astounded you bothered to apologise for what happened last night and I adore that you considered it necessary. Most in your position would not give two hoots."

"Yes, but I caused grave inconvenience, not to mention worry, and it is only right that I beg forgiveness for my thoughtlessness." Giles drew her to him and kissed her again. "Oh, don't stop," she murmured against his lips, "I could do this for the rest of the day." Giles, however, did stop. They had work to do. Grinning at her disgruntled expression, he went over to the desk and picked up two sheets of heavy paper, handing them to her. It was the letter. She skimmed through it, getting the gist of the contents before going back and reading it more thoroughly.

"It says a ring was found under one of the bodies, which had a crest on it. Was it my father's? Was he one of the dead?" Giles nodded

"It seems conclusive, my love. I'm so sorry." He paused giving her a minute, then continued. "However, it appears Stephen may still be alive, although he has disappeared, so we cannot be certain. We need to know why anyone would target your family. You have to try to remember anything and everything, even the smallest snippet could be useful."

Billie sat quietly trying to absorb it all. Processing the fact she no longer had any parents and that Stephen was now the Viscount. She refused to cry; she'd done quite enough crying in the last couple of days. Maybe later when it was all over, maybe then she might allow herself a tear or two, but not now. Mentally straightening her shoulders, Billie started talking. She still struggled to recall anything of her immediate past, the time before she awoke at Whiteoaks, but her memory of life before around four months ago was beginning to filter through the murk. Theo believed the reason she couldn't remember recent events was because they were too traumatic. Her mind had simply shut down and refused to let her back in.

She talked for what seemed like hours, while Giles listened and made notes as she spoke. He was beginning to think his first instinct was correct, that there was a French connection;

too many strange coincidences. Billie mentioned visitors arriving at their home at odd hours of the day and night, unannounced and definitely unexpected, none of whom she recognised. She remembered that Stephen and her father spent long hours closeted away in her father's study, something they had rarely done until recently, and they would stop talking whenever she came into the room, or change the subject abruptly. The atmosphere in their home had become edgy and uncomfortable and for the first time in her life she didn't feel safe.

"I don't know why I was in that carriage though, this I still cannot recall. It must have been a sudden decision though, for it appears I left with only what I was wearing. It seems I had no luggage and only the coin in my purse." Billie wrinkled her face, trying to concentrate on recovering what she had lost. Giles watched her, going over what she talked about; saddened that she was dealing with such an alarming situation.

"Do you think the answers might lie in Cornwall? At this house of which you have a vague recollection?" Giles asked.

Billie pursed her lips, considering his question. "I don't know, maybe, possibly. Why else would I be carrying those papers? What if they held instructions from my father? What if I was supposed to go to the place in Cornwall, that there is something I should be looking for, or have to give to, or hide from someone? And who is that someone? What if he entrusted me with something really important, something he wanted me to do for him? That would explain why I was in that carriage, so far from home. How am I to carry out his wishes?"

Wanting to distract her from her fears, Giles said, "Several days ago, in fact the first night you joined us for dinner, Theo and I were looking at a map of Cornwall. Maybe if you took the time to study it, you might remember a name or a place."

"Oh, that is a good idea. Where is it? Please may we look now?"

Giles smiled at her enthusiasm, and went around to a tall, thin cabinet standing against the wall behind his desk. When he opened it, Billie could see several long rolls of parchment, one of which he removed and unrolled onto the desk. It was a map of the south west of England from Dorsetshire and

Gloucestershire to Cornwall. Giles held out a large magnifying glass, for Billie to begin checking the place names scattered along the Cornish coast.

She was very methodical, murmuring every name to herself, letting it play in her head, mulling over it, before moving on to the next one. A peace descended over the room, the only sounds were the turn of papers and the pop of the wood on the fire. Eventually after what felt like an age, although was more like two hours, during which they'd enjoyed a break and another piping hot coffee but with no luck, Billie paused and straightened up. Rolling her shoulders, she tried to undo the knots accumulating there as a result of too long leaning over the desk. Giles, who had moved to the sofa to read his correspondence, noted her expression and came over.

"What is it, Billie? Have you found something?"

She looked rather stumped. "I'm not sure. There's a place whose name is resonating with me, but I can't decide whether it's just because I like the sound of the word, or it really means something."

"Where, show me?" Billie pointed to a tiny dot on the map, a hamlet called Polruan, nestling at the mouth of the Fowey River. "Polruan?" Billie nodded, adding that every time she said the word in her head another image formed.

"I think this might be it. Nothing else has jumped out at me but this place, this name, is familiar. I cannot think I would have heard it elsewhere. Maybe the word on that document wasn't 'ruin' but 'Polruan,' the first half of the word simply lost when it got so wet. Oh Giles, what if this is it, what if I am supposed to go there? What if I'm supposed to be there already?" She started panicking again, fear for her family rising like bile in her throat.

Giles grasped her hands. "Hush, Billie. Do not get so worked up. We will make arrangements to travel to this Polruan and see what is there. You cannot go alone. If there are people hunting you or Stephen, they may already know of this place. Some of my men shall accompany us and we will set off as soon as it can be organised."

Billie stared up at Giles, her head on one side as she studied his face. "You do not need to trouble yourself, my Lord. I cannot expect you to place yourself and your men in danger for me. I am just one person."

Giles let out an exasperated huff. "When are you going to accept that everything you do affects me? Do you think I could live with myself if I let you go traipsing across the country with nary a guard or a chaperone. Look what happened the last time you tried such an escapade."

"I do not think it was an 'escapade' as you so politely put it, my Lord. I may be thoughtless on occasion but I did not rush from my home with two bodyguards on a whim." Billie spluttered, pacing the floor in her indignation. "I had to do it there was no one else. They were watching my father and Stephen. No one would notice if I went for an afternoon's carriage ride. I was to go and retrieve some documents from our…" her voice trailed off as she realised she was remembering the day she fled London. Her eyes flew to his and, as there was no chair nearby, she sat down on the floor with a bump. Giles crouched down beside her, taking her hand, which was trembling a little.

"Tell me, Billie."

She stared at him, her eyes unfocused, her mind in the past, dredging up the memory that until now, stubbornly refused to be recalled and, as she began to speak, her tale finally unfurled.

Chapter Sixteen

"I was outside planting herbs in the garden. It was a glorious day, a little cool, but it was October, so that was to be expected. Alfred, our butler, came to tell me Papa needed to speak to me, and he was waiting in his study. I was a bit puzzled because I was sure Papa left for Parliament that morning. There was a bill or something, being read and he wanted to attend in case there was a vote.

I remember dawdling along the hall, a little disgruntled at having to leave my herbs half planted. I was wearing gloves, they were covered in dirt and I'd forgotten to take them off, but by the time I realised, I was already in the study. Papa didn't even notice, he was very distracted. Stephen was pleading with him about something but Papa just shook his head and kept saying that it was no good, it had to be me."

Three weeks earlier, Viscount Ashbourne's study, London.

"Papa, you cannot expect Billie to do this, it is too dangerous."

"No one will suspect her Stephen, she will be merely a young woman taking a carriage ride. I will have Havers and Banks accompany her and as soon as they are sure they are not being followed, they can leave the city through the old routes."

Surreptitiously, I slipped my dirty gloves off, dropping them under the little table I was standing beside, hoping the dirt didn't mess up the floor too much. I half-listened to my brother and father arguing, but I wasn't really concentrating, my head was still in the garden with my herbs. I had been reading about traditional remedies and believed the ones I was planting might prove beneficial in the treatment of stomach ailments and nausea. They were always arguing lately and I learned to shut it out. My home was no longer a very comfortable place to live. Suddenly Papa was shaking my shoulders.

"Billie, why do you never heed me? You always have your head in the clouds." I stared at him, his face was quite red and he seemed very angry.

"What have I done now?" I sighed, waiting for the inevitable censure. What had happened to our happy, loving home? Everyone was treading on eggshells, even the staff. It seemed as though I was the only one who tried to pretend life was normal.

"What? No, it is nothing you have done, it is what I want you to do."

I looked at him, even more bewildered. "I am sorry, Papa, but how can you be angry with me for something you want me to do?" My father gaped at me, no doubt trying to decide whether I was being impudent. He took a deep breath and asked me to sit.

"Billie, I have a very important task I would like you to undertake on my behalf. It will involve a little intrigue, some careful observation and quite a lot of courage."

I looked across at Stephen who was leaning on the mantelpiece, his expression bleak and, for no reason I could think of, a sense of foreboding came over me. "What's going on, Papa?" I whispered, grasping his hand. He pulled up a chair and, sitting down opposite me, looked me in the eye.

"I think we, Stephen and I, might be in somewhat of a predicament, my pet. It appears that some of the … errr … activities I was involved in during the war have come to the attention of the wrong people and we need to have every care." I tightened my grip on his hand. "There are…" he paused as though searching for the right word then settled on "…papers entrusted to me that should not fall into their hands and although my safe is secure, I have not dared bring them here. I cannot risk going to collect them and neither can Stephen, for I fear we are being watched."

"Why did you not just burn them, then no one can have them? Or better still give them to someone in the government? Surely they could keep them safe?" I asked curiously. Papa shook his head.

"These papers bear information of a very sensitive nature and it is the only proof I — we — have. Although at first glance they appear to be uninteresting documents regarding estate business, they in fact contain details of those involved in treachery as well as those who have been trying to bring them to justice. Foreign agents are very cunning. We believe that in their attempts to recover this list, they have infiltrated the highest levels of society and a mere word or thoughtless conversation could give them the lead they seek. I have many colleagues whose lives would be in jeopardy should these papers fall into the wrong hands."

I gaped at him. My mild mannered father was involved in something perilous? I looked over at Stephen, who hadn't moved, but whose face was very pale.

"Papa, are you an agent or some kind of spy? Is Stephen?" I asked, my voice barely a whisper. Papa neither confirmed nor denied it, but he muttered something about covert operations and the safety of England. Quite a lot of it went over my head, to be honest. I was still trying to get my mind around the whole spies issue.

"Who's this 'we' you keep talking about?"

Papa glanced at Stephen and shook his head. "I would rather not burden you with that information, pet. The less you know, the safer you'll be."

A trickle of ice-cold fear ran down my spine. "Papa, if you want me to do this for you, you need to tell me. I need to know what I might be facing or who I have to look out for. What if these people are able to figure out what I'm doing?"

My brother finally spoke. "She's right, Papa, you cannot expect her to do this for us without telling her something. You are placing her in greater danger." Stephen came over and sat in the chair next to mine. "Billie, you do not have to do this, there is some risk, but we do not know who else we can trust." I stared at the two most important people in my life, reading more from their faces than they realised. I nodded slowly.

"If you will tell me a little more about this, I will agree to help." The atmosphere in the room lightened perceptibly and my father heaved a huge sigh of relief.

"Thank you, poppet. Your decision means more than you will ever know." Then between them they proceeded to explain a little more about the men they thought were watching them and where the papers were hidden currently. I had to make my way to my grandmother's house in Polruan on the Cornish coast. There was an old cellar beneath the house, one used by smugglers not so very long ago, which was connected to the beach by a secret stairwell under the floor. The documents were concealed in an innocuous tin on a shelf. Hidden in plain sight so to speak. It all seemed rather slapdash to me, but what did I know?

"Cornwall," I squeaked. " How on earth am I going to get to Cornwall? What about grandmama, I do not wish to cause her any anxiety by arriving unannounced."

"I think you will find your grandmother is quite unflappable," Papa replied, grinning mischievously, making me think she might know more than he was prepared to tell me.

After what felt like a very long time we had a plan in place. For two men, apparently used to working covertly it didn't seem a particularly brilliant plan, but it was simple and required minimal organisation. I was to leave the house as though I was going for my usual carriage ride to the park, then once we were sure no one was following us, we would leave the city via less travelled routes. We had a black town coach without the family crest and I often used it. Unusually, I only occasionally went out with a chaperone, as generally I only left the house to call on friends or to visit the modiste. While many considered our family somewhat unconventional and probably rather eccentric, it did mean the people who lived around us would not think my behaviour to be anything out of the ordinary.

Havers would be inside the carriage before it left the stable and Banks would drive, as was the norm. That gave me two bodyguards. Both men had known me since I was a child and would never willingly let anyone hurt me. I already felt safer. I would be allowed to take only the absolute essentials in a small valise, which basically meant one change of underclothes and possibly a wrap. I would have my cloak for warmth and there would be the usual travelling rugs in the coach.

Papa wanted me to set off as soon as possible, so we arranged that I would leave two days hence. As we completed our discussions, Stephen took my hand.

"You do not have to do this, Squidge. We can work something else out." Somehow, Stephen using his nickname for me, made me feel less concerned about what I had to do. I gazed at my tall brother, four years older than I; he had always been my protector. His hair, a slightly lighter shade than mine, was sticking out in all directions because he had been running his fingers through it while we talked; and his eyes, more hazel than green, bore into mine trying to read my thoughts. My mind was already made up.

"I have to do this. I have to help. I'm sure it will be fine. Havers and Banks will not let anything happen to me. I am more afraid for you and Papa. What if they come here? What if they try to hurt you? I could not bear it if anything were to happen to you."

He squeezed my hand. "We are very vigilant, sweetheart, trust us. Now, are you certain sure?" A phrase we used as children, little realising how glad I would be of it in the not-too-distant future. I assured him I understood the risks and was prepared to make the journey.

We talked for a little longer, after which I picked up my gloves and returned to my herbs, my mind churning with what I was about to undertake. Cornwall was a long way away, several days by carriage. There was the added concern about highwaymen, but Banks and Havers would each have a gun. I think I was more worried about where we would sleep and whether I would manage to get a decent wash than the possibility of being held up by brigands. At that point it all sounded quite exciting.

By the time I got to bed that night my head was pounding, I took an herb I found useful for the rare times when I did suffer from such aches, but it was a long time before I fell asleep. I scarcely had chance to turn around over the next two days, which flew by. Papa and Stephen kept going over and over the plan with me and gave me a detailed set of instructions to the house. They did not write down where the papers were, for if on the slender chance those searching for the documents waylaid us, all our efforts would be wasted. I was to tell anyone who asked that I was travelling to see my grandmother, who was unwell.

The night before I set out, my father came to my bedchamber and gave me a strange clasp, which had been his mother's. Apparently, it was gifted to an ancestor of ours by a grateful soldier whose life she saved, and passed down through the women of our family for centuries. I did have a hazy memory of hearing about it as a child. It was a red stone, a ruby Papa said, nestled in a most unusual setting, and was supposedly a talisman of sorts. Normally it was given to the eldest daughter when she reached five and twenty years, but my father said he wanted me to have it now, hoping it might bring me safe travels, and if all else failed I could sell it for extra coin. Certainly it would hold my cloak securely.

After he left, I rolled the clasp around in my hand. It was quite remarkable, there was something very tactile about it and, oddly, I felt as though it called to me. Dismissing it as fancy, I laid it on my bedside table, but in that moment I knew whatever happened I could never give it away or sell it. It seemed to be a part of me and if it had been in my family for so long, who was I to let it go?

Maintaining the ruse of taking the carriage to visit one of my friends, I departed my home just after luncheon the next day. I bade my father and brother goodbye earlier, before they left for whatever duties required their attention. If our home was being observed, it would seem a typical Caswell day. My valise was tucked neatly away under the seat and I was glad of the rugs, as the day was cool. I remember thinking how lovely the red clasp was against the deeper red of my cloak and, unexpectedly, I was reminded of a fairy tale Maman read to me as a child — something about a young girl visiting her grandmother and a wolf and being rescued by a huntsman. I couldn't remember it properly, but for some reason it troubled me.

I don't know whether it was the memory of the tale, but as the carriage rattled along the streets my stomach was in knots. I was suddenly very aware this might not be the great adventure I persuaded myself it would be, and that fairy tales were often quite gruesome. Also, I was very much afraid we might be followed, and although this did not seem to be the case, I could not relax. Havers was still on the floor of the coach. He would not sit up until we were out of the city, for I generally travelled with the curtains drawn back and a second person would be noticed.

It felt like forever before we were out of the conglomeration that is London, but eventually green fields, trees and rolling hills took over from houses and shops. We were taking the mail route, the one terminating at Falmouth, although we wouldn't be going that far. The surface was better than some of the lesser-known routes, meaning we could travel much more quickly, but also we were a little more vulnerable. Ignoring the fear circling my senses, I kept the curtains back and enjoyed the scenery.

That night we rested at a reasonably salubrious posting inn, and to my surprise I slept like a log. Waking early, I managed a thorough wash and a good breakfast. We were back on the road by just after eight. Havers and Banks were very solicitous, making sure I was warm and comfortable, and I know they never relaxed their vigilance.

Chapter Seventeen

It was quite late the following afternoon when I heard the sound of another carriage. This was not unexpected, we passed several during the day. This one, however, was coming up behind us at a speed greater than we were travelling, and Banks tried to manoeuvre the horses to the edge of the road to allow it to pass. Strangely, it didn't overtake us, merely stayed alongside. Something about its actions unnerved Havers, and he drew his gun, pushing me down onto the floor of the carriage and dropping one of the rugs over me, telling me to stay quiet. Banks clicked the horses, and even though our pace increased, the other coach kept up. There was a lot of shouting, but I couldn't hear properly. The heavy rug covering me, and the rattle of the coach drowned out most everything, and we were still going too fast. I was terrified we might lose a wheel.

Suddenly there was a crunching sound, it was deafening and I felt the carriage tipping, everything seemed to be happening in slow motion. The horses were screaming, I think people were screaming, I just curled myself into a ball and hoped I wouldn't be thrown out, or crushed. I was hurled against the side of the coach, the heavy impact jarring through me, and I felt sick as an excruciating pain pierced my side. There was another loud noise and I imagined the other coach must have tipped also, then nothing. Once I got my breath back, I attempted to get out but the door wouldn't budge. It was jammed into a bush. I pushed the rug back and tried to work out what was going on. I think I lay for quite a while worrying about what Papa would say to all the damage — the coach looked to be ruined — and waiting to see whether anyone would help us, but no one came. It was up to me. I had to get out to make sure Havers, Banks and the horses were all right. To see whether to coach was salvageable, and then work out how to continue my journey.

I managed to shove the other door open. Climbing out proved to be a challenge especially in a cloak, and my ridiculous travelling clothes. I ached all over and fell back in several times, banging myself quite badly, realising I was going to be very bruised. Thwarted, I forced myself to stop and look around. I noticed a tear in the front of the coach where it buckled as it slipped over. It wasn't very large but I managed to crawl through it. By now I must have looked a complete wreck, but surprisingly my clothes weren't too badly torn.

Banks was trapped under the wheels. I rushed around to try and help him escape. When I got to him, I saw there was blood everywhere, and after checking to make absolutely sure, had to accept he was beyond help. I think I might have lost my head rather. I have never seen a dead body before, and this man was a friend of sorts. There was no sign of Havers or the horses. I called his name for ages, but there was no reply and it was starting to rain. I knew I needed to get away from this wrecked carriage. Whoever caused it might come back, but I had no idea where I was. So I just followed the road, keeping to the edges giving me a better chance to hide, should anyone happen by.

It got dark and I was in the middle of nowhere. There was no sign of habitation, but I found a large bush and slept under it. I felt totally useless. What on earth would my father think? Barely two days from home and already in trouble. My side hurt, making it difficult to breathe, my ankle was very painful, the whole of my body ached, and on top of all this I was lost."

Giles wanted to stop Billie, to assure her none of it was her fault, but he needed to hear the whole story and was afraid, if he interrupted her tale, she would forget again. Theo arrived to see how Billie was after her exploits of the previous night, but even his entrance did not disturb her. He was immediately caught up in her story, and now both men were listening intently. Billie's voice was quiet. She wasn't seeing them at all. She was reliving the days before she awoke in the Rose Room with no recollection of who she was.

They had to let her continue.

"I don't know how long I slept, although it was still dark when I awoke. I was very hungry, but aside from a few blackberries in the hedgerows, which were most welcome, there was nothing to eat. I just kept walking and walking, and it kept raining. Eventually the sun came out. I sat against a wall and let it warm me. It didn't last long enough to dry my clothes and I seemed to have misplaced my valise. My head was muzzy and I could not concentrate. Where was Havers? Where was I? I knew we were far from our destination. We had been travelling for only three days, not even that really. I took the clasp off my cloak. I didn't want anyone to see it. It was too costly a jewel for someone who must now look like a beggar to be wearing. They might think me a thief. Oddly enough, I didn't see a soul, but I found this a relief rather than a concern.

I didn't know where I was going. I fear I may have walked in circles. Nothing made sense anymore and I forgot I was hungry. I couldn't remember why I was here. I knew it was important but it wouldn't come to me. Faces appeared but I didn't know who they were and I couldn't decide whether they were real or in my head. The day was cold, so cold. I was struggling to walk, my foot wouldn't hold me, not even to hobble, and every time I breathed, my side felt as though it was on fire.

Then the storm hit, the rain was like stones drumming onto me and the thunder was really loud. I came to a fork in the road, I knew I'd been there before and it all became too much. I was so very tired. I just wanted to rest for a few minutes, to catch my breath, to feel warm. I saw a green bed and I did wonder why on earth it was outside, but it looked so inviting. I didn't think the owner would mind. I could pay. I got out my reticule, but my fingers wouldn't work properly, I think I dropped it. The bed was still there, there was no one else using it. I just wanted to rest for a few minutes ... I was so sleepy..." Her voice finally trailed off, large tears rolling down her face, but she was still in the past, her vision turned inward.

The two men were silenced, for although this clarified how she came to be at Whiteoaks, that she was prepared to risk her life for her father and brother stunned them. She was still sitting on the floor and Giles, now sitting next to her, was holding her hand. Theo rose from his chair quietly and, resting his hand on Billie's shoulder, spoke in gentle tones, calling her back from her memories.

Slowly her eyes unglazed and her focus returned to the present. She saw the familiar room lined with books and heard the hiss of the fire. Billie turned her head to look at Giles, her extraordinary eyes reaching for him. Her breath came in shuddering gasps, while she fought for control, her fear and distress threatening to overwhelm her. Giles drew her to him, lifting her onto his knees, cradling her against him whispering his love for her as he held her close.

Theo watched, eyebrows raised. Giles glanced up at his friend and imperceptibly, shook his head. He knew this was breaking all the rules, but right now rules be damned! Asking Theo to ring for hot drinks and maybe a light snack, Giles carefully stood up, never relinquishing his hold and carried Billie over to the chairs by the fire, which was burning low in the grate. None in the room realised how long they had been there. The fact the fire needed stoking, suggested a couple of hours at the very least.

Thomas appeared with steaming cups of coffee as well as a plate of very scrumptious-looking sweet buns and placed two more huge logs on the fire, waiting to make sure the flames caught before quietly leaving the room. Giles handed Billie one of the coffees, before offering one to Theo and then taking one for himself. They didn't speak until the cups were drained and the buns eaten. It was difficult to know quite what to say. After a little while during which they let the peace of the room envelop them, Billie said —

"I can't believe I forgot all that. It was so important. I am not much use to my father am I? It's been two weeks since the carriage accident, well more actually for I don't remember how long I walked before you found me. What if they kidnapped Havers and forced him to tell them where we were going? Maybe they've already found the papers. I still can't remember what anyone looks like. All their faces are blurred in my mind. Oh what a mess."

"Billie, we will travel to this place together. We will find the papers and we will try to find Stephen, or at the very least someone who we can trust."

Billie gazed at him. "But how will we know? Papa said even he didn't know who that might be"

"He said the documents contained the names of those trying to bring the informers to justice, didn't he?" Billie nodded. "One of those people would be a good start. However, we have to find the documents first, one thing at a time. We will do no more today. No..." when Billie started to protest, "...you need at least a day, probably longer to make sure you are not going to suffer a relapse after last night, and I need time to make proper arrangements." She knew he was right. It was sensible to travel safely rather than leave without proper preparations. Although, she thought ruefully, even the best-laid plans don't always work out. She smiled at him rather tentatively and, oblivious to Theo's presence, cupped Giles' cheek in her hand.

"Thank you, my love." Billie whispered, and for a moment there were only those two as her eyes held his, green on grey. Giles pressed a kiss to her forehead, wanting more, but a not so subtle cough from Theo brought them back to earth. "Oh, I do beg your pardon, Dr Elliott. I am behaving quite improperly," Billie spluttered, scrambling off Giles' lap, to sit in the other chair, hectic colour flaring up her face. Giles reluctantly let her go, knowing it was the right thing to do.

Theo laughed. "It is a good job I know you, Winchester, but you might want to beware of gossiping tongues. One misstep and Miss Caswell here could be ruined."

Giles grimaced, but acceded to his friend's words. They would need to persuade one of the maids to accompany them to Cornwall. A young lady travelling on her own with several men would certainly raise eyebrows, which begged the question

—

"How is it that your father allowed you to travel without a chaperone?"

Billie stared at him. He was right, that was most unusual. "I never really thought about it. Whenever I visited friends or the dressmaker, I never took a chaperone, although if my brother had no other call on his time, he usually accompanied me when I took the carriage through the park. You are correct, that is rather peculiar. I have no explanation. Maybe there is a good reason, but I find I am unable to recall. Neither can I recall what my father or brother look like, or Havers for that matter. So, I can remember what happened, just not those involved. Do you think I ever will?" She appealed to Theo. The doctor didn't hesitate.

"Of course you will, my dear. It is extraordinary that you have been able to remember these events. They were obviously very upsetting and you were in danger, yet something prompted them. It will be the same with your family. Something will just click, though I cannot give you a time frame as to when it could happen or what the trigger might be." He sounded very positive, and Billie felt herself relax. She leaned her head against the back of the chair and shut her eyes. She could hear the two men discussing the situation, but she was struggling to concentrate. All that talking had worn her out. The fire was so lovely and warm, she curled up, watching the flames dance over the log, sparks shooting up the chimney. Her eyes felt heavy and not even trying to fight it, she drifted off.

Chapter Eighteen

Giles and Theo did not notice Billie had fallen asleep, becoming engrossed in their discussions about the upcoming trip to Cornwall. Theo felt he should travel with them, arguing that having a doctor on hand wasn't a bad idea, but Giles knew the truth was, he didn't want to miss out on the excitement.

"You do realise these men are prepared to murder anyone who gets in their way don't you, Elliott?" queried Giles, frowning at his friend.

"Of course! I'm not a simpleton. I just think if you are hell-bent on rushing into the fray, another ex-soldier might come in handy."

Giles grinned. Both he and Theo saw action in the Peninsula Wars culminating in the Battle of Vitoria, where the combined forces of British, Portuguese and Spanish troops under the command of Field Marshall Wellesley — who, in recognition of his outstanding military service and after the abdication of Napoleon, was bestowed with the title 1st Duke of Wellington — overwhelmed the French. Their resistance crumbling under the allied onslaught, their defeat signifying the collapse of Napoleonic rule in Spain. Casualties were high and they lost many friends, either killed outright or died from their injuries. It was there they met Withers, who served with one of the Light Infantry Regiments.

Each had returned home a quieter, graver man, having witnessed enough death and destruction never to wish it upon another living soul. Theo, as a doctor, observed the appalling conditions under which the injured were treated — often primitive, usually unsanitary and almost certainly disease ridden. He was surprised any survived their wounds. Giles was injured during one of the battles; a bayonet to his upper thigh narrowly missed a major blood vessel. Theo saw him fall and somehow managed to get him to a makeshift hospital set up in a local villa, the state of which was not quite as atrocious as some he had seen.

Their physical injuries healed far more quickly than the psychological, but thankfully both came from loving, supportive families who allowed them the time to heal without placing undue pressure on them to re-enter society with all its foibles. Theo, as the second son of a Marquis managed to avoid the government commitments his elder brother was required to undertake, and at Giles' invitation, quietly assumed the role of local doctor in Oak Stanton, the village near Whiteoaks. He preferred the anonymity this provided rather than working in one of the city hospitals. The late Earl of Winchester died soon after his son's return, so Giles ended up back in the thick of it sooner than he would have chosen, but maybe this wasn't so bad. He enjoyed the challenge of being on several parliamentary committees, one of which was where he had come across Billie's father. His estates required him to spend much of his time at Whiteoaks anyway, meaning he could avoid most of the London Season should he so choose.

It was four years since the two friends came home and, for the most part, life returned to normal. Giles was occasionally afflicted by nightmares, and in very cold or very damp weather his leg ached. In view of how bad it could have been, however, he felt he escaped lightly.

Their conversation ran on: planning who to take; whether one coach and several outriders, or two coaches and fewer riders; how long they would likely be away; what would need doing on the estate in his absence and so on. It was early November now and as Christmas loomed closer, Giles had to consider the party he threw every year for all those who worked for him, as well as the people in the village. It was a huge affair and required considerable organisation, but he hoped they would be back long before it was time to distribute the invitations and make sure there was enough food.

Giles concluded they could leave in three days' time. It would give him enough time to discuss anything requiring attention, with Henry, his steward, and also instruct the rest of his staff. While they were talking, he drafted a missive for Withers to be mailed the next day advising him, in carefully phrased sentences, what Billie told them, and to continue his investigations into the fire and those who perished.

By the time they felt as though they had done all they could for this day, it was dark outside. Evening had fallen and a bitter wind was howling around the house. Giles invited Theo to stay the night, an offer Theo gratefully accepted. He had no pressing demands on his time and could be home early enough the next day. If anyone needed him during the night and didn't find him at home, they would know to come up to Whiteoaks.

Billie slept through all of this, but she roused as Thomas came in with a tray of drinks — brandy for the men and a glass of Madeira for Billie. She pulled herself together, shaking her head to clear the grogginess sleeping in front of the fire caused. Giles explained their plans and she agreed somewhat wearily. All she wanted to do was go to bed and find that when she woke, she would be back in her own bed at home and this was simply a bad dream. Although, as she glanced across at Giles, she decided that maybe it wasn't all bad.

He caught her gaze and smiled. Her insides melted as she smiled back, wishing they were on their own so she could be swept into his arms for a long kiss. Shocked at such shameless thoughts, she lowered her eyes, but a soft chuckle from her beloved brought them back to his, and she realised his desire mirrored hers. Forcing her mind back to their conversation, she regained some control of her emotions and managed a creditable job of behaving properly for the rest of the evening.

Billie excused herself quite early, leaving the men to their whisky and cigars, but after falling asleep almost immediately, she awoke in the early hours of the morning and now, sleep eluded her. All that napping in the chair, no doubt. After tossing for about an hour, she finally got up and, echoing her conduct of the previous night, crept downstairs to the library. Scanning through the titles, she found a copy of Virgil's Aeneid. Happy with her choice, and comfortable where she was, Billie snuggled into the chair she snoozed in less than six hours earlier, soon lost in the lives of Dido and Aeneas. It wasn't long before the warm room repeated its soporific effect, and the book slipped from her fingers to lie open on her knee.

This was how Giles found her sometime later. He too was finding it hard to sleep. Images of Billie teased him, pushing all other thoughts aside, making him want to rush into her room, wake her up and kiss her until she was breathless in his arms. He knew he could do no such thing, but it didn't seem to matter what he thought about to counter his desire, such as estate business, pig troughs, horse manure, even harvesting — nothing worked, so he'd given up.

As he entered the library, he saw her in the chair, hair hanging in a long, loose plait, curled over her shoulders, her countenance, soft in the firelight, cheeks less pale than they had been. Her dressing gown had somehow come unwrapped, revealing a simple white nightshift; one Ellen adjusted to fit Billie, so she didn't have to keep wearing the ridiculously large one they found for her when she arrived. He couldn't quite believe she loved him, nay that he loved her. He who swore off marriage fearing he could never find a bride who would love him for who he was, rather than being enamoured of his title and his lands.

Unwilling to disturb her, he went over to his desk and examined the map they looked at during the day. He traced his finger from the New Forest to Polruan, working out in his head the distance, and how long it would take, coming up with about a week, allowing for overnight rest stops for both them and their horses.

He was lost in thought when suddenly he felt a small cool hand slip in to his large one. He looked down to see Billie standing next to him, gazing up at him, her eyes heavy with sleep.

"I'm sorry, I didn't mean to disturb you." She didn't reply just kept staring at him, then turning his hand, she pressed a light kiss on his palm. He felt his breathing quicken. "Billie, you do not know what you do to me, you should return to your bed before I do something we will both regret."

"Do you love me, Giles? Will you always love me?" Her whispered questions wrapped themselves around him as he nodded, unable to speak. "Then what is there to regret?" She leant up, standing on tiptoe to kiss his cheek, the stretch causing her dressing gown to slither from her shoulders, the white nightshift in no way hiding her slender body. His heart hammered in his chest.

"You are a minx, my Willow," he ground out, his voice husky, "but you are also an innocent. I cannot and will not take that innocence here."

"You are a true gentleman, my Giles." She called him 'hers.' Heat spiralled through his body and it took all his self-restraint to keep his hands off her. "So don't make me beg." He groaned and gave up the fight, whisking her into his arms, capturing her mouth with sizzling intensity. She opened herself to him, matching him kiss for kiss, her hands roving over his body, learning, touching, teasing. Giles cradled her head in one hand, letting his other stroke along her neck and across her back, sending ripples of pleasure down her spine. He heard her moan, the sound whipping up his desire. He had never known anything like this. She utterly bewitched him. Tenderly, he cupped her breast, feeling her shudder as he did so, her gasp almost undoing him. She arched into his touch needing more; his fingers caressed her, as she slid her arms around him, moulding herself to his shape.

Billie knew her behaviour was totally unacceptable, but she was past caring. If Giles wanted to make love to her, she wasn't going to stop him; but even though she could tell how badly he wanted her and that he was fighting for control, she sensed his head would win over his heart, so she simply abandoned herself to his intoxicating touch. Allowing her own heart to rule her actions, she let instinct take over, her fingers trailing up his chest, over his shoulders, along his arms and round to his back, making him tremble. Giles was scattering butterfly kisses along her shoulder, down towards the swell of her breast and, despite the irresistible sensations this was creating, she needed his mouth back on hers. Pushing her hands up into his hair she lifted his head, seeking those magical lips that sent her to the stars. Giles lifted her and, without thinking, Billie hooked her legs around his hips making him groan again, as she felt how much he wanted her, his rigid muscle pulsing against her sensitive core.

"Oh, Giles! I never thought it could feel like this. My whole being wants you to consume me. I know my behaviour is not ladylike but you … you…" words failed her as Giles took possession of her mouth again, his hands making her body respond in a way she could never have imagined. After several minutes when she thought her heart had actually stopped, she felt Giles pull away.

"Nooooo," she muttered against his mouth.

"I want you so badly, I think there's a fair chance it will kill me if I don't take you, but you are more to me than a quick tumble in the library." His voice was hoarse with need and she could see how hard this was for him. "I love you, Billie. I wish to spend the rest of my life with you, but I still want to do this right."

Billie smiled up at him, stroking her fingers through his hair, pushing it back from his face. "Even though I would very much like you to forgo your sensibilities and make love to me here against this desk, then again upstairs in my bed and then continue to do so every day, I love that you want to wait, my Giles. As long as you don't stop kissing me, I think I might be able to cope." She winked, her cheeks colouring an alluring pink.

Giles swept her back into his arms for a long, tender and very satisfying kiss before suggesting they ought to try to get some sleep in their own beds. They walked upstairs slowly. Giles had his arm around Billie, holding her to him and she slipped her arm around his waist. It felt so right. At the door to her bedchamber, he bent his head for one last lingering kiss, then opened her door and guided her into the room. As she turned to say goodnight, he smiled his slow smile, her heart fluttered, and he was gone.

Billie got into bed and snuggled beneath the sheets, pulling the heavy comforter all the way up to her shoulders, and sank into oblivion.

Chapter Nineteen

The next two days sped by as preparations for their journey to Polruan began in earnest. Despite Billie's arguments to the contrary, assuring Giles and Theo, she was perfectly capable of making the journey on horseback, it was decided eventually that would take one coach. This would provide somewhere to store the luggage and a place to shelter if the weather became too bad between coaching inns. After more discussion, Giles chose five of his most dependable men to accompany them, making a total of nine who would travel, including Billie, and Sally as chaperone. Hopefully enough to deter any approach by highwaymen.

Clothes were packed, rugs and blankets stored neatly under the coach seats. Enough food to feed a small army was tucked into large baskets and placed ready. By nightfall the day before they were due to depart everything was as ready as it could be.

The bitter wind, which had howled around the house over the past forty-eight hours, finally blew itself out and everything was still. Those who were travelling hoped this calm interlude would continue, making their journey less arduous. Giles sent another letter to Withers, explaining what they were doing in language only his man would understand; not code as much as cryptically phrased. The last thing they needed was their plans to be scuppered by whoever was hounding Billie's family.

Billie was still very worried about her brother, but she seemed to have accepted her father died in the fire. She didn't talk about him much, although Giles did notice that all of a sudden she would go quiet and seemed to disappear within herself, lost in memories. He didn't intrude on these moments, simply made sure he was there to give her a hug or hold her hand when she rejoined the present; and Billie, for her part, was touched by his sensitivity.

Aware of how easy it would be to be swept away by their feelings, Giles and Billie somehow managed to behave with the utmost decorum in the presence of others, rejoicing in the secret joy of stealing passionate kisses on the odd occasion they were able to snatch a little privacy. Theo of course wasn't fooled for a second, but he kept his counsel, merely reminding Giles, again, how easily a lady could be ruined. This was the least of their worries, as the rumours surrounding Billie's involvement in the fire continued to circulate, especially as both Billie and Stephen were still considered missing. The story had now evolved to include Stephen in the dastardly deed, implying he helped Billie set the flames to speed up gaining his inheritance. Giles kept all newspapers away from Billie postulating that she had enough on her plate without this extra scaremongering.

In the meantime, armed with the new information Billie provided, clarifying how she came to be lost and alone near Whiteoaks, Withers had been in discussions with several of his trusted allies in the Bow Street Runners. Between them they began a surreptitious investigation into the fire, and subsequent deaths. Swearing his associates to secrecy, he explained the circumstances surrounding Billie's supposed disappearance. They agreed, in view of the timeline of her departure from London, witnessed by several upstanding citizens, it was impossible for her to have started the fire and be at a coaching inn halfway to Hampshire at the same time.

Giles also informed Withers they would be travelling to Polruan should any of them see their way to following in case the situation escalated. It was as much as they could do. One final check after the evening meal and everyone retired for the evening. Theo stayed the night at Whiteoaks, so that they could all set out together the next day. He had left his practice in the hands of a locum, a retired doctor living in the village, who was happy to help while Theo was away.

Billie didn't sleep well that night; too many things playing on her mind. She just wanted this all behind her, to find her brother alive and well, to be cleared of any blame for the death of her father and the destruction of his — their — home, and she really wanted Giles to ask her to marry him, officially. Oh yes, he said he wanted to spend the rest of his life with her, but that wasn't quite the same thing. A niggle had begun to pester at the back of her mind, that maybe Giles only wanted her as his mistress, knowing she would not be able to stand on the sidelines when he married another, far more suitable bride. Logically she knew this was a ridiculous notion — he was an honourable man — but logic doesn't tend to have much say when matters of the heart are involved.

When dawn finally broke, she had been awake a long time. Dragging herself out of her lovely, comfortable bed, Billie indulged in a thorough wash and dressed warmly. Ellen had altered some of Lady Helena's winter travel attire and Billie was very grateful, the heavier material would keep her snug during the journey. Being a proficient horsewoman, something none of her current companions was aware of, Billie hoped she might be allowed to ride on horseback for some of the time, knowing she could keep up with any man. Persuading Giles of this might prove rather difficult, but she was prepared to give it a go.

Trailing down the stairs, she wandered along to the kitchens, where Sarah was cooking up a storm — Nancy, Lucy and Kitty already attending to their morning duties. Billie loved this room, almost as much as the library, and unknown to Giles spent hours there, getting to know all the domestic staff. Having recalled she learnt the basics of cookery at her mother's insistence, despite this being unheard of among the nobility, Billie relished having the chance to put some of it into practice, delighted Sarah was happy to let her help. It was a welcome distraction while she recovered for, as much as she loved reading, it was not enough to keep her occupied during the long days, and far more preferable than sitting on her own.

Thomas came in just as Billie entered the room, grinning at her, knowing exactly why she was there, informing her Giles and Theo were dressing and breakfast would be served in the dining room shortly. Billie grinned back, thanking him, then turned her attention to Sarah who waved her away.

"Not this morning, Miss Caswell, you don't want to be getting that lovely outfit all floury and messy. His Lordship would never forgive me."

"He doesn't know I come here, Sarah, but I do concede your point. Thank you so much for providing all that wonderful food for us to take. It must have taken you ages, what with doing that as well as our regular meals." Sarah grinned at Billie's words, silently thanking the stars Giles managed to find, and fall in love with, this young lady who actually cared about the staff and worried their workload was too heavy. She just hoped he didn't blow it.

"'Tis nothing, Miss Caswell, just a few treats for your journey. Can't have any of you going hungry." Billie slipped around the huge table and gave Sarah a hug, oblivious to the fact that she had done just exactly what the cook hoped she wouldn't do and got flour all over her dress.

"You are wonderful. I hope I have the chance to come back after all this to enjoy more of your culinary delights," Billie whispered as she stepped away, brushing the white dust off her clothes, and left the room in rather a hurry, realising she may never come back. It all depended on what they found in Polruan and whether Giles really did want to marry her. Sarah watched her leave, a motherly smile playing round her lips, certain that before the year was out, Miss Billie Caswell would be Countess of Winchester and mistress of Whiteoaks — or her name wasn't Sarah Haskett!

An hour later they were on their way. It was a glorious day, crisp underfoot and, although very cold, was sunny. The frosty fields along the side of the road glistened in the morning light and the landscape was breathtaking. Giles' estate stretched as far as the eye could see, ringed by hills, woods and forests. Of those travelling with them, Billie knew Will, the groom, and George, the under-gardener, both of whom had served in the military; the remainder she had not met. Giles introduced them as Duncan, Ralph and Harry; similarly they had seen service during the wars. Duncan lost his lower left arm in battle, and the other two bore scars, but they were competent, brave men now working for Giles on his vast estates and their employer trusted them with his life.

Billie felt very safe with these men, who chatted animatedly as they rode along, making sure she was in the middle of their group. She persuaded Giles to let her ride with them for some of the journey. Under sufferance, he agreed, allowing it would be quicker if the only things in the coach were the luggage, food and rugs, as Sally — who by chance was also an accomplished rider — pronounced herself happier on horseback than in the carriage anyway. Choosing Zeus for himself, Giles suggested Bronte for Billie, who was ecstatic; she loved this horse. They made good progress and managed to travel further than they anticipated, reining in at a post-house in the late afternoon. Billie stayed in the saddle all day and was rather stiff when she dismounted, not that she had any intention of admitting to it.

Will and Duncan saw to the horses and both indicated they would sleep in the coach, keeping an eye on both it and their mounts. Giles thanked them, organising for a hot meal and a tankard of beer to be sent out. Billie found herself in a small room that she would share with Sally. The beds looked almost clean and she was too tired to care anyway. She treated herself to a cursory wash, which freshened her up, clearing her head, which was beginning to ache owing to the previous night's lack of sleep. Sally waited, walking down with her to the main room where the others were already seated. Their meal was plain fare but warm and filling, washed down with a beer. Even Billie had a tankard, which, to the amusement of everyone at the table, Giles had to finish because she found it rather went to her head.

They retired early, wanting to get on the road at a decent hour the next day. Giles walked Billie back to her door, risking a quick kiss on her forehead and squeezing her hand before he moved along the corridor to the room he was sharing with Theo. Sally, who had come up a little while before, had turned back the covers for Billie and made sure the fire was stoked up, for the night was very cold. Billie thanked her and they chatted while Sally helped Billie undress. Billie draped her clothes over the back of a convenient chair before getting quickly into bed, falling asleep almost immediately.

Waking early, Billie saw Sally was already up and about. The room was tidy, Billie's dress now hung from a hook behind the door allowing any creases to fall out, and the young maid bringing up some breakfast on a tray, for them to share. Billie indulged in as thorough a wash as possible, considering the water had ice floating in it, and the bowl was scarcely large enough to get her hand in. She ached from the long hours in the saddle the previous day, but was determined not to complain. Sally happened to have some ointment for smoothing into sore muscles, giving some respite, but Billie was smart enough to acknowledge she might have to give up and travel in the coach for some of the day. Bearing in mind it was also scarcely three weeks since she had been so ill, overexertion was not the best plan. However, because she really wanted to ride Bronte again, she wasn't about to let something as minor as sore thighs and the possibility of a relapse stop her.

By chance, it seemed Theo was not wholly unaware of Billie's predicament, for when they gathered in the courtyard prior to setting off, he suggested, not ungently, it might be sensible for Billie to begin this leg of the journey in the carriage. Frowning at this and about to protest, Billie was forestalled as Theo went on to say, if she felt up to it, he might let her ride Bronte for a while after luncheon. Bowing to the inevitable, Billie nodded and allowed herself to be assisted into the coach, her lowering expression clearly indicating how she felt about Theo's directive. She was even more disgruntled when she realised Sally would be riding, meaning she had no one to talk to. In a fit of pique, Billie snapped the curtains closed and sank back against the rugs feeling more than a little put out.

Chapter Twenty

The rhythmic thundering of the wheels, however, lulled the young woman, and before long Billie was fast asleep, belying her own belief she was completely better. Neither did she wake until they pulled up at an inn where they would take a break, to rest the horses and partake of a light meal. Giles hopped into the carriage to lift down one of the food baskets down, standing for a long moment looking down on the still sleeping Billie. Her head was pillowed on her hand and the rug, half on her and half off her, trailed over the bench seat and onto the floor. Her face was flushed and, as ever, her hair was beginning to unravel from the neat style she started the day with. Unable to stop himself, he cupped her face, his fingers caressing her cheek. She came awake instantly, grabbing his hand and sitting up, the rug slithering onto the floor.

"Oh, where are we? I didn't mean to fall asleep."

"Do not fret. We have stopped for lunch. Are you hungry?"

She smiled at him drowsily and nodded, making to stand up. Her stiffening muscles screamed as she moved and she clenched her jaw so as not to cry out.

Giles noticed her expression and chuckled. "I think perhaps it has been a good thing you have not ridden, Miss Caswell." He winked at her. Billie glared at him which had very little effect, more it made him laugh all the louder.

"I will be fine to ride this afternoon," she replied rather haughtily. "I am just out of practice." Giles wisely refrained from responding, simply holding out his hand and helping her down from the carriage. The others were all there, two of their group leading the horses over to the trough and some welcome hay, the rest lounging around the courtyard, eagerly awaiting some food. Giles handed around pies and buns, which were devoured with relish and then dug out some sweet pastries from the other basket. Duncan bought several tankards of beer and managed to procure a cup of weak tea for Billie, who thanked him gratefully.

The fresh air cleared the cobwebs and Billie wandered a little way from the others, stretching her legs, feeling the blood beginning to circulate properly. Rolling her shoulders and feeling the joints pop, she walked over to a gate leading into a field full of cows. She loved cows, such gentle creatures, their huge doe eyes and soft noses. She recalled helping with calves, it must have been when she was a child; there were no cows in London. While she stood, one or two trundled over to her, probably hoping for something to eat more interesting than grass. When the first cow reached her, it nuzzled her shoulder and, as Billie stroked its flank absently breathing in its warm scent, a series of pictures flickered through her mind. Memories of caring for injured creatures. How very odd. That didn't fit with life in London. Maybe it was when she lived in France. She frowned; it would be so much easier if her mind could just retrieve these details.

Giles came towards her, fascinated by her innate understanding of animals. Bronte was already her faithful slave, and now these cows. Although unwilling to disturb the scene, it was time to set off and he said quietly —

"Billie, we must leave, we have many miles to travel before we stop tonight." She turned, staring at him, not really seeing him, her mind still processing the images, which flooded in while she patted the cow. "Billie? Are you all right?" Concerned now, Giles grasped her hand. She looked down at their entwined fingers, then back up at him.

"I know about how to care for cows and horses, maybe even sheep. How is that possible? Horses maybe, we must have had stables, but what of the others? They are not animals that live in the city. I do not think I have lived on a farm, but how else would I know so much about them?"

Puzzled, Giles had no answers. "Maybe we will find out when we get to Polruan, maybe someone there can help you." She smiled hopefully and nodded, allowing him to draw her over to the carriage. "Do you wish to ride?"

She shook her head. "No, I think I will remain in the carriage." Her voice was disinterested. Giles glanced at her, this was unexpected. Maybe she was simply tired, but Giles wasn't sure. She seemed not exhausted as much as listless, the fiery spirit he was used to, doused. It bothered him, so after they settled Billie, wrapping the rugs around her, he motioned to Theo that he would ride in the carriage for a while and try to get to the bottom of what was bothering her.

They set off; their voices clear in the cool air, happily gossiping about this and that. Billie didn't hear them. She was still lost in thought, so lost in fact she didn't even realise Giles was sitting opposite her. Little by little, parts of her memory were returning, but it was very confusing. Why on earth would she have been living on a farm? Was she living on a farm? Was it even real? She dredged through her mind searching for the link but it refused to be pinned down.

A scene flickered into life; she appeared to be in a barn and her mother was crouching next to her explaining what to do. There was a calf lying on straw. It wasn't moving and the mother was licking it desperately, her soft lowing calling to her offspring, but her baby remained unresponsive. Billie's mother was telling her to rub the body hard. Billie was frightened she would hurt so frail a creature, but her mother said it would be fine, so she did as she was bid, rubbing and rubbing until suddenly the calf raised its head, its eyes rolling and its ears twitching, inhaling deeply.

At her mother's urging, Billie continued rubbing when to her surprise several minutes later the calf tried to rise. She helped it up, its legs were all wobbly, but it managed. The mother snuffled at her baby, licking it all over, cleaning the birthing fluids while Billie encouraged it to suckle from the cow's udder. The calf didn't need to be told twice, drawing the life giving nourishment into its body. Billie and her mother sat back and watched satisfied they had saved this little beauty. It was the first time Billie could remember helping an animal, maybe this was what inspired her love of healing.

Coming back to the present, Billie saw Giles sitting across from her, and her mouth fell open in astonishment.

"Why are you in here? Where's Zeus?"

"He is trotting alongside; he is perfectly able to manage without me on his back. I felt you needed me more." He gazed at the slight woman almost lost in the vast rug she was wrapped in. "What happened, Billie? Please tell me." His voice was warm and tender. She stared back at him, trying to gather her thoughts.

"I'm not really sure. I'm … there's a barn and my mother," she went on to describe the memory, "…thing is, I don't know whether it's even real, but if it is, maybe this is what sparked my interest in healing."

Giles couldn't help her, so in an attempt to distract her, asked what else she knew about traditional remedies. Billie's face lit up as she launched into an enthusiastic monologue about plants and herbs and how they could be blended into treatments that were most efficacious. Some were to be mixed with water or maybe a little wine and drunk; some steeped to make tisanes, and some applied topically, impressing Giles with her knowledge. Theo appeared alongside the window and started asking questions about where she found all these plants; what books had she read about the subject and if she had kept detailed notes, whether there was any chance he might get to peruse them one day. Eventually, Giles halted the carriage and swapped places with Theo, the two healers becoming engrossed in a debate about how to treat burns.

"Who taught you about these things, Billie?" Theo asked when they eventually exhausted the topic of burns. Billie shrugged.

"I'm not sure. I know my memory is still rather hazy, but I cannot recall a time when I did not know about them, so it must have either been my mother or one of my grandmothers. It is like second nature to me. At home I have my own garden where I tend all the plants I have managed to cultivate." She paused. "Of course it was probably destroyed too." Chewing her lip, then pushing that thought aside, brought her mind back to their conversation, which kept them going until they arrived at their destination for the night.

The next few days fell into a similar pattern. Early departures from wherever they spent the night, breaking for luncheon sometime around noon and covering many miles before they took their rest. Billie split her days between riding Bronte and sitting in the carriage, accepting she was not quite fit enough to spend all day in the saddle. They were blessed with decent weather for, although cold, the days were clear and dry.

On the afternoon of the fifth day, Giles reined in Zeus a little way from a small village. This was Polruan, the milepost they had passed indicating as much. Billie was rather nervous now. She had no idea what they might face. She couldn't even remember where this house was in relation to the village itself.

They found an inn on the outskirts, which, so late in the year, had enough rooms to accommodate them all, and while they were discussing meals with the proprietor, a young man maybe fifteen years of age, sidled up, eyeing the visitors with interest. The landlord was about to shoo him away when the youngster spoke.

"Miss Billie? Miss Billie! Is it really you? It has been so long since you were here. Are you going up to the Big House?"

Billie turned upon hearing her name. The youth seemed vaguely familiar but his name escaped her. "Yes, it is really me, but I am so sorry, sir I have been unwell and find I cannot bring to mind your name." Smiling at him.

"It's Joe. You used to help me Da over at Home Farm."

Billie stared at him, the memory pulling at her. A question hovered, which although seemed innocuous, needed to be asked. "You may not remember, Joe, but did I by any chance help a calf when I was there once with my mother?"

"Oh, you was allus helping, Miss. Mam worried that you would get in trouble from his Lordship, but if you did, it never stopped you visiting."

Abruptly, Billie sat down on the closest chair, still looking at Joe. "Joe," she whispered. "Please, would you show me where the Big House is? I cannot remember."

He nodded enthusiastically, taking her hand and, before anyone could stop them, they were out of the door and along the street. Giles called after her, but she either didn't hear or chose not to listen. Shaking his head in disbelief at her complete disregard for her own safety, Giles motioned to Duncan and Will and the three set off after them.

Beyond the inn, the road led down a steep hill into the village itself and they could see Billie and Joe, quite a way ahead, hurrying in the failing light. It would be dark soon and

Giles, with no idea who might be waiting for her, did not want any of them to be caught out before they had a chance to scout the place in daylight. Thankfully, the long strides of the three men were no match for a small woman and her young companion, despite the pace the two had set, and they soon caught up.

"Billie!" Giles called. She turned and he could see her face, pale and anxious in the waning afternoon. "Billie, wait, please." She stopped, still holding Joe's hand, fidgeting in her desperation to get to the house.

"What?" she demanded when the three men reached her side.

"Billie, you cannot just go rushing off without so much as a by your leave. What would you do if those men who chased your carriage were there waiting?" In his concern, Giles' tones were clipped and Billie's expression turned mulish. Joe looked at her in surprise.

"Who's chasing you, Miss?"

Billie didn't answer him, merely replying, "I will be perfectly fine. I have Joe," as though this strip of a lad could fight a group of thugs who might well be armed. Joe puffed his chest out. Giles took a deep breath and tried to gentle his tones.

"Billie, they might have weapons, guns. Neither you nor your very brave companion here..." tipping his head at Joe who grinned importantly "...would be any match for them. We need to check the house out in daylight to make sure no one else is watching. Neither do I imagine you wish to arrive on your grandmother's doorstep at such an unsociable hour."

Billie stared at the tall earl, whose fear for her was etched on his face. After a long pause, she nodded, her shoulders sagging.

"I apologise, my Lord. I was so excited to see whether this place was indeed the one of my memory, I didn't think."

"It seems to be a bad habit of yours, my Willow," she heard Giles mutter for her ears only. She smiled up at him and without thinking rested her hand on his arm.

"Please forgive me, sirs," including all three in her apology. "To cause any of you to worry was not my intent." Her coolly courteous words, countered by the warmth of her fingers, now curled around Giles' wrist. He smiled back.

"You are forgiven, Miss Caswell. Now please allow us to escort you back to the inn. We will try again on the morrow." He turned to the young man. "Thank you Joe. Please, will you return in the morning to show us the way to the Big House?" Joe grinned as Giles flipped him a coin asking the lad not to mention Miss Billie was home, as she wanted it to be a surprise." Joe happily agreed to both requests and looking back once to wave, sped off down the hill.

Chapter Twenty One

Billie turned to Giles, Will and Duncan, thanking them in her most decorous manner for their attentiveness. All three were amused at her polite words as they walked slowly back to the inn, Duncan simply reminding her why Giles felt it necessary they travel with her. While his tones were cordial, his words cut Billie to the quick. She knew she had a tendency to behave impetuously and was suitably chastened, saying little else while they walked. When they reached the inn, she thanked them again, then quickly slipped up to her room, wanting to put as much distance as she could between herself and the others. The notion they might be facing real danger, because of her, suddenly weighing heavily on her mind.

Giles followed her, his footsteps echoing on the wooden stairs.

"Miss Caswell," he called just as she was about to enter her room. "Billie, grant me a moment." She hesitated, her fingers on the handle, her head resting on the wooden door. Giles was there before she had the chance to pretend she hadn't heard. "Billie, my love, what is it?" She twisted her fingers together, unsure how to phrase the feelings plaguing her. Giles tilted her chin and brushed his lips across hers; warmth rippled through her. "Please, my sweet."

"Only now am I realising how dangerous this might be, that those watching my father may have worked out I am coming here. Giles, I do not want your men, your friends, to face this danger. It is not their fight. Surely it would be better for me to slip in on my own, find the papers and then get out. There is a chance no one will see me, and if they did, would presume I am visiting with my grandmother, placing no one else in harm's way."

"Do you think for one single moment I could live with myself should anything happen to you because we were not there to protect you? Billie, my men understand the nature of our visit here. Most were in the army and are practised in matters of stealth. You need to trust me, to trust us." He held her gaze, the truth of his words in his dark grey eyes.

Billie sighed, then, "I'm frightened," muttered, so quietly that he thought he imagined it. He pulled her close and, with scant regard for society's rules, kissed her quick and hard. Billie responded, her heartbeat quickening, and she clung to him. They forgot everything else for a minute and let their emotions take them. Giles broke away first, mindful that he had to.

"I know you are, Billie, but remember I love you and will never willingly let you come to any harm. Now, are you coming down to eat?" She shook her head, saying she had no appetite. Giles searched her face, assuring himself it was simply that she wasn't hungry, then gave her one last hug, opened the door and ushered her into the room. She glanced back and saw his slow smile curve his lips, then he winked and disappeared back along the corridor. Billie floated into the room, her face slightly flushed and her own smile teasing her mouth, uncaring that Sally was watching her.

"Is everything all right, Miss Caswell?" Sally asked, grinning delightedly, working out exactly what had just happened.

"Yes, thank you, Sally and please call me Billie? I don't know how many times I must ask."

"'Tis not right, Miss."

"Oh phish, we have shared much, and I believe we could be considered almost as close as friends. You are important to me, Sally, and it would please me greatly if you could see your way to doing so, even if it is just when we are together." Sally gave in and nodded, but would agree to do so only when the earl or any of his guests were not about, and with this Billie had to be satisfied. Smiling at the young woman, who helped her undress, after which Billie had a quick wash and then hopped into bed, saying she did not feel up to food, falling fast asleep within minutes.

The next morning, Joe presented himself just as they were finishing breakfast. It seemed that everybody had slept well, maybe for the first time since they had left Whiteoaks. Ralph and Harry had gone to check the horses, coming back as Joe appeared, reporting them to be comfortable and enjoying some fresh hay.

They gathered together in one corner of the main room, Giles asking Joe whether there had been anyone asking about the Caswell family, recently. People not known to the locals. In small villages like Polruan, everyone knew everyone else, and visitors stuck out like a sore thumb. As they talked, it became clear the Big House — built for the first Lord Chartley — had been in Billie's family for generations, all the members of which were well liked in the area. Many of the villagers worked on their lands, and Joe's father was one of three tenant farmers whose homes lay within the boundary of the estate.

Joe mentioned seeing strange men down at the harbour, but hadn't taken much notice as they seemed more interested in the fishing boats than anything else, adding that Billie's companions were the only other new people he'd seen in days. It was November now, most visitors left weeks ago for, even though the temperatures were often milder than those further inland, the howling gales that tore along the coast made spending the winter in the village, unpleasant. Billie loved the raw power of nature and remembered standing on the headland being buffeted by such winds, watching the storms far out to sea send huge waves crashing against the shore, before rushing home, racing ahead of the driving rain, which blew in ahead of the tempest.

Listening to Joe, Giles and Duncan were of the opinion the men at the harbour were likely part of the group looking for Billie, but could not be certain. They decided Billie, Joe, Giles and Ralph would go out to the Big House — or to give the place its proper title, Chartley Hall — letting Billie visit with her grandmother, while the rest took the opportunity to have a good look around. Joe knew of the secret passage under the cellar, as did most of the neighbourhood. All the local children played in the grounds of the house at one time or another, especially when Billie was there, often using the stairway in the course of their games. He readily agreed, should it prove necessary, to show Giles the concealed entrance leading up from the beach, after extracting a promise he wouldn't tell a soul. Giles, smiling at Joe's earnestness, agreed, the pair shaking on it.

The others would stay in the village, acting for all the world as though they were enjoying a break during a long journey, while taking note of anything or anyone who might seem untoward or out of place. Plans in place, all set off on their appointed tasks. Billie was quite excited, now she was so close to seeing the house, which haunted her dreams during the last few nights. Joe fairly bounced along the path, guiding them down the steep hill to the harbour, then taking a sharp left turn to follow a rutted track up towards the top of the cliffs.

It was another lovely day, bright and sunny and, although there was a stiff breeze, it wasn't uncomfortable. Billie paused halfway up the track and looked out to sea, the waves rolling in to crash along the shingle beach below where they stood, the sound familiar, rhythmic. Forgetting the seriousness of what they were about to do, she pointed out to sea and with an infectious grin on her face declared —

"Look — white horses." The two men gaped at her, what on earth? Joe chortled; delighted these men of class didn't seem to know what she was talking about.

"White horses, my Lords, the white caps on the waves." They looked out at the waves and back at Joe trying to decide whether they were being made fun of. "It's true, surely everyone knows that," Joe said, a cheeky tone in his voice. Billie was nodding, the wind whipping across the headland tugging at her clothes and tearing her hair out of the sleek twist Sally had so painstakingly fixed for her less than an hour before. Her cheeks were rosy and her eyes sparkling. Giles thought he had never seen anyone quite as captivating. She caught his eye; if possible her cheeks reddening even more and, unable to stop herself, beamed at him with unaffected joy.

"This feels like home," she cried over the sound of the sea, spreading her arms wide and breathing in the salty air. Giles moved to where she was standing, concerned at her proximity to the edge for the cliff, and grasped her hand, pulling her back onto the track.

"We must hasten, my sweet, we have much to do today." She squeezed his hand for a second, then let go, turning to Joe and asking him to lead on. Giles and Ralph left to follow in their wake as the woman and the boy swept on ahead, Joe chattering about the Big House, and the farms, and her grandmother.

According to Joe, grandmother was doing just fine, thank you. She was very popular among the locals, everyone keeping an eye on her. She had several live-in staff, as was expected. The tenant farmers made sure her kitchens were always supplied with fresh produce and during the winter wood for the fires was always stocked up. Chartley Hall was the Devereaux family seat — Lady Ashbourne's family — and she grew up here, returning to make it her permanent residence after the untimely death of her beloved husband. Unusually for a dowager viscountess, she was very much involved with the local community and never stood on ceremony. Billie could not remember the last time she visited her father's mother, but suddenly had the feeling, turning up without warning would not faze Lady Ashbourne one jot!

They trudged up the track for another ten minutes or so then they were at the top of the cliff. The view in every direction was spectacular and in front of them was Joe's 'Big House'. Billie halted in her tracks and simply stared, the local moniker rather a misnomer for the place was vast — a mansion really, almost a castle. The long gravel driveway — either side of which were meticulously manicured lawns, decorated with low evergreen hedges trimmed to perfection — opened out in a huge semi-circle stretching the width of the house. Here and there a sculpture distracted the eye, and a riot of rosebushes nestled under the front windows alleviating the view of the soft grey granite walls. It was obviously very old, its multitude of mullioned windows testament to a bygone era. It reminded Billie of a grand old lady, once the belle of the *ton,* now older and wiser, and maybe a little weary but no less beautiful.

Shaking herself out of her reverie, Billie started forward, crunching along the gravel to the great wooden doors. Grasping the oversized brass knocker shaped like a lion's head, she announced their arrival with a loud rap. Giles and Ralph scrutinised the grounds, searching for places where unwanted visitors might lurk unnoticed, shadowy spaces making concealment easy. Thankfully, there did not seem to be too many at the front of the house, although the tall cupressus trees, pencil thin and fanning out from the main gardens, might offer some camouflage against a quick glance. They would need to inspect the gardens at the rear of the house too. While they were looking, the door swung open and a wizened old man squinted in the sunlight.

"Miss Billie? Well, I never did, it's Miss Billie. Oh, my Lady, how lovely to see you. Did you send word? We weren't expecting you."

Billie smiled, his name coming to her, out of the blue, as she grasped the man's hand. "No, please accept my apologies, Humphries. This was an unplanned visit. I am very pleased to see you looking so well. How is Mrs Humphries? Are her rheumatics playing up in this cold weather?" Silently thanking her memory for dropping this information to her when it was needed, she chattered brightly with the old retainer as he drew her into the grand hallway. Giles and Ralph followed, but Joe said he needed to get home. Billie called to him, asking him to come and find her later as there was something she needed to discuss with him. He agreed cheerfully before haring off across the grounds, presumably to Home Farm.

While waiting to be announced, Billie and the two men gazed around. The entrance hall was very spacious and, although a little worn, the decor, staircase, tiled floor and furnishings were in immaculate condition. The oak banister had been polished until it gleamed a burnished brown in the dappled light from the windows, and Billie could see her reflection in the brass candelabra. An ornate rug warmed the cold floor, its thick pile inviting one to kick off one's boots and curl one's toes through the luxurious pattern.

Humphries returned saying that the dowager would receive them in the drawing room. He led the way across to a room at the far side, pushing open the elegant double doors and announcing them in stentorian tones as Miss Willow Caswell and guests. Billie bit her lip to prevent a giggle escaping as they were ushered into the room. At the far end, a tall lady stood to greet them, and for the first time in many weeks, Billie recognised a member of her family.

"Grandmama," she cried and hurtled through the room, catching the woman in a bear hug.

"Billie, my dear." Laughing, the woman pushed her granddaughter back so that she could study her face, "Be careful, you'll crush me," before holding her close again. "This is a surprise. I had no idea you were coming. Have you brought your staff? Where is your chaperone? Who are these men?" noticing the two men who lingered on the threshold.

"Oh Grandmama, I have so much to tell you, but first is Stephen here?"

Her grandmother shook her head as she motioned Giles and Ralph to join them near the roaring fire. "No, I have heard nothing from either your father or Stephen for over a sixth month. Very bad form. You men, who are you?" she asked, a little imperiously. Giles grinned.

"Lord Giles Trevallier, Earl of Winchester at your service, my Lady," he bowed, "and this is Ralph Montgomery, formerly of the Royal Fusiliers."

Billie shot a startled glance at Ralph. He seemed so unassuming and gentle, yet she had heard tales of the courage and tenacity of the Fusiliers. Ralph bowed his head and, as he straightened up, winked at Billie who smiled back at him grateful such a man was prepared to help her.

"Why are you all here, Billie?" enquired the dowager. "It seems an odd time of the year to visit, not that I do not enjoy having guests," she amended, ever the polite hostess. Billie looked at both Giles and Ralph, seeing their encouraging nods. Taking a deep breath, she began her long and rather convoluted reason for arriving so unexpectedly.

Chapter Twenty Two

The dowager listened carefully, asking questions here and there, her insight persuading Giles that while she was quick to understand the import of their situation, she was unlikely to give in to hysterics or panic.

"So, you're telling me your father thought it a good idea to send a slip of a girl halfway across England to retrieve some classified documents?" she asked when Billie wrapped up her tale. Billie nodded, saying her Papa and Stephen were very clear about the risks.

"Tosh!" expostulated her grandmother, "Edgar still believes the good in all men and assumes no one would think to harm a young woman travelling alone. He can be very naive."

"I wasn't alone, Grandmama. Havers and Banks were with me."

"And what use were they when your carriage tipped over, hey? One dead, the other gone. Ran off at the first sign of trouble no doubt. It is a good job this young man found you when he did, or you'd likely be dead," waving her hand at Giles who was looking very amused at the dowager's comments. He rather liked being called a 'young man'.

"It may be that Havers tried to find help, then when he returned discovered Miss Caswell gone," giving poor Havers the benefit of the doubt. "It seems your granddaughter walked in circles for a day or so before I came upon her. I think Havers might have struggled to find her, no matter how hard he looked. It is possible he has tried to make his way back to London to raise the alarm. No matter. We found Miss Caswell, who was placed under the care of my physician immediately." Giles paused then said in a seemingly causal tone, "Have you seen any recent reports from London, my Lady?"

The dowager shook her head. "No, I rarely bother with the London papers. They are full of gossip and scandal, barely any actual news. I must rely on letters from my friends who still live there. Why do you ask?" Curiously.

His voice compassionate, Giles explained about the fire and the belief Viscount Ashbourne died in the blaze, adding the rumourmongers were blaming Billie, or Billie and Stephen. He concluded by saying he had someone investigating the matter and, hopefully, this gentleman would be arriving in Polruan in the next couple of days to update him.

The dowager stared at him for a long time after he finished speaking, a pulse fluttering in her neck the only sign she was fighting profound distress. Gathering herself, she asked whether they had accommodation, for she would gladly open her home to them all. Billie wanted to stay with her grandmother, Giles could see it in her face, and maybe it wasn't a bad idea, but if she did, some of their number would need to keep watch over her, and the rest of the household.

"We believe there is a distinct possibility those who are after these documents have probably worked out they are here somewhere, although they cannot know precisely where. Thus, if Billie were to stay here with you, I would respectfully request that Sally — her maid — as well as I and one other stay also. The others should remain in the village where they will be able to observe any odd behaviour or to spot people who do not belong."

The dowager nodded in approval. "I agree, my Lord. Billie, ring for Jenny, she can air the rooms, they are already made up. You may have your old bedchamber, my dear. The gentlemen can sleep in the main wing, and I'm sure your maid will be comfortable sharing with Matilda." While Billie did as her grandmother asked, Ralph said something to Giles who nodded, and then as the strapping ex-soldier slipped away explained —

"Ralph will collect our things from the inn and apprise the others of our change of plans." Moments later, Humphries came in with tea and a plate of very delicious-looking sweet rolls, split and laden with jam and cream.

"Oh scrummy," breathed Billie, "these are divine." She poured the tea into delicate china cups, handing one to her grandmother and one to Giles, then gave them each a plate on which she had placed two of the rolls, before serving herself. "We're in luck, these are normally served after luncheon, but

Cook knows how much I love them." The rolls were still warm, making the cream melt, the soft mixture dribbling down Billie's chin as she devoured her portion with little regard for gentility. Giles could not help laughing. She looked like a naughty child who had found a treat she knew she shouldn't have but ate anyway.

Peace reigned while they all enjoyed the food, Giles taking the opportunity to admire the room. Charmingly appointed, it was scattered with an eclectic mix of chairs, their cushions in soft pastels, as well as the odd chaise, and between them small tables each with a trinket or decorative bowl, creating a welcoming space. While running his gaze over the paintings adorning the walls one of Lord and Lady Ashbourne when they were much younger caught his eye, and something about it pulled at his memory.

Suddenly, he realised it was the glinting red clasp at the neckline of a deep green cloak, laid loosely over whatever the couple were sitting beside. Without thinking, he got up and walked over to study it more closely. Lady Ashbourne watched him but made no comment. He stood for long moments and then, becoming aware the room had fallen silent, turned to see both grandmother and granddaughter staring at him. For a split second it was as though they were one and the same person, time overlapping; so similar were they that even their curious expressions matched. He grinned diffidently and apologised for his inquisitiveness.

"I beg your pardon, my Lady. In the painting, this clasp, your granddaughter was clutching it when I found her. It was one of the things that helped her regain some of her memory. I must profess it perplexes and intrigues me, as it seems familiar. I wonder does this trinket perchance appear on another painting of you? Billie mumbled something about it being a gift from a grateful soldier, and while 'tis a handsome piece, no soldier I know would wear such a clasp."

The dowager eyed him appraisingly for several moments before replying. "It is said that this clasp was gifted to an ancestor of ours during the siege by the Roman Army at the fortress of Masada in the first century AD." Giles raised one eyebrow somewhat sceptically. "Yes, I understand how peculiar that sounds, but it has been in our family for centuries. It is to be passed down to the eldest daughter on her twenty-fifth birthday, although I imagine some were presented with it at a much younger age, mortality rates being what they are. If there is no daughter, it goes to the granddaughter and so on. My son was apparently moved to present it to Willow rather earlier than he should have. Why did he do that, child?" turning to Billie with questions in her eyes.

"He said to take it, and if I ran out of coin, I might sell it. How could I do that though? Whatever happened, how could I sell something we have carried for so long? It is entrusted to us and it feels like a talisman, that it protects me." She blushed as she said this, aware of how fantastical it sounded; she was not living some fairy tale.

"It did not do much to protect you when the carriage rolled," Giles interjected, with a hint of irony. Billie turned to him.

"Yes, but it brought me to you." About to make light of her fancy, Giles stopped himself. It was true, it had. He already believed he and Billie were destined to be together, so who was he to question such things? It did explain why she gripped it so tightly. Lady Ashbourne then confirmed there was, or had been, a painting in their city residence in which she was actually wearing the cloak and it was possible Giles had seen it on the odd occasion when he called upon the viscount. It seemed as plausible an explanation as any and Giles nodded accepting it was so. As they were contemplating these things, Humphries came in with a fresh pot of tea, clearing away their plates. A hush fell over the room once more while they relished the delicate flavour of the hot drink, each lost in thought; the only sounds being the ponderous tick from the grandfather clock and the hiss of the flames as they devoured the great log.

A little while later, Lady Ashbourne broke the quiet saying, "Billie, I suggest you go and find these documents now. I rather think I have an idea, which might gain you some time. Lord Winchester, go with her, she will likely fall down the stairs or trip over her own feet if left to her own devices,"

Billie spluttered indignantly, but Giles chuckled, the dowager obviously knew her granddaughter very well.

"Have no fear, Lady Ashbourne. I will keep an eye on her." He stood and waited for Billie to show him the way. She hopped around the low table between the chairs they had been sitting on and kissed her grandmother.

"Thank you, Grandmama. Somehow I thought you might know what to do." Lighting a spill before she left the room, Billie nodded to Giles and led the way along the halls and passageways, past the green baize door that led to the domestic quarters and out through a heavy wooden door almost hidden at the end of a dark corridor. A steep set of stairs fell away and Billie picked up a candle from a pile conveniently placed on a small table just inside the doorway, using the nearly burnt out spill to light it.

The glow was just enough to see the stairs. They made their way down cautiously, taking care to listen, on the off-chance someone had beaten them to it. All that met them was silence and the muffled swoosh of the waves far below. It was cold. Neither wanted to stay any longer than necessary, but neither had they any clue as to where the documents were secreted.

Giles spotted several rush lights dotted around the cellar, which although smelly would at least give them brighter light. Then he placed the candle in a holder on a wooden bench, and they began a systematic search of the room. Nothing came to light, so they continued on into the adjoining room. This was the one with the trapdoor that led down to the beach. The pair searched everywhere and Billie was becoming convinced she had been sent on a wild goose chase, when Giles called her over to a heap of books stacked haphazardly on an old shelf. He pointed to the book at the bottom of the heap and Billie could see it wasn't a book at all; rather it was a shallow box or tin. Giles lifted the rest of the books away, both coughing as the dust plumed around them.

Billie slid the box off the shelf. It felt quite light, in fact it felt empty and it was with no little amount of unease she pried open the lid. Breathing a sigh of relief they saw a scroll of papers bound with red legal ribbon. Removing the papers, Billie replaced the tin on the shelf, leaving Giles to pile the books back in their original position. Quickly, they made their way up the stairs into the relative warmth of the main house, making sure they doused the rush lights and the candle on the way.

Billie was shivering with tension as well as the cold by the time they were back in the drawing room. Lady Ashbourne was still ensconced by the fire and they hurried over.

"Did you find what you were looking for?" she asked. Billie nodded, undoing the ribbon and unrolling the papers, placing them on the table. It looked very complicated to her, but there was no mistaking the lists neatly inscribed at the bottom of two of the sheets. Billie handed them to Giles, unable to make head nor tail of it. The earl scrutinised them diligently, then sat for a long time pondering the implications.

Eventually he said. "This is incredibly sensitive information. Many lives could be in danger if the men who we think are looking for you are indeed French agents and manage to get hold of these documents." A cold finger trailed down Billie's spine. "I am stunned your father entrusted this to you. If these were discovered in your possession…" Not wanting to frighten her any more than she already was, Giles stopped himself from finishing his sentence but Billie realised what he was about to say and barely prevented a terrified whimper from escaping her lips. "I think, however, there are enough of us here to handle the situation and Withers should be arriving soon."

"Back to my idea, Lord Winchester," intervened Lady Ashbourne. Giles waited. "Why don't we copy these documents, but instead of reproducing the actual names, replace them with ones we have made up, adding a 'lord so and so' here and a 'duke such and such' there. If the spies are anything like the ones we dealt with during the wars of the 70's, they have no clue as to who's who in our aristocracy. They simply hand over to their masters any information they are able to glean." Billie's jaw dropped and she gaped at her grandmother, her fear turning to shock. What was going on with her family? "Close your mouth girl. You look like a stranded fish."

"Grandmama, what do you mean 'we had to deal with'?" The dowager viscountess shook her head.

"Never you mind, my dear, it is probably better you don't know. Suffice it to say I am the reason your father became involved in covert operations."

Well, this just got better and better! It appeared that her whole family were up to their armpits in secret intelligence work. How was it she missed out?

Her grandmother smiled at Billie, and reading her mind continued, "Your mother didn't want you to be involved. She knew the risks your father and brother were exposed to and did not want that life for you, even though being half French you would be a great asset. No one expects a lady to be a spy," winking at her granddaughter.

Billie's head was spinning. This could not possibly be happening to her. Giles and the dowager ignored her, talking over her head, discussing the replica documents and how they would make the paper look aged. They were supposed to have been hidden for at least two years. As she became aware of the conversation flowing around her, she forced herself to concentrate.

"Tea works very well. Dip a cloth into diluted tea and rub a small amount over the parchment, it turns it a dirty yellow. That should work. We'll smear some dust over the roll to make it appear as though it has been languishing on a shelf for a while. Then we will need to leave it in a more obvious spot. In order for us or, actually you, to prove they are stealing confidential papers, we have to let them find what they are seeking. I will keep the originals in my bedchamber. I have several places such things can be hidden where nobody would ever think to look." Lady Ashbourne grinned, and Giles saw a flash of the young woman she had been, again reminding him very much of her granddaughter. He glanced over at Billie, his heart catching at her bewildered expression. Without thinking, he reached over and touched her hand.

"Everything will work out, Billie, trust us."

She stared at his hand, then at his face then back at his hand, turning hers and squeezing his fingers. For a moment they forgot where they were, caught up in each other's gaze. A discreet cough brought them back to reality and Giles, dropping Billie's hand, apologised for his unseemly behaviour.

166

"Are your intentions towards my granddaughter honourable, Lord Winchester?" the dowager asked pointedly. Giles smiled at her, then looked at Billie.

"They are, my Lady and please, call me Giles" Lady Ashbourne inclined her head. "I wish to marry her, but since it appears that Viscount Ashbourne has perished, I am hoping Stephen will grant me permission to court Billie, Miss Caswell. If only we knew where he was." Billie beamed at him, her eyes like stars. He had made an open admission of his intent; he must really mean it.

Chapter Twenty Three

A little while later, after the three had enjoyed a light luncheon, Ralph returned with the carriage and their belongings. He was shown to one of the guest rooms, a bedchamber far more opulent than anything he had ever been in. Rather overwhelmed, he simply placed his small travel bag on the floor and hurried out, intending to ask Giles whether it would be more appropriate for him to sleep in the domestic wing. Giles laughed when Ralph made his plea.

"No, I need to you to stay close by. You will be too far away and unable to be of assistance should anything happen during the night. How are the others?"

"They are comfortable with the arrangements. As far as they have been able to determine, there has been no sighting of these strange men lately. One of the fishermen, however, did mention that he overheard a conversation in the taproom about them being interested in checking out the old smugglers' routes. He also said one of the men 'talked funny,' but let's face it they would think anyone who was not from around here talked funny, so that didn't necessarily mean anything." Giles nodded, filling in Ralph on what they were going to do with the documents. Ralph was happy to help. He worked in a barrister's office before the war and was proficient in the copperplate style of handwriting used in many legal documents. After brief discussions with Lady Ashbourne, Giles and Ralph disappeared into the library, spending the remainder of the afternoon working on the replica documents.

The dowager took this opportunity to have a heart to heart with her granddaughter. Until the death of her mother, Billie's life had been divided between Cornwall and France, rarely spending any time at the London house. When she was younger she played with the local children, never behaving like the child of status she was, tumbling back into the house after a long day with her friends, looking as though she had been dragged through a hedge backwards — which wasn't actually wholly unlikely — with much of said hedge still stuck in her clothes and her hair.

Often found helping in the kitchens or over at Home Farm, and when she happened to be staying over Christmas, Billie would organise huge hampers full of mouth-watering treats for all those who worked on the estate. Never one for the more refined pastimes expected of ladies, Billie was happiest learning about things of a practical nature: how to look after a poddy calf or an abandoned lamb, how to bake, how to patch a hole in a hedge, and learning about which herbs or plants were suitable for healing either animal or human.

It would also have come as a shock to her society friends if they learned it was the elegant and sophisticated Elizabeth Caswell, Lady Ashbourne herself, who taught Billie about traditional remedies. As a child, the dowager, then simply called 'Lizzie' by all who knew her, had a friend Abby whose mother Lilias was considered to be the local wise woman. Some even whispered that Lilias was a witch, although never dared say so to her face. The child of absent parents, Lizzie found it easy to give her governess the slip, sneaking out of Chartley Hall and running all the way into the village to meet up with Abby. The two would spend hours sitting with Lilias, learning about the old ways with plants and herbs, what to mix them with, what was safe and what was poisonous.

This came in very handy when, as an adventurous young woman, Elizabeth quite by chance became entangled in a political conspiracy that might have had far reaching consequences had she not employed her knowledge to good effect. The perpetrators were brought to their knees by a mysterious ailment allowing the powers that be to swoop in and, for want of a better description, remove them from harm's way. On the bright side, during the operation, Elizabeth met the man whom she would marry — a loving and devoted, if not rather lively match, and the dowager preferred her impetuous granddaughter find the same contentment.

She studied Billie now, noting a slight tightness around her mouth, a posture rather more tense than the relaxed surroundings warranted, and a wariness in her eyes.

"Billie," her granddaughter glanced over. "Billie, I think you need to tell me everything that has occurred." Billie shook her head, not really wanting to burden her grandmother with what had transpired over the past month or so, but to share it would be such a relief. Even though Giles had been so very supportive, he didn't know Papa or Stephen. "Come on, precious," using the endearment she used to invoke, when Billie had needed persuading into something as a child, "I think you will feel better if you do."

Giving up any pretence of being stoic, Billie moved to sit on the ottoman near the dowager's feet and, leaning her head on her grandmother's lap, told her everything. Billie cried several times during her tale, especially upset that she still couldn't remember what her father and brother looked like. Her grandmother was stroking the rich chestnut hair curling boisterously over Billie's head while she talked, both appalled at what her young granddaughter had faced and amazed at her courage. Just as she was coming to the end of her story, there was a knock at the door and Giles poked his head around. Taking in the scene at a glance, he started to retreat, giving the two a little more time together, but Billie called him in.

"You may come in, Giles. I am done." She looked all in and muttered something about going to her room. As they passed, she reached out, her cool fingers brushing Giles' hand, sending tingles along the earl's arm. He stared down at her, wishing he could kiss her anxiety away, but made do with a gentle smile, then she was gone, her feet light on the thick pile of the rug, and he heard the door click behind her.

"So, young man, how did you go?" Giles grinned at Lady Ashbourne, his long legs taking him across the room in four strides to hand her the document, which she unrolled, scanning the contents. To the unsuspecting eye it looked like details regarding the running of an estate with two lists of names, one supposedly relating to the tenants of that estate, the other those of the surrounding landowners. Even to the more discerning eye it appeared to be thus, except the names were completely fictitious, but anyone unfamiliar with the aristocracy would be none the wiser. It was hoped that it would be enough to distract the foreign agents until the real list could be handed over to someone they could trust.

The tea had done its job for the document did indeed look aged, and Giles commented that he and Ralph were about to go and replace the papers back in the cellar in a less obscure spot. All that remained thereafter was to maintain their vigilance. Lady Ashbourne nodded and bid him do just that, then mentioned hot chocolate would be served shortly, or something stronger if they preferred.

Taking another taper, Giles and Ralph ventured back down the steep staircase, this time taking a good look around, placing the documents on a shelf between two other items, not quite hidden, but enough that anyone searching wouldn't come across them too quickly. Carefully rubbing some dust on the parchment, Giles found an old cobweb and ingeniously hooked it above the papers, making it appear as though they hadn't been disturbed for quite some time. Satisfied with their efforts, the two men made their way back to the drawing room, reporting to the dowager.

Then they took their leave, saying they wanted to have a quick scout around the grounds, just in case. Lady Ashbourne informed them that dinner would be served at seven as, being on her own, she usually dispensed with supper, and that there was no need to change. Giles thanked her mentioning that as their luggage was very limited and they had not expected to be staying in such refined surroundings, none of them had brought eveningwear. Lady Ashbourne watched them leave the room, smiling at the thought of her firebrand of a granddaughter becoming a dignified countess. She hoped Giles wouldn't try to change her, Billie was quite special just the way she was.

The evening passed pleasantly enough and the meal was delicious, a light soup followed by roast beef with all the trimmings, and fruit compote for dessert. Billie was quiet throughout. The reality of what she was involved in, along with the revelations of the afternoon, as well as how quickly events were overtaking them, becoming somewhat overwhelming. She was not bothered about her own safety as much as worrying t her grandmother might get hurt or worse. Regardless of the dowager's youthful exploits, she was getting on in years, no longer quite as spritely. As soon as it was polite, Billie excused herself and trailed wearily up to her bedchamber.

As she reached the top stair, Billie heard a familiar footfall, turning to see Giles following her, his expression one of tender concern. She waited for him in the shadows.

"Please do not fret, my love. Everything is in place. As long as you heed my words, you will be safe," Giles said quietly. "Ralph and I will take it in turns to keep watch tonight, so you may sleep peacefully."

"You shouldn't be here, we are alone," she murmured tiredly, drinking in his face, fighting the urge to lean against him and feel his arms around her.

"I won't tell, if you don't." He smiled, winking mischievously. "Your grandmother knows I'm here. She sent me after you."

"Oh." So he hadn't come of his own volition. She felt her shoulders droop, but Giles knew her better than she thought.

"I would have come to check up on you anyway, Billie, but it is rather nice your grandmother trusts me." Billie sighed and gave into her desire, leaning against Giles breathing him in, his scent soothing her ruffled mind. Giles drew her close, kissing the top of her head. Billie lifted her face and gazed at the tall, handsome man whose eyes mesmerised her. Her heartbeat quickened and, without thinking, she lifted one hand running it lightly over his jawline and into his unruly hair. Giles turned his head, brushing her palm with his lips causing a tremor to run through her. "Although I admit to finding it rather difficult to warrant that trust," bending to capture her lips with his.

Billie sank into his embrace, matching him kiss for kiss, moulding herself to him, as ever drawing strength from his body. Heat coiled around her stomach as their passion flared. Giles' hands roved over her, teasing and caressing and she thrilled to the potent pleasure of his touch. Still very much an innocent, Billie wasn't sure how to reciprocate, simply letting her hands swirl across Giles' clothes, cool fingers catching his heated skin at the 'v' of his shirt, delighting in the groan her tentative gestures elicited. Emboldened, she slid her fingers down his body and over the fall of his trousers, aware of his need for her in the pulsing muscle barely contained within.

"Oh God, Billie, I am powerless when it comes to you," he growled, his voice catching as she brushed her hand against him. "We must stop. This is madness."

"Must we really?" she questioned wickedly, pulling his head back down to her mouth. He laughed softly, as he was effectively persuaded not to stop for just a little longer. Long moments passed, Billie felt her knees buckling, but Giles held her to him, never allowing her to fall; the restless heat between them igniting a fire they might well have struggled to put out had not the sound below of a door closing cut through their ardour. Aware of how compromising a situation he was placing Billie in, Giles broke their kiss without relinquishing his hold immediately, steadying her against him until their breathing resumed something resembling a regular rhythm.

"I love you, my Willow, and I am counting the days until I can prove to you just how much." Billie giggled, at his expression, which was rather like that of a starving wolf having just spotted its prey.

"You look as though you might quite like to eat me, Giles."

"That would be the least of your worries, love," he muttered rather hoarsely against her ear. Her breathing hitched as she stared into his eyes and they risked one last kiss before Giles reluctantly let her go and she walked sedately along the hall to her bedchamber, feeling a whole lot happier than she had done less than an hour before.

Chapter Twenty Four

The next day was overcast. Out to sea, dark clouds were amassing; a harbinger of bad weather later in the day, and the blustery wind was bitterly cold. Billie slept very well considering the tumult of emotions racing through her just before she went to bed, presenting herself in the dining room not long after eight. Her grandmother, always an early riser, had already eaten and was in the library, going over some business with her steward, so Billie ate in isolated splendour. Just as she was finishing her second, very tasty, coffee, Giles strolled into the room. Her heart did an odd flip-flop in her chest and she sat back secure in the knowledge they were alone, drinking him in, much tastier than the coffee. His tall muscular physique, his dark hair and those grey eyes stormy as the clouds building in the distance. Oh, how she loved him.

She smiled a slow smile, her glorious eyes aglow in her elfin face. Giles grinned back asking how she had slept to which she informed him most politely that she slept like a top, how about him; the mundane topic distracting them from what they really desired. Seemingly, both he and Ralph managed a fairly decent night between watches, and nothing untoward happened. He wanted to go into the village to meet up with the others that morning, to share what they knew or had discovered. Then, he would bring them back to Chartley Hall to show them the lie of the land, and the passageway from the cellar. If the men whom Joe overheard really were agents, their interest in smugglers might well have led them to the other end of the secret stairway.

They chattered while Giles had his breakfast, Ralph joining them shortly thereafter, mentioning he had already eaten, in the kitchens. Billie frowned at him, but he forestalled her comment, saying that he was out very early and it was easier to eat with the staff. Billie, realising Ralph was a little uncomfortable in such opulent surroundings, wisely left it, merely saying he was welcome to help himself from the sideboard if he was still hungry. Grinning, he thanked her, pouring himself a cup of hot coffee, topping up Giles' cup at the same time. The two men fell into conversation about their plans for the day.

"Would it be acceptable for me to accompany you into the village?" asked Billie when there was a break in their chat. The two men looked at each other, silent communication passing between them, then Giles nodded slowly.

"I believe it would be all right, as long as you promise to stay with us, and that if you suddenly decide that there is someone you just *have* to see, you will allow one of us to go with you. We cannot risk you being alone." Giles spoke in serious tones, holding Billie's gaze in the hope she understood the import of his words, and after a minute, she nodded.

"Thank you, Giles. I will be on my best behaviour."

Ralph spluttered with laughter and Giles bit his lip, both knowing how unlikely this was. Shortly after, she went to get ready, popping into the library to apprise her grandmother of their intentions.

"…and I will instruct Humphries not to answer the door to anyone he does not recognise Grandmama." Lady Ashbourne inclined her head as Billie kissed her cheek. "We won't be very long, but do not hold up luncheon for us," slipping out and quietly closing the door behind her.

She ran lightly along the hallway and through the baize door into the domestic quarters seeking Humphries, which was where Giles found her half an hour or so later. Sitting on the table, swinging her legs, Billie was telling the staff all about life at Whiteoaks. He stood back a moment listening to her gossip, struck once again by how much knowledge she gained about his household just three short weeks. Giles deliberately coughed as he walked into the room and she turned her head, immediately introducing him using his proper title, at which point everyone either bowed or curtseyed. Giles acknowledged them in his friendly manner and then said it was time to leave. Billie jumped down from the table hurrying after him, waving goodbye in a distracted fashion, hearing gurgles of laughter from the room as the door swung shut behind them.

"Miss Caswell, you are far too familiar with the staff wherever you happen to be staying." Giles intoned, intending to sound jovial, but it came across as rather pompous. Billie stopped in her tracks, glaring at him, trying to decide what he was on about.

"I am as familiar as I choose to be, your Lordship," she replied, her voice cool. "I have always been on good terms with our staff and I have no desire to change, so should you decide our — whatever this is…" she waved her hand between them, "… is worth pursuing, then you will just have to accept it. I will never be one of those simpering, insipid ladies ignoring the people tending to their every whim, while they fritter away the day doing needlepoint or talking about the weather. I like to be outdoors riding or walking, tending my plants and herbs, helping to treat sick or injured people and animals — and yes, I like to talk with our staff. If I recall correctly, you are on similar terms with your household and I really do not think the way I behave is any of your business."

Billie swung past, unconsciously tossing her head. Realising his mistake, Giles reached for her, grasping her arm and pulling her back to him. She shrugged his hand away and stood stiffly, annoyance bristling out of her. He spread his hands in a gesture of apology.

"That came out badly," he said ruefully. "Truly, I meant it to sound as though I was speaking in jest." He paused. "Sarah keeps telling me that my words bear more weight now than they used to, yet I keep forgetting. Maybe I need you to help me."

"Maybe you do, but your attitude confuses me, Giles. One minute it appears you wish me to share your life, the next you seem to push me away, not with actions but your words suggest you are less than certain. I am who I am but mayhap that is not enough for you. I know I love you, but you need to be sure. Half-hearted is not enough, I need it all," watching him as she spoke, as despite his words of the previous day, a small corner of her brain persisted in telling her this was all too good to be true. Head held high, she braced herself for what she suddenly feared might be the inevitable let down. Giles moved towards her, cupping her face in his hands, staring into the emerald depths of her eyes, now cloudy with apprehension.

176

"You have owned all of my heart since first you awoke in the Rose Room, all in a panic because you had forgotten who you were and why you were there, your incredible eyes dark with fear. It was all I could do not to drag you into my arms right then in front of Theo and my staff, and kiss away your terror. I fought against these sentiments, as I never expected to care for any woman enough to want to share my life with her and the sheer depth of feeling I have for you scares me. Sometimes, I fail to consider my words and very, very occasionally, fail to see the consequences of my actions. But whatever happens, my love for you will never fail. I am eternally bound to you. The first time I saw you, I believed I recognised you and, although as far as I am aware we have never met, I feel as though I have known you for a lifetime, maybe several lifetimes. I cannot explain this but it is as though we were meant to come together. That this is our fate."

Giles halted, grimacing a little, knowing if anyone else heard him they would think him addled, his words much too poetic for a respectable earl. This connection, this emotion he felt for Billie, had caught him off guard, leaving him vulnerable, exposed. Then it dawned on him, this same vulnerability plagued Billie. She too was coming to terms with a whole gamut of new feelings, easily crushed with a careless word or thoughtless action.

They had not spent enough time talking or simply being together to understand the finer nuances of the other's speech or body language — what actually made them tick. Passion and desire, however seductive, are not sufficient. Their love needed to be strong enough to sustain them their whole lives. Not only a blessing in joyous times, but also to fortify if life threw obstacles their way, to protect if others sought to pull them apart. Together they should be greater and more durable than they were as individuals.

He noticed Billie staring at him, her mouth in an astonished 'O' and he repeated his thoughts to her, still cupping her face, determined she trust his words.

"I know that sounds rather hackneyed, for we cannot deny our physical attraction, but you are not just a body to me, I want to know your mind, how you think, what makes you happy, what hurts you, I…" Giles never finished his sentence. Billie drew his head down to hers, kissing him with everything in her, pressing her slender body against his muscular frame, letting her kiss tell him what she doubted she could ever articulate. Time slowed and the house around them seemed to melt away, several minutes ticking by until reality invaded their senses and they broke apart, breathing ragged, hearts aflame.

"That is my greatest wish, Giles. I want to share everything with you. I do not wish to marry a man who governs me, who expects me to bow to his whims, or who wants to change me — to crush my spirit, for that would be akin to a slow death. I want a man who will love me just as I am, with all my faults, the same way that I will — that I do — love him for his." She paused. "I realise 'tis unconventional, but I would rather live a lifetime alone than lose myself." Billie held his hand as she spoke, her fingers entwined with his. Giles lifted her hand and kissed the inside of her wrist, sending delightful quivers through her body.

"I want that too. Do you think we might start again?" Billie nodded shyly. Giles bowed over her hand "Good morning, my Lady. Giles Maximilian Trevallier, Earl of Winchester at your service. It is a pleasure to meet you." Billie giggled at the formality, but played along, inclining her head and dropping a curtsy.

"Good day to you, my Lord. My name is Miss Willow Caswell, daughter of Viscount Ashbourne, and I am very happy to make your acquaintance." All very genteel, then she blew it by standing on tiptoe to kiss Giles full on the lips. "So sorry, my Lord. I found I was unable to help myself, I was quite swept away by your astounding good looks." Laughing openly now. Giles grinned and, kissing her on the forehead, said they really must get on with their day. Ralph would be wondering what on earth had happened to them.

Ralph was in no way concerned. In fact he hadn't realised the morning was slipping away, engrossed in conversation with the dowager regarding the value of investing money into a new shipping line plying trade to the Americas. Standing, he thanked Lady Ashbourne for her time, and the three took their leave. Despite the fact Ralph brought the carriage up the previous afternoon, the three decided to walk into the village. The clouds, although low, were not too threatening as yet and they imagined they would be back at Chartley Hall before the storm arrived.

It didn't take them very long to reach the inn where they found the others waiting for them. Sally and Will had enjoyed a short stroll around the village earlier and reported there didn't seem to be anyone acting suspiciously. Giles explained what they had done with the documents, and Billie extended the dowager's invitation to anyone who wanted to join them at the Big House, as her guests. It was obvious they were torn, especially as Giles considered having some of his men in the village was important. Duncan did point out that surely it would be more sensible for them to be together up at the Hall, as that would be the focus of any threat. On top of this, the thought of luxury over the spartan accommodation of the inn was very tempting.

In the end, luxury and of course common sense, won out and those lodging at the inn, paid their account and collected their horses from the stables, hitching bags to saddles. Before leaving the village, however, Giles wanted a proper look around, so while he along with Duncan, Sally and Billie toured the locale, the others waited patiently in the taproom, the delay tempered with plenty of hot chocolate and a pile of fresh sweet buns. Billie enthusiastically pointed out places of interest: the long jetty, the slipway for the boats, the small yet colourful fishing fleet sitting at anchor today owing to the incoming storm, the quaint thatched cottages painted white, their pristine windows framed with bright curtains, currently flapping madly in the breeze.

It was an idyllic setting, even on such a dull day. Here and there people were chatting over garden hedges. Many called out to Billie as they strolled past, she was obviously well known. One even asked after her brother. Careful not to give too much away, Billie merely said he had not been able to accompany her this visit, but did introduce those with her. The presence of a tall and very handsome earl along with his equally attractive soldier friend, proved distraction enough, and would keep the gossips happy for days to come.

It was not a large village and soon they reached the far end, the houses giving way to fields and woods gently sloping up and away from the coast. There was barely a track leading away in this direction, too hard for anyone with ill intent to follow, either in or out of the hamlet. This meant anyone looking for Billie or the documents would almost certainly enter the same way they had done, along the main road, making their surveillance rather easier.

As they wandered back to the inn, they were gossiping about who would walk and who would ride, when Joe suddenly appeared begging Billie to come over to Home Farm. His mum really wanted to see her, and apparently there was a very early — or maybe extremely late — set of twin lambs abandoned by their mother that he was looking after. Billie excitedly agreed saying she would walk back with Joe. Duncan, noticing Giles' expression, muttered that he would follow them discreetly, thus ensuring her safety, leaving Giles and Ralph to lead the way to Chartley Hall.

Joe took Billie's hand and the two rushed away, leaving Duncan in their dust. Giles shook his head at Billie's impetuousness; recognising life with her would never be dull. He watched them disappear up the track, then he and Sally turned towards the inn to collect the others, and not long afterwards the remainder of the group set off up to the Big House.

Billie and Joe burst into the kitchen of Home Farm, chatting nineteen to the dozen about life on the farm and life in the city. Joe desperately wanted to visit London, but his parents did not have the money; and even if they did, they couldn't up and leave the farm. Billie was saying when she returned home, maybe he could come for a while and work for her — maybe as a groomsman in the stables, completely forgetting that currently, she had no home. Joe's mother, busy baking bread, turned at their entrance, a huge smile wreathing her face.

"Well, if it isn't Miss Billie. My, my, you never change Miss, always so bright and happy. Like a breath of spring you are there's no mistake. Come in, come, take a load off and let me have a look at you." Mrs Penhaligon brushed the flour off her hands and spun Billie to face her properly, taking in her rosy cheeks, windswept hair and shining eyes. "Doubtless young Joe wants to show you his lambs. Go on with you, child, they're by the fire," relinquishing her hold. Billie gave her a quick hug and dropped to her knees by the hearth.

Two tiny lambs were fast asleep curled up in a basket, an old blanket thrown over them for extra warmth. Joe picked up one very carefully and handed it to Billie, who crooned over the precious bundle, stroking its curly head. The creature made little mewling sounds and Joe gave her a cloth soaked in milk that the lamb could suckle on, while he did the same with the second lamb, letting them feed to their heart's content. Eventually replete, the small orphans snuggled into the respective shoulders of Billie and Joe.

Billie sat cross-legged on the rug cuddling her lamb, filling Mrs Penhaligon in on her life, and they spent a happy hour or so chatting about this and that. Billie had just caught up on all the local gossip when they were disturbed by a quiet knock on the door. Duncan poked his head around, apologising for the intrusion, indicating Miss Caswell was expected up at Chartley Hall and the afternoon was getting on. His jaw dropped at the site of Billie cradling a baby lamb, while sitting on the floor, with scant regard for her clothes. Billie grinned at him, placing the lamb gently back in its wrappings, and scrambled to her feet, thanking Mrs Penhaligon for her hospitality. Joe and his mother saw them to the door calling after them that they hoped Billie would return soon. She shouted she would love to, Duncan and she hastening home along the track.

The sky was darkening, heralding the storm, the wind buffeting them as they walked. The air, heavy with a pungent zing — the distinctive aroma promising lightning and rain, fairly sizzled. They were about to enter the main gardens of the Chartley Estate, when a hooded figure loomed up out of the waning light, standing directly in their path. His sudden appearance made Billie jump, and she let out an involuntary squeak as Duncan moved to stand in front of her. The man dropped his hood and spoke directly to the young woman.

"Well, my sister," he drawled, smiling wolfishly, "it has been too long. I was out of my mind with worry. Where have you been?" Billie stared at the man. He seemed somewhat familiar but she couldn't be certain, unable to see him clearly in the half-light. Surely, if her was her brother, she would remember him? "I see you are coming from Home Farm. How are Joe and the Penhaligons? I trust they are well."

Billie was confused now. How could he know about those at Home Farm if he wasn't her brother? Moreover, if he *wasn't* her brother, why would he think she would assume he was? Light dawned: unless he knew of her memory loss. She needed to play along until she could work it out without giving too much away.

"Stephen!" she said, quite pleased her voice sounded full of relief rather than fear. The man inclined his head. Billie still wasn't convinced. Too much had happened to her in the last little while to trust immediately. "How did you know I would be here?"

"I assumed you would come to Grandmother's," was his only response. Billie edged closer to Duncan, who was resting his hand on his coat pocket. "Who is this?" jerking his head at Duncan.

"This is Mr Barrington." Suddenly unwilling to mention the others and hoping Duncan would guess what she was up to, she continued, "You must remember him from the village." The man raked his eyes across Duncan then nodded.

"Of course, I did not see you properly in the gloom."

At this, Billie knew he definitely was not her brother. That begged the question — who was he? His features pulled at something in her mind. More to the point, how dangerous was he? She soon found out; for, without thinking, she moved closer trying to see his face more clearly and the man seized her by the arm, yanking her to him while drawing out a gun from under his cloak, motioning Duncan away from Billie's side. Duncan refused to move; but Billie was not going to let him take a bullet for her. It wasn't worth it.

"No, Mr Barrington," she cried, raising her voice over the howling wind. "Please, do not worry, Stephen is just worried for me aren't you, my brother?"

"I find it wise to trust no one, sister dearest."

Billie nodded, telling Duncan to leave them, to go back to the village, that she would be safe with Stephen. Duncan stubbornly shook his head, but despite the newcomer's grip, Billie was able to take a step closer to the ex-soldier. Grasping his hand with her free one, she looked him straight in the eye.

"Please, Mr Barrington, I will be fine." Then dropping her voice, "I will lead him to the fake papers, go and find the others, we do not know how many accompany this man." Raising her voice and instilling a note of irritation into her tones, "Oh, just go, you know they'll be waiting for you in the taproom." Squeezing his hand, she let go, turning back to the stranger who called himself Stephen, completely ignoring Duncan who shrugged apparently unconcerned and, turning on his heel, seemed headed towards the village, leaving Billie alone with a dangerous stranger.

Chapter Twenty Five

As Duncan disappeared into the gloom, Billie said in what she hoped were indignant tones. "He is on his way. Now, who are you, for you most certainly are not Stephen?" They were moving into the shadow of the trees bordering the gardens, whereupon the man tightened his grip on her arm, almost lifting her off the floor and making her yelp in shock and pain.

"Now then you little strumpet, where are those papers your father so kindly told you about?" he snarled, his face an angry mask.

Billie gulped and tried to brazen it out. "What papers? Who are you and how on earth do you know who I am?"

"Never you mind, Miss Caswell," he sneered. "Suffice it to say I am aware of your carriage accident, and subsequent memory lapse. Shame you didn't die along with your driver, but at least you led me here and I nearly had you believing I was your worthless brother." His tone was full of contempt. "I had a suspicion Ashbourne would think to secrete the papers in Chartley Hall, it's nicely off the main routes. I've been in the area for several days hoping either you or Stephen would show up. Your timely arrival merely confirmed my conjecture. My preference would have been to use one or both of you to force your father to show me where they are hidden, much more entertaining for me. Sadly, it seems he no longer walks this earth…" not sounding particularly sad at all. His words jarred Billie, grief for her father threatening to spill over, "…however, his daughter is a very pretty substitute and this way I get two for the price of one."

The young woman shivered, unsure what he meant precisely, as he gripped her chin with his free hand, tilting it so the fading light illuminated her face.

"To have made it thus far shows a considerable amount of mettle, Miss Caswell," he said sounding almost surprised. "I would enjoy keeping you for myself, you have spirit."

Billie tried to prevent the revulsion she felt from showing on her face, merely responding rather sarcastically, "Why, thank you for your kind words, good sir. I am flattered. How do know of my father's death? Did you perchance have anything to do with it?"

"Now that would be telling. Enough with your questions, you will not distract me. Now where are the papers? It will be the worst for you if you do not tell me." He squeezed her arm where he still held her, making her whimper as his fingers bit into her flesh. She took a deep breath, trying to steady her nerves.

"To the best of my recall, they are hidden in a cellar under the house, but where exactly I have no clue. I can show you the cellar, you will have to do the searching yourself."

"Take me now. I will not be letting you out of my sight until I know these documents are the ones I am instructed to recover. Even then I may decide that to release you is too risky."

Billie clamped her jaw tight, concerned he would hear her teeth chattering. She could only hope Duncan was able to double back and tell the others. Gripping Billie's arm, the man moved quickly across the gardens and around to the back of the building, taking care to hug the shadows. His movements were stealthy and when Billie tried to drag her shoes on the gravel he hauled her back to his side, nearly pulling her over.

His voice, close to her ear, was full of menace. "Do not draw attention, Miss Caswell. Now I know the whereabouts of the papers, you are of little use, more a bonus, you might say, a gift for my master. I could just as easily drop you over the cliff." His inflection was stilted, his words chosen with care, almost as though English was not his mother tongue.

Billie stuttered something unintelligible trying to be brave but failing dismally. This man was very strong. She knew there was no chance of escape until they were in the cellar, then he would have to let her go in order to search for the papers. A gift for his master — that really did not sound like fun — oh, please let Giles find her quickly.

"Will you behave?" he hissed. She nodded, unable to speak. He studied her for a long moment and then turned back towards the house. "Which doorway?" She pointed a trembling finger towards the domestic entrance.

"That way is closest to the cellars. If we are careful, no one will see us. There is a corridor separating the kitchen from the main house, the entrance to the cellar is just beyond the baize door."

He hurried them towards the house, keeping against the walls, ensuring that they were completely invisible to anyone who happened to glance out. Billie tried to see whether anyone else was with this man, but even though there were strange shapes in the gloom, she was unable to distinguish whether they were people or trees. They reached the back door, and Billie pushed it hoping it might creak and draw someone out to see who it was, but it was well oiled and swung open almost silently. The man's hand still clamped around her arm, the two crept along the corridor and through the connecting door to the hallway beyond. Billie showed him the door leading to the cellar, muttering it would be pitch dark down there, so how would they be able to see what they were doing?

The man glanced around — telling her to move if she dared — then quick as a flash shot along the hallway, snatching a candle from one of the holders on a small corner table and was back gripping her arm before she had time to blink, never mind run or scream. The flickering light was barely enough but when they went through the door, Billie picked up one of the larger candles from the pile, holding it in hands that shook so much, it took the man two attempts to light it. At least they were not likely to fall down the steep stairs now. He grunted a thanks, a gesture so completely at odds with his behaviour that Billie was confounded, but unable to question it, because he pushed her in front of him to lead the way. She made her way cautiously, lifting her skirts and cloak so she didn't trip, taking the steps as slowly as she dared in the hope if she could delay him long enough, someone might get to her.

Eventually they reached the first room and Billie made a great pretence of searching.

"What will they look like?" she asked plaintively. "Is it a wad of papers or a small roll?"

"It is a roll of parchment you stupid woman. Are you too dim-witted to recognise parchment when you see it?"

"Sir, I am just a girl. What would I know of official documents?" Knowing they would find nothing, Billie kept up the act, looking in the most ridiculous places, stalling for time. Then they moved into the next room and it didn't take the man long to spot the roll Giles and Ralph placed on the shelf the previous day. The layer of dust and cobweb seemed to convince him this was what he was searching for. He removed them from the shelf and unrolled them, telling Billie to hold the candle so he could check their authenticity. He gave each sheet a cursory glance and then, apparently satisfied, tucked them inside his cloak.

"Now, madam, you are coming with me." He was about to start back up the stairs when a sound from above caught his attention. He growled angrily. "Someone's coming! Now how would they know we're here?"

"How should I know? You're the smart one, I'm just the dimwit, remember." Billie said impudently. He shoved her against the wall, banging her head against the cold stone with such force her teeth rattled. She could feel tears forming but was determined not to cry in front of this man. She tried to gather her scattered wits and thought quickly.

"There is a trapdoor..." she stammered, "...in the other room, the one where you found the papers. It leads down to the beach. You could escape that way."

He gripped her face in his large hand, fingers bruising the soft skin and, removing the candle from her nerveless fingers, held it close to her cheek. "You had better not by lying to me, woman, or you will pay dearly," shaking her so hard, she staggered.

Billie remained silent, but led the man back to the chill room, pointing out the trap door. He gave her the candle and heaved the door. The hinges screamed as he pulled it up, and just as it fell back to reveal a dark staircase cut into the rock, the cellar door flew open and footsteps thundered towards them.

Cursing Billie, he shoved her hard into the rickety shelves, which began to collapse, swamping her in all manner of rubbish. The candle — knocked from Billie's hand — flickered and went out, the room suddenly blacker than a night with no moon, as the man dropped through the trapdoor and shot off down the steep stairs far faster than was sensible. Billie didn't care; he was gone and that was all she was bothered about. The room lightened perceptibly as three men tumbled in, almost falling on top of the debris under which she lay. She could hear voices and things were lifted off her but she couldn't respond; her mouth didn't seem to be able to form the words. Everything sounded very distant, muffled; then nothing as darkness claimed her.

She could hear voices and she tried to answer, but it was all too hard. She imagined she was lifted clear, but couldn't really be sure. Faces swam across her consciousness but she didn't know whether she was awake or dreaming. She did remember a man chasing her through the house and just when she thought she had escaped his clutches, he found her at the top of the stairs, laughing maniacally as he pushed her. Her feet went out from under her, her arms flailed as she tried to propel herself up to no avail, tumbling backwards the sound of her own screams echoing around the hall.

"Billie, Billie, come on child, wake up." A familiar voice, she just couldn't quite place it. A hand curved around her cheek, cool and slender, stroking her face. "Billie, poppet, you must wake up." She groaned and turned away, brushing the hand off her face.

"Leave me alone," she muttered, which actually sounded more like "lerm mphnerf" as she was muttering into the pillow. She heard a smothered laugh from someone with a deep voice, also familiar and very dear. Her head was all swimmy, and she struggled to fight her way through what felt like layers of cotton wool. After what seemed like an age, she managed to open her eyes, meeting four pairs of worried ones staring back at her. Her grandmother, Giles, Theo and Sally were sitting around her bed. Oh, she was in bed! That was weird. Wasn't she in a cellar?

"Billie, sweetheart, do you know who we are?" Giles asked. Billie nodded, then winced as pain lanced through her head. Groaning, she ran her hand over her hair, catching a large bump at the back of her head. Nausea roiled around her stomach.

"Feel sick," she managed, and a bowl miraculously appeared as she was very violently sick, wondering why someone would be as rude as to be banging her head with a mallet, "stop the hammering, please." She moaned, before calmly throwing up again. Someone held her around the shoulders and helped her drink some fresh, cool water, which did make her feel a little better. "What happened?" she asked groggily.

"I fancy you'll have to tell us that, but it can wait," Theo said, patting her arm. "I think you'll survive; just a nasty crack on your skull and some bruising. I don't believe anything is broken, despite ending up under a shelf-load of stuff."

Billie stared at him, images flooding into her mind of a strange man who wanted her to think he was her brother, of papers and of the cellar. "He told me he was Stephen, but he was going to shoot Duncan. Stephen wouldn't do that. I couldn't let that happen, but he knew me, he knew us."

Lady Ashbourne hushed her granddaughter, who, now she had finally woken, wouldn't be shushed. It all spilled out, most of which they already worked out for themselves, but her description of the man was vital. It transpired that as Duncan skirted back round to the front of the house, he came across three other men and, despite having only one good hand, the ex-soldier knocked two of them unconscious, the resulting furore bringing out George, Harry and Ralph who had cornered the third, all three now securely under lock and key in one of the outhouses. They would be removed to the local magistrate on the morrow.

Duncan told them about Billie, so they rushed through the house; now surmising they probably arrived at the top of the cellar stairs just as the agent opened the trap door. As they entered the first room, they had seen him push Billie into the shelves before disappearing down the secret stairs. There was a chance they might have caught up with him had they followed, or risked going around to the beach, but it was pitch dark, making it easy for anyone to slip past them. With the storm now raging overhead, there was more likelihood they would break their necks on the treacherous paths or slippery rocks. They had a description. They would find him sooner or later.

Chapter Twenty Six

The four surrounding the bed could see Billie was fading again and Theo, after examining her thoroughly, confirmed that she wasn't badly hurt, but ought to rest. Giles desperately wanted to sit with her and had asked the dowager whether, if Sally stayed too, it might be permitted. Lady Ashbourne gave up worrying about this man, and his intentions with her granddaughter, when she saw him carrying her up from the cellar, his face grey with fear. Cradled in his arms, Billie was unresponsive; her face, white under the angry bruises, and it took all of Theo's powers of persuasion to get the earl to place her on the bed. For Giles it was too close to Billie's last illness. She nearly died then. He couldn't lose her now. None of this was helped by the knowledge that the man who hunted her remained at large. Giles would not relax until he was tracked down and, preferably, hung.

The other two left the room and Sally curled up on one of the sumptuously large wing-backed chairs dotted about the bedchamber. Giles sat on the edge of the bed holding Billie's hand, talking to her about anything but the current situation. He blathered on about Whiteoaks, about the Christmas party he was supposed to be organising, about the gardens and about whether she would like one set aside for her herbs and plants after they were married, distracting her from the events of earlier. Billie tried to listen, but was struggling to concentrate, exhaustion singing its siren's song and in the end she succumbed, falling asleep still holding Giles' hand.

At some point in the night Billie woke, and turning her head, noticed that although Giles was fast asleep, his head resting at an odd angle against the side of the chair, he hadn't let go of her hand. She smiled, and looking around, spied Sally also sleeping in what must have been a most awkward position. Carefully, and making sure she didn't disturb him, Billie slipped her hand from Giles' grasp and scooted out of the bed, waking Sally gently. Sally murmured something and Billie whispered that she was taking her somewhere more comfortable, helping the tired girl up and through into the adjoining room where a bed lay ready-made. Ignoring Sally's protests, Billie guided her to the bed, helping her in and pulling up the covers. The young maid was back in the land of nod before Billie was at the door.

Going back to her own room, she placed a huge log in the grate, then sat on the bed for long moments studying Giles, admiring his carved features in the glow of the fire, the flames highlighting and softening his slightly angular face. His hair lay in an unruly mop, his shirt was open at the top, his cravat — untied — hung loosely around his neck, his waistcoat unbuttoned. He looked the epitome of a rake, yet she knew he was not. Her heart hitched and warmth ran though her as she imagined him naked on the rug in front of that same fire, his hands running over her, making love to her. Dragging her mind back to reality, she got back into bed and then attempted to slip her hand back into his.

Giles came awake immediately, reaching for her.

"Hush, my Giles, 'tis just me. Come, you cannot sleep like that, lie here. This bed is big enough for two and the blanket can separate us." Giles stared at her through half-closed lids, sleep fuddling his mind, making him think he was dreaming. Billie leaned over and took his hand. "I know what I'm doing and I really want you to hold me." Glancing around the room, he realised Sally wasn't there. Billie put her finger to her lips. "She is next door I have put her in the other bed."

"Well, aren't you a little minx?" He smiled, feeling his heart quicken. Billie had no clue her nightgown was almost transparent, and in the flickering light little was left to the imagination. "You might want to pull the covers up," he added roughly. Billie glanced down and realised what he meant, blushing as she snatched the sheet up to her chin. Giles chuckled. She reached for his hand again and pulled him onto the bed. This time he gave in, settling under the thick coverlet, but making sure two layers of bedding were between him and Billie. She snuggled down, lying on her side and moulding herself against him, her head resting on his chest. She could hear his breathing and feel his heartbeat and finally she felt safe. Without thinking, she stretched her arm over his waist while Giles put one arm around her, anchoring her to him. Their hands met and entwined on his stomach.

"I love you, Giles," she murmured. "Thank you for rescuing me…" she yawned prodigiously, before continuing tiredly, "…if this was a fairy tale, I think you must be the huntsman…" She was asleep before explaining her comment and it took Giles a moment or two to work out what on earth she was talking about, remembering the bang to her head. He smiled to himself as it came to him and kissed the top of her head.

"Any time, my love, any time."

The next morning, Giles woke very early, dawn still an hour away. He was lying on his side, Billie wrapped in his arms, her back to his chest. He had no clue how that happened, but her slumber was undisturbed by nightmares, something he was thankful for, and he slept the sleep of the just. He wanted nothing more than to kiss her awake and then make passionate love to her until she begged for mercy. Her slender body fitted against him, her curves slotting neatly against his hollows, as though she was meant to be there. He was right, sentimental as it sounded, she was his destiny.

While he was thinking this, Billie stirred, turning in his arms, bewildered for a moment until she realised where she was. Then she smiled gently and, in complete disregard for propriety — not that propriety seemed to rank very high on Miss Caswell's list of how the daughter of a viscount should behave — pulled his face down for a kiss.

"Good morning, Giles," she whispered when they finally paused for breath.

"Good morning, my Willow," Giles replied, tucking a wayward curl behind her ear and tracing her jaw with his finger. "You are a marvellous sight to wake up to." Billie smiled again and raised herself up on her elbows to kiss him again. A tremor ran through him and he knew he had to put a distance between them. It was hard enough when they were both fully clothed, but all that stood between him and her skin was a gauzy nightgown his fingers itched to tear off. He began to get up, but Billie was having none of it.

"Don't leave, Giles." Without breaking eye contact, she took his hand and deliberately placed it just above her breast, his fingers splaying around her shoulder, feeling the warmth of her body through the flimsy material. "I know this is forward of me, but I am beyond caring," she murmured. "I wish to feel your touch. My body is crying out for you and although I realise you are too much of a gentleman to grant me this wish without my asking, in this instance I am willing to beg." His own thoughts echoed in her words, "Please teach me how to make love." She held his gaze, her eyes fathomless green, his greyer than a restless ocean under winter skies. Giles attempted to dissuade her — half-heartedly, it must be admitted — but at least he tried.

"Your head?"

"Is fine," she responded, her fingers brushing his face, feather-light.

"Your grandmother?" Still trying to divert her, but aware he was fighting a losing battle.

"Understands." Her eyes bewitched him. His resolve shattered and bending his head, kissed her with all the pent-up desire he had been trying vainly to suppress. She moaned against his mouth, opening her lips to meet the onslaught. He kissed her nearly senseless, before moving on to her neck and down her throat. His hands roved across her body finding their way under her nightgown, discovering every part of her, caressing and stroking, making her arch into him. His cool fingers reached her breast, cupping first one then the other making her quiver and cry out, following his fingers with his mouth, his tongue swirling around the sensitive peaks, teeth nipping gently, while his hands continued their hypnotic dance over her skin.

Billie wriggled beneath him sending little shock waves up his body. She was dragging at his clothing and somehow her nightgown along with his shirt and waistcoat ended up on the floor. Her hands were all over him, tracing the hard planes of his chest and stomach, swarming up his back and thighs, kissing him wherever her lips could reach, fingers curling through the smattering of dark hair curling over his chest, brushing out over his nipples, making him tremble with desire.

Giles let his hands trail over her hips, sweeping down towards her centre, teasing across heated flesh, searching, tantalising. Gently he parted her legs, letting his fingers work their spell. She shuddered underneath him but did not ask him to stop, continuing to enthral his body with her own sorcery, somehow unbuttoning the fall of his trousers, inquisitive fingers gliding around his throbbing muscle, her touch, exquisite torture. Pleasure rippled through Billie as Giles slowly set alight a firestorm that rocketed through her, everything spinning out of control until she was certain the universe had erupted in an explosion of light and colour. It was several minutes before she was able to speak, her breath coming in gasps, her heart pounding. As the planets realigned themselves, she realised Giles held her close, she was cocooned within his arms and he was still kissing her.

"Giles!" When she finally caught her breath. "Oh my, that was the most wondrous feeling imaginable. Do other people know about this?"

Giles started smiling, his own heart drumming a very rapid tattoo and his voice not quite steady. "Yes, my love, it is a well-known phenomenon, but I am not sure every couple is this lucky. I think maybe only those who care very deeply for each other ever achieve such ecstasy."

"Oh, that's such a shame, poor things. Can we do it again?"

Giles was laughing now. "My darling girl, we can do it as often as you wish, although I feel it my duty to warn you that it gets better."

Her face reflected her disbelief. "Really, how is that even possible?"

Giles pulled her to his chest and whispered in her ear. She flushed bright red and stared at him. "Err, so this," she said encircling him again and squeezing lightly making him groan, "fits inside me?" He nodded, biting his lip at her expression. "Well let's do it then." Giles shook his head, almost helpless with mirth, amazed at how she could be so naive yet so wanton all at the same time.

"No, my sweet, we should wait until we are wed, that is as it should be." She grumbled at him, but was wise enough not to push it, simply went back to caressing him, delighting that she could make him tremble so. Just as Giles thought he had regained control, her gentle ministrations sent his heart rate back up and his breath came in short, ragged bursts.

"Billie, you should not...urrgghhhh" as her fingers tightened a fraction. Flicking a glance at him, she relaxed her grasp, concerned she was causing him discomfort.

"Giles, I'm sorry, I didn't mean to hurt you." He cupped her face.

"It doesn't hurt, my Willow," he muttered, his voice sounding tightly wound, "but the more you do that, the harder it is for me to maintain any kind of restraint and I do not wish to mess up these fine sheets."

She gaped at him, puzzled yet intrigued. Why had no one ever told her about these things? How would she have ever known what to do if she hadn't been as lucky as to find Giles, who cared and was patient enough to explain? She supposed her mother would have done, but she died years ago, and now Billie felt like an idiot and rather at a loss. It seemed as though Giles desired she continue yet also wanted her to stop.

"You must think me utterly stupid," she whispered, feeling gauche and awkward. "Please help me understand what to do. Your body tells me you like this, but then you ask me to stop. I'm sorry, no one ever … how do … what … how could you possibly mess the sheets?"

Giles stared at Billie, who was chewing her lower lip and frowning in an agony of uncertainty. His heart clenched in sudden sadness for this young woman who, having lost her mother, missed out on so much. Recalling Billie would have been only about fifteen when her mother died, he realised no one else had thought to prepare her for a life beyond her childhood. He hugged her to him, in a way rather pleased he would be the one to tell her, however sensitive the topic.

"Oh, my love, one thing you could never be is stupid. You are one of the most intelligent women I have ever met. It is just that normally, your mother would have taught you such things as she readied you for adulthood. You do not have an older sister who might have taken her place, so certain things have been left unsaid." He went on to explain the finer points of lovemaking, never loosening his hold of her and by the time he'd answered all her questions, of which she had many — much to his amusement — he had managed to contain his own desire for the time being.

"Now," he said, changing the subject completely, "it is high time I returned to my own bedchamber to prepare for the day. I think we must leave for London, which is where I believe the man who took the papers will be headed. Hopefully, we will meet Withers on the way at which point we can furnish him with a pretty detailed report." He slipped out of the bed and pulled on his shirt and waistcoat, searching for his cravat, which had ended up on the floor behind the chair he slept in. Coming back over to the bedside and handing Billie her nightgown, he leaned in, running his fingers through her hair, which was adorably awry and, cupping the back of her head in his hand, kissed her again. Reluctantly he pulled away. "I will see you at breakfast." He was almost out of the door when Billie asked wistfully —

"Will we be able to come back here? I do not wish my love for this place to be clouded by fear."

Giles turned as she spoke, the pale light of the breaking dawn silhouetting her in its pearly glow. A wave of emotion so powerful, he felt weak at the knees engulfed him and he went back to her, lifting her from her pillows and crushing her to him.

"We will come back as often as you want, my darling Willow," and for a few more minutes gave into his desires. Breathless — this was becoming a habit — he finally released her and dropping a wink, he forced one foot in front of the other and left her room.

Billie lay back on her bed hugging herself, then pulling the covers right up to her chin, fell fast asleep, a secret smile curving her very well-kissed lips.

Chapter Twenty Seven

A few hours later everyone gathered for breakfast, all having slept soundly. Giles outlined their next move, suggesting they leave that day and make haste to London, stopping briefly at Whiteoaks to collect an appropriate assortment of clothing. They were all in agreement, except Billie who mourned the fact their visit had been cut short. Her grandmother, however, urged her to comply with Giles' plan. She was worried her granddaughter was still in danger and preferred they not be in so isolated a place.

Billie bowed to the inevitable and truly she did not want to be apart from Giles for any length of time. After a hearty meal, they packed their belongings and soon were ready to depart; the carriage, and horses ready. Billie was determined to begin the journey on Bronte and no amount of sweet-talking would dissuade her. Theo agreed she showed no ill effects from the run-in with her assailant, besides the bump on her head and bruising to her face, and could see no reason why she shouldn't ride. Giles was just being over-protective.

Goodbyes were said, promises to hurry back were made and the entourage set off. The storm that raged for much of the night blew itself out in the early hours, and the day was calm, a weak sun breaking through a thin layer of cloud. The sea was still ruffled from the tempest but not unduly so. As good a day for travel as could be expected for this time of the year. November was nearly half way over and thoughts of Christmas were beginning to clamber for attention.

They made good time, and their journey was uneventful, taking as long as it took. Thankfully the weather remained kind, and the sight of Whiteoaks five days later was most welcome. Will and George went on ahead to notify the staff, and Giles could see smoke curling white in the dusk from several of the chimneys. Windows glowed softly from the many candles Lucy and Nancy had no doubt lit in anticipation of their master's return.

All would be staying overnight, as all would accompany Giles and Billie to London. Initially, Giles was determined Billie should stay at his city home but, tactfully, Theo persuaded him it would be less controversial if she stayed with Theo's mother. Her home was in the same square as Giles' residence and in this way no one could question their relationship. Eventually, Giles acquiesced, acknowledging the sense in Theo's argument.

As they rattled into the courtyard, Will came out to take the horses, with Ralph and Duncan offering to give him a hand. Giles was just about to assist Billie down from Bronte, when a voice called his name. A figure unfamiliar to Billie strolled out of the back door. Giles turned and a huge smile wreathed his face.

"Withers!" Giles exclaimed. "So good to see you, my friend! What news?"

The man grinned at Giles who clasped the hand of the tall stranger in a tight grip. Striking up an animated conversation, the pair strode off, leaving Billie glaring at their backs as they disappeared into the house. Feeling righteously ignored, she dismounted, and led Bronte into the stables, handing the mare into Jake's capable hands. Thanking him, she then made her way into the house, popping into the kitchen and calling a greeting to Sarah and the other staff. Unsure what to do now, and cross at such cavalier treatment, she stomped up to the Rose Room, where several outfits lay on her bed ready to be packed. Lucy followed, saying she would assist Miss Caswell as Sally had been given leave to prepare her things for the onward journey. Unobtrusively, the young maid began to fold the clothing into a trunk, brought down from the attics for the purpose.

Tired from long days of travelling, Billie wasn't feeling up to being nice to someone else she didn't know, asking Lucy to inform his Lordship she would not be joining the company for dinner. Admittedly, she was more than a little disgruntled he just left her sitting on Bronte, and weariness made her churlish. What was it he said about thoughtless actions? Lucy helped her out of her travel clothes and Billie, after indulging in a thorough wash, pulled on a freshly laundered, lavender-scented nightgown and got into bed.

She must have dozed, for the next thing she heard was her door crashing open. Unable to get her bearings, she shrieked in terror, thinking, in her half-awake state, the agent had found her. She hurled herself off the bed, crawling under it, and squeezing her eyes shut.

There was dead silence, then —

"Billie? Why are you under the bed?" It was Giles. Oh, the relief! Then, remembering how annoyed she was with him, stayed put. "Billie, sweetheart, please come out. There are some people downstairs I think you should meet."

She refused to budge. "Go away," she growled. She heard footsteps and the swish of material, and then a face appeared under the flounces surrounding the bed.

"What on earth are you doing under here, my love?" Clearly perplexed, Giles put his hand out to her. After a brief debate with herself, she took it, albeit grudgingly, and he was surprised to feel tremors running through her. He drew her out, brushing the dust off her clean nightgown, and lifting her chin so she had to look him. "What's wrong, Billie? Why did you scream?"

"The door, I thought..." she was unable to finish her sentence, fearing she would sound feeble. She shrugged his hand away and made to climb back into bed.

"Oh no, Miss Caswell, you just hid under the bed. I think I deserve an explanation," his tone jovial as he smiled at her. Billie, tired from all the travelling, and continuing to feel overwrought, did not return his smile, her nerves frayed to their last thread. She knew that under normal circumstances she would likely have laughed along with him, but tonight wasn't one of those circumstances, and she exploded.

"Oh, you think you deserve an explanation, do you? You, who just burst in here without so much as a knock! Well, my Lord, here's your explanation. You left me sitting on Bronte because someone more important turned up. Yes, I know I'm perfectly capable of getting off a horse, but you just turned your back on me and walked away. Is that how it would be if we were to wed? I am fine as a piece of entertainment, when we are alone, but the moment one of your colleagues or friends or basically anyone else turns up, I am banished to the sidelines?" Billie spat the words at him, exhaustion, fear and fury battling with her senses.

Giles' jaw dropped in shock at her outburst, and he started to speak but she was having none of it, continuing to rage at him.

"Then, despite being advised I did not intend to join you for dinner — as clearly, you have no need of me — you ignore my wishes and, apparently, forgetting there are still those who might quite like to separate me from my life, crash through my door and wonder why I scream! Do you ever, for one single moment, stop to think?" Blithely ignoring the fact she was the one who rarely thought before she acted. She was crying now, her chest heaving as great sobs tore at her.

Stunned at the force of her anger and distress, Giles realised, in his eagerness to persuade her to join them downstairs, he behaved heedlessly. Muffling an expletive he caught her to him, running his hands over her back trying to soothe her shattered nerves.

"Oh God, Billie! I'm sorry, you are right. I was so surprised and pleased to see Withers I forgot everything else that is important to me. It did not occur to me you were still so fearful, especially here where I presumed you felt safe. Surely you must believe it was never my intention to frighten you."

She pulled away from him, pacing the room in her agitation, giving Giles the full benefit of her lissom body. He could see right through the flimsy nightgown, stirring a familiar heat in his loins, making him want to take her right there in front of the fire — to hell with her anger and his guests.

"Oh, I know you did not intend to frighten me, Giles…" she muttered, gesticulating wildly, "…and if you had not walked away, *that*…" waving her hand towards the bed, "…would not have happened, *that* was just adding insult to injury; but you did walk away and it gave me pause. Giles, we live in a world where women have little autonomy, where it is preferred they are seen and rarely heard, or at least kept in the background, their only joy gossiping or going to dances. I cannot live like that. I would rather spend all the days of my life alone than be anyone's second thought." Billie hiccuped as she strove to get herself under control, but for all her pluck, she was still just a young woman who had faced many challenges these past few weeks and she felt as though everything was unravelling. "I want a partnership. To be involved in the day-to-day life of whomever I marry. To spend time together, to not find him at his club or with his mistress — oh and I cannot share my husband with a mistress, it would kill me — while I sit at home, alone, sewing some frippery or trying to play the piano. I thought — I believed — you understood that, that it was one of the things, which attracted you to me. Maybe I misread the situation."

Giles made an inarticulate sound and dragged her back into his arms.

"Willow, my beautiful Willow, firstly and most importantly I love you more than my own life. You never have been and never will be anything other than my first thought. Secondly, and just as importantly, I have no desire to change you but you must remember, all this is new to me too. Until we met, except when I served, I never had to place another's expectations, wishes, concerns, fears or needs before my own. I am trying hard but it may take me a little time to figure it all out. I do not wish to be apart from you unless absolutely necessary, and just to be clear I do not nor do I ever intend to keep a mistress. I would like us to have a partnership too. I know you are interested in how the estate functions and in the lives of those in my service, this I will share with you gladly. Certainly, I cannot imagine you sitting quietly in the corner of the parlour sewing. You are much too spirited to be satisfied by such genteel pastimes."

He chuckled suddenly, an image of Billie trying to be refined popping into his head.

"How about we help each other to adjust?" He searched her face. His eyes held Billie in thrall, so dark they were like pools of night, yet she could see his incalculable love for her reflected there, and so deep she thought she might actually fall into them.

She heaved a huge sigh, then released a breath, which would have blown a lesser man over —

"Oh Giles, could we? That would be perfect. Are you sure you would be happy for me to be involved in your life to that extent? I warn you, I will not be a biddable wife. If you do or suggest something I disagree with, I shall not hesitate to tell you." She looked up at him gauging his reaction, but he simply grinned down at her, commenting he expected nothing less; and with that swept her back into his arms, kissing her into silence.

Several sublime minutes later, Billie stood in his arms, staring up at his ruggedly handsome face, again reading in his expression the truth in his heart. Suddenly, all her fears, questions and nonsense fell away, and she relaxed against him. He held her close, just held her, for what seemed like a long time, but was probably only a minute or so. Her own heart stopped fighting and warmth blossomed through her.

"My Giles, I do love you, more than I can ever express in words and I hope that soon I may demonstrate just how much."

Giles gazed at his love, murmuring this was also his fervent wish, kissing her gently and tenderly, as they stood wrapped together — finally on the same page. "Now, please will you come down to the library with me? You really should meet these people."

Billie nodded, pulling on a very decorous, winter-weight dressing gown and, sliding her feet into warm slippers, accepted his arm. They made their way along the hallways and down to the library. As they entered, a young man so like Billie they had to be related jumped up from the chair he was lounging in. Billie faltered and gripped Giles' sleeve. The man in Polruan looked so similar. A shiver ran through her.

Feeling the tremor through her fingers, Giles glanced down.

"What is it, Billie?"

"He looks like … that's why I thought … how can be I be sure?" Her voice fell to a whisper. She turned to Giles, saying under her breath, "The man who wanted the papers led me to believe he was Stephen. Obviously it wasn't him, but he had the look of this man, and I cannot trust my eyes."

The man came a little closer, speaking in gentle tones, tones she felt she should know. Still, caution made her hesitate.

202

"Billie, Giles explained about your memory but surely you must recognise me?" His face, his voice, the way he was tilting his head, so familiar, but she had been caught out before.

"Maybe, but how sure are you that I should know you?"

He pondered her question for less than a minute before replying. "Certain sure, Squidge." Then he winked. Billie bit her lip. Only her brother would dare to call her 'Squidge' or use this special phrase, theirs since childhood, and only he and their father were privy to that conversation in the study. Was it really only a few weeks since? It felt like a lifetime ago.

"It's really you?" she whispered, hardly daring to believe her eyes. He nodded. "You didn't die in the fire?"

"No, I didn't die in the fire, Billie. It's really me." She ran to him then, and he hugged her tightly. "You have been very brave, I am so proud of you."

"No, I haven't," her words muffled against his chest. "The carriage crashed. I got lost. His Lordship had to rescue me, and I forgot what I was supposed to be doing. I was sick, then we went to Polruan, and the agent still got away. I don't think I'm cut out to be a spy." She felt his chest rumble with laughter and he hugged her again.

"I think you did fine, Billie." Her brother responded, his voice a mix of amusement and relief.

"So do I." A very deep voice spoke from the shadows. Billie froze, realising she had suddenly lost her ability to function. Moving into the glow of the candlelight, another figure as tall as Stephen although much broader, smiled and held out his hand. "Hello, Pet."

"Papa?" Billie stuttered. Her breathing stuttered, and she felt her knees begin to buckle. She heard a peculiar gulping noise and realised she had made it. There was a roaring in her ears. Everything began to recede, and seemed to be dissolving. For such a large man, he moved surprisingly quickly, catching his daughter as she did the most sensible thing she could think of right then and fainted.

Chapter Twenty Eight

Billie came around almost immediately, mortified she fainted in front of all these people. She was cradled on her father's lap, her head resting on his shoulder. Giles handed the viscount a glass of brandy, the whole of which he insisted Billie swallow. It did the trick, and everything came back into focus. She sat for a little while silently contemplating this momentous event. Her father was not dead, he wasn't lying on a cold slab somewhere, and her beloved brother was here too. How was all this even possible?

"Papa, how did you escape? How on earth did you and Stephen know how to find me? Whiteoaks is not what you might call on the beaten track."

"It's quite a long story. Are you sure you are up to it tonight, poppet? You seem rather tired." Billie nodded, glancing under her lashes at Giles, who knew exactly what she was thinking, and smiled his slow smile, making her heart melt.

"I'm fine, I don't think I could sleep now even if I wanted to, this is all too huge. I have lived the last month believing both of you dead, later finding out that apparently Stephen was alive but missing. Then the consensus was I, or both Stephen and I, murdered you. I am most anxious to hear what actually happened." Lifting her head from her father's shoulder, Billie glanced around the room, spotting several people she did not know. Withers and his men, no doubt. She turned to the man she saw come out of the house when they arrived.

"Major Withers," she exclaimed, and he bowed, "I am very pleased to meet you. I am sorry we were not introduced earlier. It seems his Lordship was so excited to see you, he quite forgot he had guests," looking at Giles pointedly when she said this, her tone belying the teasing smile playing around her lips. Giles grinned rather sheepishly, knowing he was forgiven, and spread his hands in tacit apology. Billie continued, "Thank you for your hard work. I believe it was you who was able to clear my name. I am most grateful." The man smiled at her, saying it was his pleasure to assist. Then she added a greeting to the other men circling the library — lounging against window ledges or propping up walls. The room seemed full of people, including her father and brother but in actual fact there were only eight extra. All were listening intently.

Then Billie nestled back against her father's shoulder, as she did when a child, while he told her what happened.

On the afternoon of her departure, the weather turned very cold, prompting the staff to stoke up the fires in all the rooms. He was expecting visitors in the evening — two colleagues on one of his committees — who wanted to discuss an upcoming bill. They arrived as anticipated, the three engaging in a lively debate regarding the bill. The meal, and evening as a whole, was enjoyable, if uneventful, until the viscount's two guests were about to leave. They were standing in the entrance hall saying their goodbyes when, at the same moment Brookes — the footman — opened the door, three rough-looking men burst in, flattening poor Brookes, who fell cracking his skull on the bottom stair. The sheer force of the impact killed him instantly.

Paralysed with shock, the viscount and his guests, remained motionless, while the thugs demanded money, rings, tiepins, anything they had of value. Presuming that this was just a robbery — there had been a few in the area — and once they had some items of monetary worth, they would leave, Edgar Caswell complied, handing over his family ring and a few other trinkets, his two colleagues doing the same. Then, one man stood guard over the two guests, and one watched to make sure they were not disturbed, the third forced Edgar into the study, whereupon he demanded the papers.

Realising this was no simple robbery, Caswell was very thankful Billie was long gone and the papers were well hidden. Telling the man, in no uncertain terms he had no idea what he was talking about, he warned him to leave now would be in his best interests, as doubtless the Watch would be doing their rounds shortly. Laughing nastily at this suggestion, the crook again tried to force the whereabouts of the documents from the viscount, who continued to deny all knowledge.

Eventually the stranger lost patience and struck Edgar, in the face dazing him momentarily, threatening to return once he had located the papers, to finish off the family, referring to the Caswell children by name. It seemed curious this man knew so much about the viscount's family, and Edgar thought him vaguely familiar but assumed he'd seen a likeness drawn in one of the papers. The man's speech was odd too, as though he knew English well but did not speak it often. One of his cronies, who brought the other two into the study, had a similar inflection.

The robbers, or whatever they were, shut the three men in the study, and Edgar discovered later they tucked a chair up under the door handle preventing them from giving chase. Withers and his colleagues surmised it was at this point the three men moved through the lower rooms pulling smouldering logs out of each grate, before skedaddling, leaving the house, and everyone in it, to burn to death.

Billie shuddered at the telling, imagining the horror of that night. Edgar rang for his butler, Alfred, who came directly and released them, but by now it was too late. The fire had taken hold, and it was all they could do to get everyone out. As it was, two others from his household, missed in the melee, were overcome by smoke and perished in the flames. The viscount, obviously still very shaken, struggled to finish his story.

The next day the papers were full of the fire, reporting the death of Viscount Ashbourne, his body identified by a ring found under the elder victim — in reality Brookes, who was of similar stature to Edgar. Bearing in mind the viscount felt his life to be in danger, he decided to let society believe he was dead until such time they could catch the perpetrators. As luck would have it, Stephen had been visiting one of his friends, who agreed to keep quiet as to the young man's whereabouts.

Three days later, Havers turned up with Billie's valise, giving an account of what occurred along the road. By this time Edgar, appalled when he realised the lengths to which these agents would go to get the papers, wished heartily that he had never heard of the secret service.

Havers explained that when the two carriages came together, he jumped onto the offending one, to try to divert it away from the Caswell coach, but was unable to prevent the collision. Further down the road, the other driver shoved him off, and although momentarily stunned, Havers escaped relatively unscathed. By the time he returned to the scene of the accident, however, Billie had disappeared, and Banks was dead. All that remained was the little case. Havers managed to round up the terrified horses but, despite spending hours trying to find Billie, he was unsuccessful. He decided his best option was to return to London to report the incident, and hope Miss Caswell had somehow managed to make her way home.

So, now his daughter was missing, his house had burnt to the ground, three people were dead and at least three men, possibly more, were on the hunt for Billie, with Stephen likely in their sights also.

Unsure whom to trust, the viscount eventually risked speaking to the Bow Street Runners. Not usually the most helpful people but in this instance they already had an inkling all was not as it seemed with the fire at Ashbourne House and, to cut a confusing and convoluted tale short, a few days later he was introduced to Withers. From this point it was plain sailing. Withers told what he knew, including that Giles found Billie injured, unwell, and without recall as to why she was so far from home.

Shortly thereafter Withers had received word Giles, and his entourage, were headed for Polruan, and from there on in, their stories were the same. Withers informed Edgar of his intent to journey to Whiteoaks to meet up with Giles and then to accompany him back to London, where they presumed the man with the papers was headed. The viscount was relieved to hear the stolen papers were fake, and grateful the originals were now safely stored away. They could be left at Whiteoaks until it could be determined who might eventually take possession of them.

Giles took up the story, telling those who didn't already know all that had happened since he found Billie unconscious in the roadway up until the last night in Polruan, including that the dowager was the one to suggest placing a set of fake documents in the cellar. Edgar Caswell chortled with laughter at the image of his mother gleefully planning to trick foreign agents, commenting he knew something of her background and it was through her, he was approached to work covertly for the English government.

Billie continued to be astounded at all this secret undercover intelligence stuff, admitting it was rather too much for her. She still feared once the man realised the documents were not authentic, he would come looking for her. Mentioning this now, she was assured a close guard would be keeping watch over her, until he was caught, although they considered it unlikely he would bother to search for her.

By now it was late, dinner a forgotten meal. Thomas came in with some platters of light supper and plenty of hot chocolate. Billie, fatigued beyond words, was barely able to keep her head up, but didn't want to leave the security of her father's arms. Noticing her pale face, however, Giles murmured something to Stephen, who nodded and approached his diminutive sibling.

"Billie, love, I think you should go to bed." She stared at him, so tired she could not comprehend his words. He took her hand, and asked Giles to direct him to the Rose Room. Giles escorted them upstairs, leaving brother and sister at the bedroom door, wanting to kiss Billie goodnight but knowing it was not possible. Stephen was virtually carrying Billie by this stage and was about to help her into bed when Lucy appeared. The maid took over, removing the dressing gown and tucking in the young woman. The last glimpse Giles had, as the door shut, was of Billie's enchanting face framed by those untameable chestnut curls — fast asleep.

While the two men walked down the stairs, Giles broached the delicate subject of Billie's marriage, asking Stephen whether anyone had asked their father for her hand. There had been a few suitors, but Billie never encouraged any of them and so far, refused even to contemplate marriage. Stephen was unsurprised at the questions, having already figured out this tall earl was enamoured with his sister. He seemed a genial man, Billie trusted him, and as long as Giles promised to treat her well, that was all Stephen could ask for, giving the man his blessing to approach their father.

Before sitting back down, Giles asked to speak to Lord Ashbourne in confidence, the two men disappearing into Giles' private study adjacent to the library. They were gone for quite a long time. A second round of hot chocolate, and whisky brought in before they rejoined the others. Neither man commented on their conversation, but both looked satisfied with the result, especially Giles who looked as though all his Christmases had come at once. Being men, the rest made no mention of it, engrossed in a spirited discussion about their upcoming scheme to catch the foreign operative.

Withers kept circling back to what both Billie and her father said, that the man who confronted them seemed familiar. So much so, Billie was almost persuaded he was Stephen. He mentioned this now while ideas were being tossed around, asking the viscount whether there was even the remotest possibility he could be a relation.

Lord Ashbourne was about to discount such a suggestion when something stopped him. He rolled the concept around in his mind, going over every minute of that fateful evening, remembering the man knew his children's names. It struck him as odd at the time and this, along with the fact the man looked enough like Stephen to fool Billie in low light, made him think a familial connection was indeed something they must consider.

Withers asked the viscount for a list of all the men in his family, regardless of whether he thought them capable of treason. Lord Ashbourne, with assistance from Stephen, jotted down several names. Then Stephen mentioned they had family on their mother's side, in France. As he said this, Edgar Caswell snapped his fingers.

"I know who it is. It has to be Victor. His father, Mathieu, originally hoped to marry my Vivienne, but she told me her father considered him crass, and a bumbling fool. Vivienne married me, and Mathieu married the daughter of some minor noble. Mathieu never forgave her or her father for refusing his overtures, and has since hated me with a passion for being granted what he expected to be his. The last time I saw Victor must have been…" Lord Ashbourne tapped his chin, "…at least four years ago, but I remember thinking then how like Stephen he was. Even so, I am shocked he would betray his family and mine in such a heinous way. His father's hatred for me, for us, must have manifested itself in his son. Although how he knew I was dealing with classified information is a mystery."

Withers was not in the slightest surprised, commenting that if the motivation was strong enough, unscrupulous people had ways of digging up the most closely guarded secrets. The discussion dwindled; the men were weary and so retired for the night, agreeing to pick up where they left off the next morning. It wasn't long before everyone was asleep, and silence blanketed the house.

Chapter Twenty Nine

Billie awoke the next morning and stretched, feeling her joints pop and settle. The events of the previous evening tumbled into her mind and she smiled to herself, supremely happy with her life. Ignoring for a moment, that very pesky cloud on the horizon in the shape of a French agent likely bent on revenge. Making herself believe this was a minor complication, she pushed it aside and got up. After a proper wash, she dressed, managing perfectly well without Lucy, who appeared when Billie was already halfway through pulling her clothes on, and the young maid tut-tutted at her haste.

"Oh, Miss Caswell, you should have rung for me. I'd have been here in a jiffy. Please take a seat while I fix your buttons and your hair." Submitting to Lucy's ministrations, Billie managed to sit just long enough for Lucy to pronounce herself happy with the result, and then after thanking the girl, grabbed her cloak, shoved her feet into warm, kid leather boots and whirled out of the room, flying down the stairs to the kitchens.

She peeped around the door, calling a 'good morning' to them all, mentioning she was going for a walk. Thomas tried to stop her, saying she should wait for one of the men, but she was gone before he got the words out. Sarah raised her eyebrows, and the butler went across the courtyard to the stables, asking Jake to keep an eye on Miss Caswell. Jake was about to follow Billie, when a tall figure intercepted him. Giles appeared saying he would make sure Miss Caswell was able take her constitutional unmolested by bandits and robbers. He winked at Jake, who grinned and went back to cleaning the tack.

Giles strode out after Billie who was walking briskly along the paths, the frosty ground crunching under her boots, swinging her arms to keep warm. He soon caught up with her, calling her name as he drew close. She spun around on her heel, her face lighting up at the sight of him, causing his heart to skip a beat. He covered the last few steps to her side quickly, and bowed over her gloved hand.

"Good morning, Miss Caswell. I trust you slept well?" Gazing into her breathtakingly green eyes, glimmering in the morning light. She regarded him for a long moment before nodding, affirming she had indeed enjoyed a restful night and then they continued with their walk. For once, Giles seemed at a loss. He started to speak, fumbled his words and then tried again. Billie slowed her pace and glanced at him askance, wondering what on earth was the matter. Whatever he wanted to say must be very important. He tried again. "Willow, last night I spoke with your father…"

"…I know you did, Giles, I was there," she interrupted. He placed a finger on her lips, and started again.

"Last night I spoke with your father. I asked him whether he would be as gracious as to allow me to court his daughter with a view to marrying her."

Billie stopped so abruptly, Giles nearly tripped over her.

"You did what?" she asked, her voice barely a whisper. Giles repeated his words. "And what did my father say?"

"He said the three of us might discuss it this morning before we depart for London, and although he saw no reason to reject my suit, the final decision was yours." He held her eyes, all the love he felt for her clearly written on his face along with a tinge of fear that even now she might decide to turn him down. Billie stared back; hardly daring to believe her wish might be on the verge of coming true.

"You definitely want to marry me then?" she queried. "Despite the fact I am rather headstrong, stubborn, somewhat contrary and impulsive, with a tendency to get the wrong end of the stick. Oh, and a really bad spy."

Giles chuckled. "They are precisely the reasons why I want to marry you. That and the fact you are intelligent, courageous, caring, utterly irrepressible, and the most beautiful woman I have ever seen. Oh, and I love you more every day."

She gulped, her hand fluttering towards him, then back to her heart. Very formally she began. "Oh Giles, I'm terribly afraid…" he stared as panic began to course through him. Dear lord she was going to turn him down, then he noticed her smile, "…that you might be stuck with me forever." His heart began to beat again and although there was nothing he wanted

212

more than to swing her up into his arms and kiss her, he managed to contain himself to a simple —

"Willow, my darling Willow, you have just made me the happiest man on earth."

"I would say the feeling is mutual, my Lord." She winked at him, her eyes sparkling. "Just one question." He raised an eyebrow. "Do we have to wait? I mean, is there a given or an expected period for courting, like a month or six months, or can we marry sooner?" Giles shrugged, no better informed than she.

"I have no idea, love, I have never been married before."

Billie giggled. "I hope we can marry quite quickly, there are..." she stopped, colouring slightly. Giles grinned as she spoke, immediately working out to what she was referring, and took pity on her.

"Me too, sweetheart, me too." He crooked his arm and she curled her fingers around it, both the very models of propriety, but Giles could feel the warmth from Billie's hand even through her glove, and she could feel the slight tremor running through his arm.

"Giles," she paused. He turned.

"Yes, love?"

"When we're married, would it be possible to spend most of our time here? I love it, 'tis preferable to the city, and being uncomfortable in large crowds of people I find the constant partying and late nights rather tiresome. I think I could be of use on your estate, with my remedies and such, or maybe help in the schoolroom." She paused, crinkling her nose in thought, making Giles want to kiss her all the more. "In fact, I'd rather like it if we could marry here. It would wonderful to be able to share our happiness with all those who have been so kind to me."

Giles gave up trying to be decorous and bent to kiss Billie on the tip of her now not so crinkled nose. She moved her head slightly as he did so and he caught her lips. They locked eyes and for several minutes simply fell into each other's gaze.

"Do you know, my Giles, I sometimes think I'm going to wake up and find this was all a dream."

Giles removed his glove and cupped her cheek, feeling the muscle in her jaw pulsing to his touch. "This is no dream, my beloved, and to prove it I will be there next to you every time you wake up."

She sighed and pressed her lips to his palm, sending a frisson down his back. Then suddenly she became very purposeful. "Come on, let's go and see whether my father is up and about. I should very much like to be called your betrothed." She grinned at him and, in full view of anyone who happened to glance out of the windows, Giles kissed Billie on the lips, catching her to him. She wound her fingers into his hair and revelled in the sheer joy of the moment. She giggled as he lifted his head and, conveniently forgetting they had been quite intimate less than a week previously, said happily. "Oh dear, now you'll have to marry me."

Giles laughed along with her, tucked her hand under his arm and they strolled back to the house surrounded by an aura of soon-to-be wedded bliss.

Lord Ashbourne, and most of the others were already partaking of a hot and very delicious breakfast when Billie and Giles entered the dining room. Joining them, the two piled their plates with all manner of tasty morsels, thanking Thomas as he poured out large cups of steaming coffee. The mood was jovial; they were all looking forward to returning to or visiting the city. The viscount was staying at his club, so was happy to fall in with Theo's suggestion Billie stay with his mother. The conversation circled around upcoming Christmas celebrations in London, glittering events hosted by the most important families of the *ton*.

Billie was worried about returning to Society. She managed to avoid most of the parties, balls and banquets so loved of the aristocracy, because she always felt awkward in company. Although perfectly able to hold a conversation about absolutely nothing, she was somewhat of a wallflower, preferring to observe from the sidelines. Now she was faced with the prospect of attending several functions, and to make matters worse all her clothes were destroyed in the fire. Until she had the chance to organise a new wardrobe, she was reliant on the selection of Lady Helena's clothes, kindly altered by Ellen.

Beautiful though they were, she feared Lady Helena might not be as accommodating as her brother when she came face-to-face with the woman who was not only going to marry said brother but was also wearing her hand-me-down dresses. Not the best introduction. Added to this was the knowledge many considered her responsible for the fire at their town house. Even though Withers proved it could never have been her, some liked clinging to scurrilous gossip, and it was hard to recover from that kind of scandal. She hoped it wouldn't cause problems for Giles. She would prefer to continue to avoid these events, but acknowledged Giles might quite like to, or was expected to, attend. She surmised it was probably a good idea to discuss the situation with him before it all got out of hand.

As soon as it was polite, Giles asked Lord Ashbourne whether he might accompany Billie and him to the library, and the three left the room. The remainder watched them go, their expressions astute, and proceeded to place bets at least one celebration during the Christmas season would be a wedding. The three were gone for less than a half an hour, returning to the dining room where everyone was waiting expectantly.

Viscount Ashbourne took the floor saying it was his very great pleasure to announce that his daughter, Miss Willow Caswell was now betrothed to Giles Trevallier, Earl of Winchester — the wedding to take place just before Christmas. The room erupted in cheers, the men patting Giles on the back and shaking his hand, then bowing over Billie's hand and wishing her all the happiness in the world. Stephen held back until the others finished, and then hugged his sister, whispering that in his opinion Giles had won the prize of the era. Billie's cheeks flared with hectic colour, completely overwhelmed, but in a rather lovely way.

Eventually everyone calmed down and Billie murmured something to Giles who grinned and nodded. The two excused themselves and hurried away, leaving the rest rather bewildered, but waiving it aside, went off to prepare for the journey. Billie asked Giles whether they might tell the staff, the couple now heading to the domestic quarters. Everyone, save Will and Jake, were there. Giles asked for a moment of their time. Sarah took one look at him and then at Billie and knew, without them saying a word, what was coming. Quietly, Giles told them Billie had agreed to become his countess and they would be having the wedding there at Whiteoaks.

As with the men in the dining room, the staff was delighted. They had come to love this slip of a girl who arrived in such a sorry state. She wheedled her way into their hearts with her sunny demeanour, her obvious love for Giles, and her warmth and respect for the household at large. Sarah enveloped Billie in a motherly hug saying how glad she was, and the others followed suit. Then they went around to the stables to tell Will and Jake who had much the same response.

Inordinately glad everyone seemed pleased with his choice of bride, Giles pulled Billie into a corner of the courtyard for a long and very tender kiss. Billie responded with interest and they savoured the moment — well, actually it was more like several moments. Coming up for air, Giles smoothed a long curl off her flushed face.

"I love you, my Willow."

"I love you too, my Giles." Holding hands, each was transfixed by the other's gaze, oblivious to everything else around them, until the sound of approaching voices brought them back to earth. "We should get ready, I think the men want to leave soon," Billie whispered reluctantly.

"Hmmm…" Giles replied in undertones, "…I suppose we should." Neither moved, not wanting to break the spell, hearts thrumming. The kitchen door swung open and Duncan and Ralph came through carrying their luggage

"Come on you two, plenty of time for that when you're married," Duncan laughed, winking at Billie who blushed yet again. Giles grinned and ushered her inside, saying he'd be waiting for her at the bottom of the stairs when she was ready, before turning to assist with the horses.

Billie discovered Lucy had organised her luggage, so all she had to do was pull on her thick cloak. As she did so, she noticed someone, she presumed it must have been Giles, had placed her clasp on the bedside table. She touched it, tracing the intricate design of the metal, the deep red of the stone twinkling in the soft light from the window, causing her to wonder how so costly a trinket had stayed in her family for so long without some avaricious relation selling it or having the ruby cut into smaller stones. She pinned it to her cloak, the blood red and burnished metal of the clasp standing out on the forest green of the material. It did feel like a talisman, a guardian angel in solid form.

Smiling at her vivid imagination, Billie quickly checked that the room was as it should be and, thanking Lucy for everything, wandered back down the stairs where Giles was waiting. He turned to watch her descend, his heart lifting when she smiled at him. He offered his arm and she linked hers through it. Squeezing her hand, he said he would be riding Bronte, as she was better than Zeus in the city, but thought she might like to travel with her father and brother. Grateful for his foresight she thanked him demurely; her shining eyes contradicting her formal tone. Chuckling, he escorted her out of the grand front door and down the few steps to where the carriages stood. Giles held her hand while she stepped into the first one, and tucked the warm rug over her knees. Sally was already seated, with Billie's father and brother arriving forthwith. Moments later the rather large group had set off.

Their journey was mostly without incident. The weather became inclement and they were obliged to stop once or twice due to a build-up of snow on the roads, arriving in London two days later. With open arms, Theo's mother, the dowager Marchioness of Beaumont, welcomed Billie. She was an extremely elegant yet very down to earth lady and aware Billie's mother was dead, was looking forward to helping that young lady not only prepare for her wedding but also to organise a whole new wardrobe. In anticipation, she already had appointments booked with the modiste for fittings and hoped Billie would attend many of the upcoming social gatherings. Billie glanced at Theo who was trying not to laugh at her desperate expression.

"Mother, I think you might let Miss Caswell settle for the night before you have her tripping all over London. You must remember she has not been well and too many outings would not be good for her."

Billie smiled at him gratefully and, taking the Marchioness' hands in hers, thanked her hostess for everything but commented she would need only a small wardrobe, and the fewer gatherings she was required to attend, the better. Lady Beaumont was a little nonplussed but hid it well. She was not used to young ladies of the elite who didn't like to spend money or go to parties.

Billie, fatigued from the long day's travel asked whether she might be permitted to retire for the night. Sally was summoned, whereupon Billie followed the maid upstairs to a very feminine room decorated in soft yellows; it was like a touch of spring on this winter's night. She did spend a brief moment wondering what Giles was doing, but was so tired that she fell asleep as soon as her head touched the pillow.

Giles, meanwhile, arrived at his town house to be welcomed by what appeared to be a gaggle of women, but in fact numbered only three. Even Charlotte was there, she and her husband deciding to visit with her mother until after Christmas. They were surprised to see him, as he generally refused to come to town in the winter; however once he explained his reasons and that his newly betrothed was with him, they were intrigued. They, of course, knew of the disastrous fire as well as all the gossip surrounding it, and admitted to some reservations regarding Giles marrying into such a family. Giles tactfully suggested they should not believe every morsel of gossip doing the rounds and Miss Caswell was cleared of any wrongdoing, reminding them, she nearly died trying to help her father and brother.

There was a winter ball to be held three evenings hence, it would be here when they would meet Billie and her family. It was certain to be an interesting party.

Chapter Thirty

In the event, Billie was introduced to her betrothed's family two days after her arrival in London. Giles deemed it less nerve-wracking for her to meet them in the informal surrounds of his home, than at a ball in front of countless others. Billie had been very anxious, especially as she had still had no option other than to wear Lady Helena's clothes. She need not have worried, Lady Winchester welcomed her warmly, giving her no chance to feel uncomfortable, and Giles' two sisters pronounced themselves charmed by their brother's bride-to-be. Lady Helena was most gracious about the clothes, remarking that they suited Billie far better than they ever did her. The afternoon flew by and, as Giles escorted her home, Billie managed to express her thanks in a stolen yet scorchingly fervent kiss.

The rest of the time was spent in a flurry of shopping, fittings and afternoons sitting in the drawing room, smiling at people she didn't know, the majority of whom she never cared to. Most just wanted to gawk at the woman whom the rumour mill accused of burning down her home. It was becoming rather tedious and she was eternally grateful when Giles appeared, as though on cue, to invite her out for a carriage ride through Hyde Park, or a stroll around one of the museums or an art gallery. It was taking all her patience not to scream and rant at the scarcely veiled barbs thrown at her by some of the social set.

On the day of the ball, Giles called at Lady Beaumont's to speak with Theo and as he passed the open door of the drawing room, noticed how pale Billie looked. He stood for a moment, running his eyes over her. Billie was sitting quietly among a group of gossiping women, outwardly paying attention, but her jaw was clenched and her hands were twisting the material of her dress, crushing the delicate fabric. He mentioned it to Theo who was enjoying a relaxing brandy in his study with an acquaintance. The poor man was in need of a stiff drink, having failed to find an excuse not to accompany his wife when she had come to call — ostensibly to ensure the unfortunate Miss Caswell was none the worse for suffering such a calamity. Theo headed to the parlour, and when he was able to make himself heard over the babble of voices, asked that Billie be excused for a moment. Taking her by the shoulders, and asking a few pointed questions, the doctor gave her a quick check over.

"Billie, are you feeling all right?" he asked solicitously.

She shook her head as though trying to clear it. "I will be when all these women leave me in peace. How do they do it? Nobody is listening to anybody else. They are like a flock of geese. My head is pounding, and I am struggling to maintain my composure. Most are dreadfully rude with their 'Oh Miss Caswell, how did you manage to snare Lord Winchester after being accused of arson?' and their 'Really, you lost your memory? How upsetting for you, yet it turned out to be so convenient didn't it?' all the while simpering and giggling behind their hands. Grrrrr … I hate it. I'm very sorry, Giles, but I do not think I can attend that ball tonight. If this is what it means to socialise with the *ton*, I think I would rather have my finger nails pulled out without laudanum." She was almost in tears, and Theo suggested Giles take her for a nice long walk along the river. There was a winter carnival and it might help lift her spirits.

It had become almost a tradition now, at this time of the year, for entertainers and stallholders to ply their trades along the banks of the Thames between Blackfriars and London Bridges, attracting thousands. A less dramatic version of the Frost Fairs which sprang up when the river was frozen solid, these bright, gaudy and short-lived festivals were still very popular. A pleasant diversion during the long dark days of winter

Giles was more than happy to and after ringing for Sally, the three departed in Giles' carriage. Billie breathed a sigh of relief and leaned back against the seat, rubbing her forehead distractedly.

"I wish I could get into my garden," she muttered. "I have herbs there that would clear this megrim. Do you think it's possible?" she entreated Giles.

"I think it is probably too dangerous, sweetheart. I understand that the house is barely standing. To try to get through to your garden would be very risky. What herbs do you need?"

"Lavender works, but better still is feverfew. I was tending some, which I placed under glass for protection, but maybe they were all damaged in the fire." She sighed and leaned into Giles' shoulder, before realising she probably shouldn't. As she moved to sit back up, Giles shifted so his arm went snugly around her, drawing her against him. Sally merely grinned at them both. There was nothing really unacceptable going on; they were, after all, betrothed and she was sitting right there.

By the time they arrived at the Embankment, Billie felt less discombobulated and the three enjoyed a long walk past the sideshows and performers, who must have been chilled to the bone. Sally was fascinated for, until their trip to Polruan, she had never travelled further than five miles beyond Whiteoaks, and the sights and sounds of this vibrant city enthralled her. She was intent on soaking up everything so she could tell the others when she returned home.

Giles treated them to a large cup of steaming hot chocolate and the three shared a bag of roasted chestnuts, taking care not to burn their mouths. They admired the performers, and the two women pottered around the stalls picking up ribbons and trinkets — nothing they wanted to buy, but it was nice to look. Soon the afternoon began to wane, and Giles knew they should return home, to allow Billie time to dress for the evening. He was pleased to note that Billie's cheeks were flushed from their walk in the chill air. As they approached Lady Beaumont's residence, Billie thanked him for rescuing her from the gaggle of women, affirming she felt much better, and was looking forward to the ball. Giles dropped a quick kiss on her forehead and squeezed her hand, confirming he would be back to collect her at eight.

It seemed to Billie she scarcely had a moment to blink before it was time to depart for the ball. She bathed, had her hair washed, suffered lightly scented cream massaged into her skin, and allowed a maid to tame her tousled locks into a very ornate bun with loose ringlets framing her face. Refusing any facial cosmetics, Billie was eventually persuaded into a touch of something, which despite it's grand title of Rigge's Liquid Bloom — apparently all the rage — merely added a delicate pink shimmer to her lips.

She chose the deep emerald silk gown, one of the first dresses Ellen altered for her. Pale jade gauze, so fine it was like cobwebs, overlaid the darker silk of the dress, the colours merging into one another, and almost the same shade as her eyes. The gown suited Billie's chestnut hair and creamy complexion perfectly, the material flowing around her, whispering as she moved. Sally twisted matching ribbon through her curls, and Lady Beaumont lent her a string of lustrous pearls, which complemented the slightly plunging neckline. Billie was concerned the dress was too revealing, but Lady Beaumont assured her it was exactly right. Sliding her feet into wonderfully soft, matching leather evening slippers, she was ready. For a few minutes, she stood in front of the mirror trying to control her nerves. Sally came in with Billie's velvet cloak, telling her that Giles had arrived and was waiting downstairs. Billie picked up her clasp from the bedside table — its solid coolness going someway to steady her trepidation — and made her way to the top of the stairs.

Talking to Theo, Giles was lounging against the balustrade, looking devastatingly handsome in black, his tailcoat unbuttoned to reveal a crisp white shirt under a deep wine, brocade waistcoat, the same colour as his cravat. As he heard footsteps, Giles straightened up and turned to watch her descent, causing Billie's heart rate to increase, a soft blush staining her cheeks. Giles' face was a picture, making Billie giggle, totally ruining the elegance of the moment, as she came down the stairs taking care not to trip over her skirts.

When she reached him, he took her gloved hand and rolled the cuff back a little, kissing her on the inside of her wrist, making her shiver in delight.

"Good evening, Miss Caswell. May I say you look quite ravishing?" he murmured, his smile making her toes curl.

"You may, my Lord," Billie replied demurely, the formality of their greeting lost when she winked at him. Sally dropped the cloak over Billie's shoulders, and Giles secured it with the clasp. They stood for a moment drinking each other in, before Lady Beaumont coughed and they came back to reality.

"Come on you two, time to go. Thank you for collecting us, Giles. You are a dear." Theo's mother patted Giles on his cheek as though he was still a youth, rather than an earl who sat on government committees and ran a vast estate. Theo grinned, complimenting Billie on her gown as the four got into the carriage. The ball was within walking distance but the night was cold and the ladies certainly did not want their dresses getting damp on the frosty ground.

Held at the very opulent home of the Duke and Duchess of Allingham, it was obvious this ball was one of the events of the winter season. The entire house was blazing with light. Huge vases of flowers were scattered throughout the rooms, their delicate fragrances evocative of warm summer afternoons, banishing the bite of winter for just a little while. Billie was awestruck; never in her life had she been to anything quite as extravagant. Lady Beaumont escorted her to the retiring room where they left their cloaks with the attendant and made sure their finery was as it should be.

Their party was announced and a hush fell over those who heard, for this was the first time Lord Ashbourne and his family had been seen in public since the fire. Necks were craned and fans were whispered behind as they entered the ballroom; but attentions were easily diverted, and the moment passed. Once the party greeted their host and hostess in the proper manner, they were almost immediately gathered up by loyal friends, and swallowed into the festivities.

Theo claimed the first dance with Billie but Giles insisted on the rest, taking great delight in twirling his betrothed around the dance floor. There was food aplenty, crystal bowls full of fruit punch, and glasses of cool lemonade or ratafia. It was all colour, music, laughter and chatter. At some point during the evening, Helena and Charlotte whisked Billie away, telling Giles in mock severity he should not be monopolising her time.

Giles could not keep his eyes off Billie, however, she mesmerised him. He knew exactly where she was at all times, even when apparently deep in conversation with his friends; which was how a little while later, he noticed Billie, who was standing with his sisters chatting animatedly, suddenly stiffen. Her face flushed bright red before paling to white, hands fisting against her dress in agitation. As he watched, a look of indefinable sadness descended over her features and his heart wrenched. He nudged Theo with whom he had been talking, the two men making their way across the room.

By the time they had fought their way through the throng and reached Charlotte and Helena, Billie was nowhere to be seen. Charlotte said that a huddle of young women were gossiping gleefully and somewhat maliciously about Billie's family, and the fire and how surprised they were Giles would risk his reputation by dancing with a woman to whom rumours of murder still clung. And wasn't it quite scandalous she deemed it appropriate to be at this ball when her father was homeless. Surely she could only be on the hunt for some gullible, rich nobleman who might marry her thus saving her family from destitution.

Billie had quietly excused herself, saying she was going to the retiring room. Helena and Charlotte tried to stop her, but she thanked them for their concern, said she was fine and slipped away. Scathingly, Charlotte rebuked the four girls, telling them exactly what she thought of them and that they should know better than to spread scurrilous gossip without considering anything as fundamental as the facts. Giles asked Helena to go and find Billie, his sister hurrying off.

While they were waiting, Giles could not shake a sense of foreboding. Helena was taking too long. Where was Billie? Finally, Helena reappeared looking very worried. She had not been able to find Billie, but the attendant noted a small lady wearing a green dress collected her cloak not five minutes past.

Giles growled his frustration. *Now* where had she gone? He and Theo found their respective mothers and explained what they thought had happened. The two dowagers knew the girls, and decided a quiet chat with their parents might be the next order of business, sweeping along the ballroom like avenging angels in pursuit of their quarry. A gratifying response, but didn't really answer the question as to where Billie had disappeared.

In the meantime, Billie who unobtrusively left the party was standing on the path hugging her arms around herself in the chill night air, wondering what to do next. Had she paused for one moment, she might have remembered the Winchester carriage was available, driven by Will who would know exactly what to do; but, as was her habit, she didn't think. The hurtful words continued to swirl around her head and all she wanted was to get away. How could she place Giles in that position? He didn't need a life where scandal constantly whispered at his heels.

She was walking rather aimlessly in no particular direction when, out of the blue, she realised her old home was not too far away. Crossing the road, her delicate shoes silent on the frosty path, Billie headed towards it. She did not see a tall figure detach itself from the shadows to follow at a discreet distance, nor did either of them realise a third person seemed to be tracking their movements. It was late, close to midnight. The sky was clear and the stars were out in abundance, and if not so focused on her destination, Billie might have taken time to admire their ethereal beauty. Less than twenty minutes later, she came to the gate, about the only part of the house remaining intact.

She stared at the destruction in shock, having little idea as to the scale of the damage. When she pushed the gate, it grated on its hinges, the sound loud in the quiet street. She hesitated, but no one opened doors or windows to see who or what caused such a racket. Gingerly, she found a path through the debris. Beams, and large chunks of stone lay haphazardly over what was once the ground floor. Here and there scorched material fluttered, a cushion lay damp and moulding, a piece of furniture completely undamaged sat amongst charred ruins, the staircase now leading nowhere. She was flabbergasted. Everything she had ever owned was gone; she hadn't really registered how much the fire had consumed until now. All that remained of the once elegant town house was a grotesque silhouette.

Billie picked her way to the back of the house where her garden had been. Her herbs lay battered on the flagstones. The glass, which once covered her more delicate plants, was smashed, shards sticking up out of the plant pots. Without thinking, she sank onto the ground, scooping up the soil, trying to save something from such devastation. She was so engrossed in her task she didn't hear the crunch of footsteps behind her, nor did she notice a tall man was now standing right in front of her. When he spoke, she nearly jumped out of her skin, and bit off a scream. Initially thinking it was Stephen, she started to ask how he knew she'd be here. Then she realised it wasn't her brother; it was Victor.

"Well, well! Who do we have here? A young woman all alone in a burned-out house. Tut tut, my dear, you should know better than to wander the streets of London on your own, you never know what might lurk there." His voice was silky smooth, yet his tone held an underlying threat. Billie took a breath and tried to control her panic, glancing around to see whether she had any escape route. All she could see were broken beams, crumbling walls and darkness.

"What do you want with me?" she demanded, pleased to note her voice didn't shake.

"The papers."

"You have them. I saw you take them!" she retorted, her tone rising a notch.

"They were fakes, as well you know."

"How could I know?" Feigning astonishment. "I had never seen them before that day." Which was almost true. He took a step closer to her, speaking in very low tones.

"You will lead me to the original documents. If you don't, you will never see your family or your beloved earl again. There is no one to rescue you now."

Billie was still sitting on the ground surrounded by her plants and she curled her fingers around a pot while contemplating the possibility of hurling it at Victor's head.

"How can I possibly lead you to documents I have no knowledge of?" she retorted, infusing incredulity into her voice. She sat back on her heels regarding him warily; suddenly curious as to what motivated his actions. "Why Victor? Why are you doing this? What has my family ever done to deserve such animosity?"

Victor stared at her, a frown creasing his forehead. "Because your mother betrayed France."

Billie gaped at him. "Don't be ridiculous!" she expostulated. "How on earth could Maman betray France? She loved France, nor would she ever have done anything to hurt Grand-père, and anyway she spent most of her time here in England with Papa and us."

"There were numerous occasions when she came upon information, confidential material, which she subsequently shared with your father. He passed everything on to his government. It was enough for them to decipher certain military strategies and operations."

Billie was floored. No way could she imagine her mother doing such a thing. How would she even come by such sensitive information? A question she posed to Victor, with some hauteur, it must be said.

"At balls, at parties, at soirees, anywhere a large number of people gathered, and it seemed her friendly nature encouraged all manner of confidences. Your family mixed with the highest levels of French society before your remove to England. To be scrupulously fair, she was very good at it." Victor sounded almost impressed. Billie still didn't believe it, but another thought tickled at her consciousness.

"Did you kill her?" she whispered, holding her breath.

Victor shook his head. "No, she fell off her horse. My father told me, as far as they could work out, something spooked the creature and it tossed her. She landed awkwardly and broke her neck. It did save me a job," he added meditatively. "Now, tell me where those papers are."

"I do not know. Honestly, Victor, Papa took them."

Victor stiffened, his face reflecting his confusion at this news. "Your father? No, no, he is dead, I read the papers."

"Sadly your scheme didn't work, Cousin. It was our butler who was killed. Neither my father, nor my brother, nor either of the two men you shut in that room died. Three others, however, were not as lucky, for which you will be held accountable in this life or in the next," the last muttered under her breath. "So all this is in vain. Despite your best attempts, my father lives, the papers are safe and even if you kill me you will not get them. As for the earl, he can never be mine. The scandal attached to me by your actions means I will never be able to marry. Maybe knowing I am forever shunned will be a balm for the embarrassment of your own failures." Her voice was filled with loathing and no small amount of pain.

The two glared at each other across the ruined garden. Victor declared that Billie lied, that her father died in the fire and she was trying to trick him. He spewed forth a string of dire warnings if she refused to help him. All the while Billie railed at her cousin, calling him a vagabond, a traitor and a sorry excuse for a human being. In any other circumstance, their argument would have probably sounded very amusing.

While this was going on, Giles, Theo, Lord Ashbourne, Stephen and Duncan, along with Withers, were approaching the two cousins as quietly as possible. Duncan, the second man in the shadows, saw Victor follow Billie, and asked Will waiting in the carriage, to inform Giles, he would tail them. Giles and the other three men came pounding down the steps of the Allingham residence less than two minutes later looking for Billie. Will passed on Duncan's message, but it took several minutes for them to decide where Billie might be headed. Then Giles remembered their conversation about the herb garden and asked Edgar whether he thought she might go there. Billie's father thought it conceivable, especially as the garden was her sanctuary, the house relatively close to where they stood.

The four men hurried through the night, taking care on the slippery pathways, the frost hardening as the temperatures continued to drop. They arrived at the gate not long after Duncan, who updated them in undertones. As they pondered their next move, Withers loomed up out of the darkness; one of his subordinates reporting there seemed to be some funny business going on involving Miss Caswell.

The gate remained open, so they were able to enter stealthily. It was harder to pick their way through the debris-ridden building without drawing attention, but they were careful, and managed to reach the rear of the house. They hung back trying to work out who was who. In the moonlight they could see Victor towering over Billie, who was difficult to distinguish from all the other wreckage, for she was still huddled on the ground, her dark cloak camouflaging her.

Their conversation was clear, however, and they heard enough to know that Victor was at the very least responsible for the attempted theft of classified documents and most likely the fire, the carriage accident and the deaths of four men, including poor Banks — they just needed to catch him.

Giles also heard Billie say why she could not marry him; her voice full of regret and his heart ached. Nothing would stop him making her his bride; he just hoped he would get the chance to prove it to her. They crept closer were nearly upon the cousins, who continued to berate one another, when one of the group stood on a piece of charred wood. It cracked underfoot, the noise echoing like a gunshot in cavernous space. Billie and Victor stopped arguing, the sudden silence deafening. Victor peered towards the sound, but the men were smart enough to shelter against what remained of the building and he could not determine how many were concealed in the shadows.

"I see your protectors have arrived, Cousin," Victor drawled. "This should be fun." He reached into his pocket and, withdrawing a gun, raised his voice. "There is no escape for her tonight, your Lordship. She refused to give me what I want. She will pay, which means you will also pay. I imagine her death will prey hard on your soul."

Billie heard a muffled oath, and recognising Giles, nearly giggled, hysteria tickling at her senses. *He had come for her! How did know where to look?* It mattered not. He was here. Her heart soared.

Determined to distract her cousin, she said. "I think you will find you are hearing things, Victor, it was probably a fox. Lord Winchester has no desire to come looking for me. He accepted his suit is pointless. When I left the ballroom, he was already dancing with another. He will forget me soon enough." She stood up, still clutching the pot plant. Her face was white in the moonlight, but her eyes flashed green fire. From his position, Giles could see how furious she was, and realised her intent with the pot. If she threw it, they would only have seconds to help her.

Victor was laughing, but it was not a happy sound and he waved the gun at Billie who stood stock still, her anger bubbling up. She was not going to let this man destroy all that was dear to her. She flexed her shoulder, and was about to throw the pot when a voice reverberated through the darkness.

"Victor! How dare you threaten my daughter? You have already done enough to be hanged, do not compound your folly by murdering an innocent woman."

Victor's jaw dropped, then his hand dropped — the gun hanging loosely by his side. "Ashbourne? It cannot be! The fire, you perished, I saw the bodies."

Lord Ashbourne came out of the shadows and confronted his nephew. "No, sadly it seems that all who have died by your hand were guilty of nothing more than being members of my household staff. Your scheme to destroy my family has failed. You are nothing but a scoundrel, unable even to complete the task for which your masters appointed you."

Victor's face flushed with anger and he pointed the gun directly at Billie's father. The other men all moved then, and Victor realised that he was surrounded. Resolved not to go down without a fight, and knowing he only had one shot, he swung the gun back towards Billie.

"Maybe not," he snarled, "but I can still make your life a living hell."

"No!" shouted Lord Ashbourne — too late. Victor cocked the hammer and took aim, but in that split second, Billie hurled the pot at her cousin's head with all her strength, hitting him in the face. Simultaneously, the pot shattered and the gun went off, the sound deafening Billie who dropped to the ground covering her ears and muttering —

"Mustn't snap, don't snap." The shot went wide, ricocheting off a ruined pillar, and a swarm of men filled the small space, taking down Victor before he had a chance to flee.

Giles ran to Billie, crouching next to her. He peeled her hands from her ears, as she continued to still exhort herself not to snap. He lifted her from the frozen ground, holding her to him, running his hands over her, checking to make sure she was unhurt. Murmuring her name, he rained kisses down on her face, telling her she wasn't broken she was still his Willow. Billie did giggle then; relieved she was safe and more importantly Giles came for her, tilting her face so she could look at him. He brushed an errant strand of hair off her cheek and, in full view of all seven men, kissed her fully on the lips.

"Oh, my love! Why on earth didn't you come and talk to me, instead of rushing away like that? You might have been killed. You nearly were killed. I could not bear it if I lost you. The only scandal attached to your name is the one in the minds of mean-spirited gossips; and even if there was, it would not stop me from marrying you. I am completely and irrevocably head over heels in love with you." He kissed her again, and when Billie finally had a chance to reply, she blushed rather prettily and to the amusement of all, responded with her now familiar cry —

"I'm sorry. I didn't think."

Epilogue

It was early morning, a few days before Christmas. The sun was only just peeking over the horizon, changing the sky from grey to pink. Snow blanketed the ground and all was quiet. The previous week had seen the annual Christmas Ball, a night of splendid festivities and deemed one of the best ever by all who attended. Whiteoaks was decorated within an inch of its life. Boughs of fir and twists of berry-laden holly, mixed with ivy and bay, adorned every available surface; their deep green hues brightened by huge bows of red and gold ribbon.

Today was for another celebration, and by choice a much quieter affair than the uproarious party. A small figure slipped out of the house, warmly wrapped up in a heavy cloak, boots and gloves. She loved this time of day before anyone else ventured abroad; it was as though she were the only person awake in the whole world. The air was icy cold and very still. Occasionally there was a crack as a branch gave way under the weight of the snow, and the odd twitter from a bird disgruntled at the lack of bugs.

Her footsteps were muffled in the deep snow as she trudged across the gardens. It was her wedding day and she wanted a moment to herself, before everything went crazy, to take stock and prepare herself for the next and, she trusted, happiest phase of her life. She walked over to the low fence separating the gardens from the rest of the estate and looked back at the house, which from today would officially be her home. Even though she had been living there on and off since Giles found her a little over two months before, she had only really been a guest, a very loved and pampered guest, but a guest all the same. It was still rather overwhelming.

Billie drank it all in, gazing at the magnificent house nestled in the snow, its soft red brick walls edged with stone quoins, warm and welcoming. Its slender chimneys with smoke curling lazily up to the brightening sky. The multitude of windows already glowing from the candles lit within. Smiling at the scene, which looked like a painting, she turned to gaze the other way, out across the Great Park and on towards the forest, shivering a little as the cold seeped through her cloak. The quiet was disturbed by the thud of heavy footfalls. She glanced over her shoulder to see Giles striding towards her. As happened every time she saw him, her heart did its familiar hiccup, heat coiling through her and she beamed at her very soon-to-be husband.

"Goodness me, Willow! What on earth possessed you to come out here on so cold a morning? Shouldn't you be doing whatever it is women do on their wedding day?" Coming up to her, taking her hands in his and leaning in to kiss her cheek.

"I wanted a minute before it started, just for me..." she paused, "...but I am very pleased to share it with you."

Giles pulled her close, the heat from his body penetrating her outer clothing and warming her. It was a month since that fateful night in London. Withers and Duncan escorted Victor to the lock-up from whence he was taken to face a judge who declared execution to be the only just punishment. Although Lord Ashbourne intervened, asking it be commuted to imprisonment — for despite his nephew's heinous crimes, he could not countenance the man's death — the judge had yet to announce his final verdict. Despite life in prison being a far harsher penalty than the gallows, most believed Victor would hang.

Billie, her father and brother spent many long hours closeted in Giles' study going over recent events and the impact on their family, but eventually they just had to accept and move on. What was done was done. The papers were in safe hands, and Withers was leading the investigations, which aimed to bring to justice, those considered to have contravened the security of England and its government.

Three weeks ago, Giles brought his bride-to-be — along with her father and brother — home, to the delight of his household. Billie helped with the preparations for the Christmas Ball and organised all the gifts for the staff, which would be presented on Boxing Day. Three days prior, people began arriving for the wedding. Billie's grandmother; Giles' family; Theo and his mother; as well as Withers and his wife —

a lovely young woman called Jemima, with whom Billie was fast becoming friends. Duncan, Ralph and Harry and their respective families, were also invited, but they lived close by and would be arriving that day. Billie asked that the entire staff be allowed to join them, for they had been unfailingly kind taking her to their hearts before they even knew her name. Giles was more than happy to agree.

Giles and Billie revelled in the tranquillity of those few stolen moments, which set the tone for the whole day. They chatted about this and that, nothing earth shattering, just the mundane everyday conversation of two people whose lives were now bound. At some point Giles, once again ignoring the rules of propriety, kissed his bride until she was gasping for breath, not that she complained — merely returned his kiss — with interest!

It was a good hour before they strolled back, by which time it seemed that the whole house was bustling about. Guests coming downstairs to partake of the sumptuous breakfast served up by Thomas and Lucy, while the remainder of the staff handled the final preparations for the day's celebrations. On the way to her room after breakfast, Billie popped her head through the kitchen door to thank Sarah and Mrs Grey, declaring the smells emanating from that bastion of culinary triumphs were divine. They shooed her off, smiling in delight.

After that, the day flew by, almost too fast for Billie who wanted to savour every moment. The bride looked breathtaking in a forest green velvet gown trimmed with red, which clung to or flowed from her slender frame in all the right places, the train rippling out behind her. Long, rich chestnut curls framed Billie's radiant face; the rest of her unruly hair pulled, pushed and twisted until Sally, who cleverly affixed Billie's ruby clasp into the intricate hairstyle, was satisfied it might hold at the very least until the end of the official ceremony. A snowy white cloak for the journey to and from the church completed her outfit. Giles wore dark grey trousers and tailcoat, the shade matching his eyes almost exactly, his crisp white shirt under a striped green and cream waistcoat and his cravat the same colour as Billie's dress.

They were married in the village church and the ceremony itself was short but very moving, at the end of which Giles begged their guests' indulgence for a brief moment. Both he and Billie wanted to share the import of this moment with those closest to them: a few words from their hearts and something more than the solemn dignity of the liturgy. Billie spoke first, her voice trembling just a little.

"My darling Giles. I never put much stock in fairy tale romances and although I believe in love, I never imagined it could happen to me, that someone would come into my life and sweep me off my feet. Then I met you, or rather you found me, literally sweeping me up…" gentle laughter echoed around the nave, "…and even though we met but a short time ago, I feel as though I've known you forever and that my life truly began with you. So in this moment, as we bind our lives together, I want to say that maybe there are such things as fairy tales, for my happily ever after, is all because I happened once upon an earl." Giles grinned at his bride.

"My beautiful Willow. Your mother named you for a tree that never breaks merely bends with the tempest to stand tall again once the storm has passed. You are well named, for you have faced many trials with a courage most men do not possess and you remain unbroken. I have loved you since the first time you looked at me, with no memory of who you were or how you came to be unconscious on my driveway, dripping water all over me and my home." The gentle laughter gave way to outright mirth and Billie twinkled at her new husband. "In front of our families and friends, I hereby affirm that I will cherish you for the rest of our lives, and promise always to be your fairy tale earl."

Gathering her into his arms, Giles kissed her tenderly, to the satisfied sighs of all the women in the room. Billie clung to him, sinking into his kiss, her insides melting. Then, he lifted his head, and they turned to face their guests who cheered with joy. The celebrations began in earnest, a string of carriages transporting the guests back to Whiteoaks.

As the day wore on, Giles found it harder and harder to keep his hands off his new wife, and she didn't help matters by smiling beguilingly at him and winking when she caught his eye. Every time they passed each other, he grasped her hand or touched her back. When they stood together his fingers entwined with hers, his thumb rubbing over hers, his touch making her tremble. Finally, after all the food had been eaten and they had chatted and smiled and danced and when no one seemed to be looking, Giles took his wife's hand and led her quietly away, oblivious to the knowing looks of several of their guests.

Still holding hands, they stole up the stairs, Giles steering Billie to his bedchamber where they would both now sleep. During the last few days, Sally and Mrs Grey moved all of Billie's things into this room, adding a touch femininity to a room whose decor was quite masculine and austere, their thoughtfulness duly noted.

They stood together in the peace of the room, then Giles cupped the back of Billie's head, twisting his fingers through her curls, removing the clasp and undoing the elaborate hairstyle, letting it tumble in chestnut richness around her shoulders. Tilting her face, he kissed her. Billie leaned into him; her heart beat increasing as the familiar slow burn coiled around her stomach. Her fingers fumbled with his cravat and waistcoat, while he began to unbutton her gown, slowly peeling away the layers of delicate material between his touch and her skin, each piece whispering to the floor to pool at their feet. Shrugging out of his shirt and trousers, he gently removed the last of Billie's clothes, then they stood for a moment drinking each other in.

Rather stunned at the man standing before her, Billie reached out to touch him, but shyness took over, making her drop her hand. Giles traced her cheek with one finger, resting it under her chin, raising her head back up so he could look into her eyes.

"My adorable wife, I'm not sure you have yet realised just how deeply you affect me." Reverently spoken. Unable to stop herself, Billie glanced down. Giles chuckled. "Well maybe you do, but you have nothing to be shy about. You know my body and I know yours, we're just going to…" he paused, then

236

delicately, "...extend that knowledge a little more." Drawing her against him, Giles cradled her body against his, fitting her to him curve for curve and Billie felt the slow burn smoulder into life, heat coursing through her veins. Giles lifted her, carrying her over to the huge and very comfortable-looking bed, laying her gently on it before resuming that heart-stopping kiss.

The leaping flames from the fire seemed to match their ardour, as Giles' hands roved over Billie's body rediscovering her slender shape. Brushing his fingers over her hips, and her stomach, and upwards to her breasts, his tender caress like the beat of a butterfly wing. Billie moaned against his lips as her hands, of their own volition, stroked across her husband's taut frame. She began skimming her cool fingers over his back, up onto his shoulders and down through the hollow of his neck, feeling him shudder against her. His lips trailed along her jaw, down her throat and to the slope of her breast.

Under his masterful touch, the smouldering heat flared into incandescence and Billie felt as though her whole being was consumed by liquid fire. She arched into him, yearning for his mouth on her flesh and Giles, using his tongue to great effect, tormented her until she was almost delirious, her body becoming molten while at the same time his hand stroked down her stomach, teasing across the sensitive skin between her thighs. Billie gasped, and in response grazed one hand over his back, bringing her other down to wrap around the muscle pulsing against her leg, fingers squeezing gently, gratified by the guttural moan forced from Giles' lips. With an effort, he stilled his movements and lifted himself up on one elbow.

"Billie..." he muttered hoarsely, tucking the hair off her face, "...do you know what you're doing to me?"

"Oh, I think I have a pretty good idea," she smiled, before pushing him onto his back, kissing all the way down the long length of him. As she came back up, Giles caught her to him, moving her under his body and holding himself above her, bending to capture her lips again, while Billie's hands continued to weave their magic over his fevered skin. Giles knew he was close, but he didn't want to hurt his wife any more than he would need to.

In a voice ragged with longing, he murmured, "Billie my love, I need to take you, but it will hurt. I will be as gentle as possible, just trust me."

Billie, her heart thrumming and her breath coming in short gasps, was beyond speech and simply nodded — her eyes holding his green on grey — her desire to feel him inside her intense, her arousal making her ready. Almost undone by the expression on her face and to make it as painless as possible as well as for the enjoyment of both, Giles caressed her skin, the feather-light touch making her tremble with wanting him before trailing his hand across her abdomen and down to her core, his fingers stroking her until she was crying out for him. Only when he was sure she was on the brink did he settle himself between her legs, slowly sliding into her, adjusting his position carefully, allowing her body to open up for him.

Billie was writhing under him, her movements making it difficult for Giles to maintain any form of control. She lifted her hips, welcoming him further in, as her heat swallowed him. Billie experienced a spasm of pain, but almost before it registered, it was obliterated by the waves of rapture that crashed over her, as Giles took her up to the edge of the precipice. Letting instinct take over, she curled her legs around his back pulling him in deeper, matching his rhythm as he took her higher and higher, rising towards a crescendo that seemed to take forever. Quite certain a full orchestra was playing and thousands of fireworks were going off in their bedroom, they reached the zenith together and Billie felt sure she must have touched the stars as the world exploded.

Slowly everything reformed around them and they floated back down to earth on a cloud of euphoria. Giles kissed Billie tenderly and languorously, whispering his love for her as she nestled against him, pliant in his embrace. After several minutes during which they tried to get their breath back, she murmured —

"You were quite right, my Giles." Giles raised an eyebrow. "You did say it gets better, and I will want to do this quite frequently I imagine." Giles smothered a laugh, as his wife stretched like a cat and moved against him, lifting her face for another kiss. Happy to oblige, Giles captured her lips and, forgetting about everything else — including that they were supposed to be acting as hosts to a houseful of guests — made heady, intoxicating love to his new bride for the rest of the afternoon.

Rather later than they anticipated, looking delightfully sheepish and maybe a little tousled, Billie and Giles rejoined their guests — all of whom knew exactly why the happy couple slipped away, but were polite enough not to mention it. More food and wine appeared and the evening passed in a haze of laughter and good cheer. It was very late before their guests retired to their beds or departed for home and, still rather overwhelmed with the abundance of good wishes, the newlyweds stood in the magnificent hallway revelling in the sudden quiet.

Giles murmured that they should probably go to bed, a wicked light in his eyes. Billie giggled at his expression, gladly letting him take her by the hand and escort her upstairs. Someone had very thoughtfully re-made their bed, just in time for them to muss it all up again in the most delectable fashion.

It was maybe an hour before daylight when Billie awoke, lifting herself up on one elbow and admiring her very handsome earl in the light of the fire, still not quite believing he was hers. Giles must have sensed her gaze, as his eyes opened, a slow smile lighting up his face, and he moved to kiss her very satisfactorily.

"Good morning, my bewitching wife," he whispered, kissing her nose.

"Good morning, my irresistible husband," she replied. "Come, I have something I wish to show you." Hopping out of bed and sliding her feet into warm boots, Billie shrugged into her thick winter dressing gown, waiting for Giles to do the same. Somewhat perplexed, yet becoming used to his wife's unusual ways, he did as he was bid and followed Billie down the stairs. To his surprise, she took his hand, drawing him into the library and over to the huge French windows. The candles had been snuffed out hours before, the only light coming from the dying embers in the fireplace. Opening the curtains, then the doors, Billie stepped out onto the flagged patio, pulling Giles with her. He was looking rather bewildered — it was, after all very dark and very cold, but she simply grinned at him.

It was snowing, the delicate flakes adding to the thick carpet of pristine whiteness blanketing the ground. The world around them slept and all was still.

"Why are we here, Billie?" Giles questioned curiously, wrapping his arms around his wife to keep her warm.

"There is something very magical about being abroad at night in the depths of winter; they call this the witching hour," she murmured. "It is as though time is holding its breath, poised irresolute at the threshold of a new day, undecided whether it will usher in the dawn or let the darkness retain its dominion over the earth. I wanted us to be here, at this moment, in the dark, in the snow and in the silence, for you and I are also poised, at the beginning of our lives together and I thought you might like to feel its spell."

Giles gazed down at his love, drowning in the luminous green of her eyes as she was mesmerised by the dark grey pools of his. The inky blackness enveloped them as their shadows became one with the night. Rocked to the core by the intensity of his emotions, Giles drew Billie close and kissed her for the longest time with an exquisite tenderness, Billie's shivers nothing at all to do with the chill air. Slowly their embrace deepened, bursting into a passion that would have felled her had Giles not been holding her so tightly, and they lost themselves in each other. If they had been listening, which of course they weren't being rather preoccupied, they might have heard a hushed sigh as time released its breath, allowing the frosty iridescence of dawn to peek over the horizon heralding the new day.

And as with all fairy tales, they lived happily ever after.

Thank you for purchasing this book, I do hope you enjoyed it. If you have a moment to write a quick review on Amazon I would be most grateful.

The synopses for my other books follow.

I hope we meet again soon,

Rosie

You can find me on,
Facebook:
https://www.facebook.com/RosieChapelTheAuthor/
Twitter: @RosieChapel2015
Website: www.rosiechapel.com
Goodreads:
https://www.goodreads.com/author/show/14759605.Rosie_Chapel

The Pomegranate Tree
Hannah's Heirloom - Book One

Hoping to trace the origins of an ancient ruby clasp, a gift from her long dead grandmother, Hannah Wilson travels to the fortress of Masada with her best friend, Max. Strange dreams concerning a rebel ambush begin to haunt Hannah and following a tragic accident, she slips into the world of Ancient Masada.

A woman out of time, Hannah must rely on her instincts and her knowledge of what will befall this citadel to survive. Will she escape, or is she doomed to die along with hundreds of others as Masada falls – and what does any of this have to do with an ancient ruby clasp?

Echoes of Stone and Fire
Hannah's Heirloom - Book Two

Pompeii - a vibrant city lost in time following the AD79 eruption of Vesuvius. Now rediscovered, archaeologists yearn for an opportunity to uncover the town's past. Some things however, are best left alone - revealing the secrets hidden beneath the stones could prove perilous. Hannah and Max are brought to Pompeii by a surprise invitation to join an excavation team who are trying to uncover the city's long history.

After entering an excavated house that bears a Hebrew inscription, Hannah's two worlds collide and she falls back through time to ancient Pompeii. A place where her ancestor is a physician to gladiators engaged in mortal combat, where riotous mobs run amok and where a ghost from the past returns to haunt her.

Will Hannah and her loved ones manage to escape the devastation she knows is coming, before the town is engulfed in volcanic ash? Will she ever find her way back to Max the love of her life, waiting not so patiently millennia away? Or will echoes be all that remain?

Embers of Destiny
Hannah's Heirloom - Book Three

AD80 - Hannah and Maxentius must embark on a new journey to Northern Britannia. This harsh frontier is far from the comforts of Rome and danger lurks where least expected; a garrison of soldiers, some unhappy with their isolated posting; local tribes, outwardly accepting of their Roman occupier, but who may still resent the seizure of their lands.

Millennia away, Hannah Vallier finds a familiar item while working in a museum near Hadrian's Wall. It is the pomegranate; carved by Maxentius on Masada. Before Hannah can discuss it with Max, disaster strikes! Believing her husband has been killed, Hannah retreats into the past, her soul melding with that of her ancestor, but with little idea of what they could face. Is the risk from the conquered tribes, or much closer to home?

As rebellion threatens to shatter a fragile peace, Hannah's heart whispers that just maybe Max isn't dead and that he is calling her home. Can she trust her heart or will she remain caught out of time, her destiny floating away like embers on a breeze?

Etched in Starlight
Hannah's Heirloom - Prequel

Maxentius - a Roman soldier fresh from the battlefields of Armenia, arrives to take command of the military outpost of Masada, Herod's isolated citadel in the Judaean desert. A seemingly mundane posting after years of warfare, Maxentius finds it more challenging to maintain a focused garrison than to face the wrath of the Parthians across a disputed frontier.

Hannah - a young Hebrew physician spends her days dealing with injuries from street brawls, deprivation, disease and loss. As her beloved Jerusalem plunges into chaos; her brother — who belongs to a band of rebels determined to drive out their Roman occupiers — tells her of their plans to storm a desert fortress and steal the weapons stored there, persuading his reluctant sister to go with him.

Masada - following the ambush, Hannah finds and treats three badly wounded Roman soldiers. In the aftermath and against impossible odds, Hannah and Maxentius realise that they are more than healer and captive, their fate already etched in starlight.

Prelude to Fate

For Lucia, staring into the jaws of an horrific death, escape seems impossible.

Rufius Atellus, a veteran Roman soldier, is appalled when he recognises one of the victims about to be executed. Surely this is a ghastly mistake?

A ferocious she-wolf, anticipating a tasty meal, suddenly finds herself under a human's control.

In an unexpected twist, and as danger threatens, the lives of all three become inextricably entwined. Was it chance brought them together in that theatre of bloodshed, or simply a prelude to fate?

To Unlock Her Heart
A Regency Romance
Linen and Lace - Book Two

After being caught in a scandal with a duke, Grace Aldeburgh has been shunned by everyone ~ family, friends and Society. To shield herself from the trauma she was subjected to, Grace buried her heart away, so deeply that she wasn't sure it could ever be found.

Two years later, with little hope of ever being free of the stigma, relief seems at hand in the guise of a bequest from her Great Aunt. Grace has inherited a house in a tiny village, far from prying eyes and malicious gossips. Once there, she meets Theo Elliott, the village doctor and what begins as a tentative friendship, blossoms into something more enduring. Fearing further censure, Grace knows she must tell Theo her secret, but the doctor is no fair-weather suitor and has already resolved to be the man to unlock her heart.

Just as happiness appears to be within her grasp, her erstwhile tormentor once again stalks Grace. After a failed kidnap attempt, the duke's quest culminates in an acrimonious confrontation with Grace and suddenly the reason for his venal pursuit of her becomes agonisingly clear.

Love on a Winter's Tide
A Regency Romance
Linen and Lace - Book Three

Lady Helena Trevallier is in no hurry to marry, unwilling to allow a man to dictate her life. She has a secret, one that would probably horrify her social set and one any prospective suitor would demand she curtail. Every day, Helena disappears into a world few acknowledge, helping the poor, downtrodden and abused.

Hugh Drummond avoids most of the Society events he is invited to; events stalked by mamas seeking husbands for their daughters. A state of wedded bliss is something that holds no interest for him. Busy managing his shipping line, he sees no need for a wife, whose only joy is dancing and frivolity. If — and it was a huge if — he ever married, he would want a woman as capable as he, not some giddy society Miss.

Then, Hugh meets Helena and despite their resolve, fate, it seems, has other ideas. As their attraction deepens however, treachery threatens to tear them apart. Will they uncover the perpetrator in time or will their love be swept away, lost forever on a winter's tide.

A Love Unquenchable
A Regency Romance
Linen and Lace - Book Four

Jessica Drummond, a bright and cheerful young woman, rarely gives romance, let alone love, a thought. Long hours working in her brother's shipping office affords little chance of her ever meeting an eligible bachelor.

Duncan Barrington, veteran of the Napoleonic Wars, believes himself wounded in both body and soul. He has no intention of inflicting his demons on anyone, certainly not a beautiful and, in his opinion, irresponsible city lady.

One cold and snowy morning, the plight of a bedraggled puppy throws Jessica and Duncan together and, as a spark of something indefinable yet wholly unquenchable begins to burn, it is unclear who rescued whom.

A Hidden Rose
A Regency Romance
Linen and Lace - Book Five

After witnessing his mother's grief at the loss of his father, Nick Drummond resolved never to cause someone he loved such distress. Even the happiness of his siblings would not sway him – until he met Rose.

Rose Archer was almost content assisting her doctor father in a tiny fishing village in the north of Yorkshire. To experience the world beyond, a tantalising dream – until she met Nick.

Unexpectedly, the impossible becomes possible, and the renounced – desired above all things, but the shipwreck that brought them together, may yet tear them apart. Will Nick learn to trust his heart, or will his love for Rose remain forever hidden?

His Fiery Hoyden
A Regency Novella

"Please inform your master, Sasha is perfectly happy here with me and there is more chance of hell freezing over, than of my brother dancing attendance on his Grace."

A plea for help ignored. A child left to bring up her baby brother.

Livvy has no respect for the nobility; they let her down when she most needed them. Why should she accede to their demands now?

Philip, Lord Harrington, is stunned to discover the young heir to the dukedom lives a stone's throw away in a ramshackle cottage, and resolves to restore the child to his birthright.

They meet in a clash of wills, but just when it seems Livvy might surrender, the victory Philip desires, may not taste all that sweet.

Of Ruins and Romance

While escorting a group of tourists around the ancient Roman port of Ostia, Kassandra Winters bumps into someone she first met in less than auspicious circumstances two years previously. The encounter leads to a job offer - to be the assistant guide for a three-week tour of ancient sites in and around Rome. Unable to resist such an opportunity, Kassie agrees.

Kassie has intrigued Gabriel St Germain since he accidentally knocked her flying outside her university professor's office. Her face haunts his dreams, yet he never expected to see her again. So, he is surprised when she appears, as though destined to do so, in the middle of a ruin, and he concocts a plan to win her heart.

Gabriel's old-fashioned courtship touches something deep inside Kassie and, although struggling to believe someone as handsome as Gabriel could possibly be interested in her, she soon realises she has fallen irrevocably in love with him. However, just as Kassie shares everything of herself with Gabriel, her world comes crashing down. Can their romance survive or will it fall in ruins, like the relics of antiquity that brought them together.

All At Once It's You

When Alex arrives in the small village of Rosedale Abbey, to take up a position as a research assistant for a renowned archaeologist, the last thing she is looking for, or expects to find, is love.

Jake was perfectly happy with the status quo. When it came to relationships, he didn't do committed or long term. He called the shots, and if his current flame didn't like it, she knew what to do. A philosophy, which served him well - until he met Alex.

Romance blooms, but even as the untamed wilderness of the North Yorkshire moors weaves its spell, a long buried secret might yet jeopardise their happily ever after.